CRITICAL ACCLAIM FOR DONNA LEON

A Venetian Reckoning
'A splendid series . . . with a backdrop of the city so vivid you can almost smell it' *Sunday Telegraph*

'An excellent sense of location, strong characterization and a murky but believable plot. I look forward to number five' *Independent*

'An evocative peep into the dark underworld of the beauteous city' *Time Out*

The Anonymous Venetian
'A finely organized, stylishly told story about how crime gets done in Venice. No travel agent will recommend it' Julian Symons

'Venice is the perfect backdrop for a crime novel and there can rarely have been one so compulsively readable' Frances Fyfield

Death in a Strange Country
'This series has become one of the adornments of current crime fiction . . . a gem' *Scotsman*

'Commissario Guido Brunetti, most charismatic current Euro-cop, uncovers deadly ants' nest of corruption. Highly accomplished, scary read' *Guardian*

Death at La Fenice
'Venice, that eerie, beauteous city where things are rarely what they seem . . . first class' *Ms London*

'Intriguing – with an excellent denouement' *Mail on Sunday*

A VENETIAN RECKONING

Donna Leon is a professor of English Literature at a university near Venice and visits England regularly. *A Venetian Reckoning* is her fourth novel to feature Commissario Brunetti, following *Death at La Fenice*, *Death in a Strange Country* and *The Anonymous Venetian*, and is followed by *Acqua Alta* and *The Death of Faith*.

DONNA LEON

A VENETIAN RECKONING

PAN BOOKS

First published 1995 by Macmillan

This edition published 1996 by Pan Books
an imprint of Pan Macmillan Ltd
Pan Macmillan, 20 New Wharf Road, London N1 9RR
Basingstoke and Oxford
Associated companies throughout the world
www.panmacmillan.com

ISBN 978-0-330-51660-0

1

A CIP catalogue record for this book is available from
the British Library.

Phototypeset by Intype, London
Printed and bound in the UK by
CPI Mackays, Chatham ME5 8TD

Questo è il fin di chi fa mal!
E de' perfidi la morte
alla vita è sempre ugual.

This is the end of evildoers.
The death of the perfidious
Is always the same as their lives.
Don Giovanni
Mozart/DaPonte

For Toni Sepeda and Craig Manley

Chapter One

On the last Tuesday in September, snow fell for the first time in the mountains separating northern Italy from Austria, more than a month before it could ordinarily be expected. The storm arrived suddenly, carried by fat clouds that swept in from nowhere and with no warning. Within a half-hour the roads of the pass above Tarvisio were slick and deadly. No rain had fallen for a month, and so the first snow lay upon roads already covered with a glistening layer of oil and grease.

The combination proved deadly to a sixteen-wheeled truck bearing Romanian licence plates and carrying a cargo manifest for 90 cubic metres of pine boards. Just north of Tarvisio, on a curve that led down to the entrance to the autostrada and thus into the warmer, safer roads of Italy, the driver braked too hard on a curve and lost control of the immense vehicle, which plunged off the road moving at 50 kilometres an hour. The wheels gouged out huge trenches in the not yet frozen earth, while the body of the truck cannoned off trees, snapping them and hurling them about in a long swath that led to the bottom of the gully, where the truck finally smacked into the rock face of a mountain, smashing open and scattering its cargo in a wide arc.

The first men on the scene, drivers of other heavy transport trucks who stopped without thinking to help one of their own, went first to the cabin of the truck, but there was no hope for the driver, who hung in his seat-belt, half suspended from the cabin, one side of his head battered in by the branch that had ripped off the driver's door as the truck careered down the slope. The driver of a load of pigs being brought down to Italy for slaughter climbed over what remained of the hood of the truck, peering through the shattered windscreen to see if there was another driver. The other seat was empty, and so the searchers who had by then gathered began to look for the other driver, thrown free of the truck.

Four drivers of trucks of varying sizes began to stumble down the hill, leaving a fifth up on the road to set out warning flares and use his radio to summon the *polizia stradale*. Snow still fell heavily, so it was some time before one of them spotted the twisted body that could be seen a third of the way down the slope. Two of them ran towards it, they too hoping that at least one of the drivers had survived the accident.

Slipping, occasionally falling to their knees in their haste, the men struggled in the snow the truck had crashed through so effortlessly. The first man knelt beside the motionless form and began to brush at the thin layer of white that covered the supine figure, hoping to find him still breathing. But then his fingers caught in the long hair, and when he brushed the

2

snow away from the face, he exposed the unmistakably delicate bones of a woman.

He heard another driver cry out from below him. Turning in the still-falling snow, he looked back and saw the other man kneeling over something that lay a few metres to the left of the scar torn by the truck as it plunged down the hill.

'What is it?' he called, placing his fingers softly against her neck to feel for life in the oddly positioned figure.

'It's a woman,' the second one cried. And then, just as he felt the absolute stillness of the throat of the form below him, the other called up to him, 'She's dead.'

Later, the first driver to explore behind the truck said that he thought, when he first saw them, that the truck must have been carrying a cargo of mannequins: you know, those plastic women they dress up and put in the windows of shops. There they were, at least a half-dozen of them, lying scattered over the snow behind the shattered rear doors of the truck. One even seemed to have got caught in the lumber that had been tossed about inside the truck and lay there, half hanging from the back platform, legs pinned down by stacks of boards so securely wrapped that the impact of the truck against the mountain had not been sufficient to break them open. But why would mannequins be dressed in overcoats, he remembered wondering. And why that red in the snow all around them?

Chapter Two

It took the *polizia stradale* more than half an hour to respond to the call and, when they finally arrived at the scene of the accident, they were forced to set out flares and deal with the kilometre-long rows of traffic that had backed up on both sides of the accident as drivers, already made cautious by road conditions, slowed even more to gape down through the wide hole in the metal railing, down to where the body of the truck lay. Among the other bodies.

As soon as the first officer, unable to understand what the truck drivers shouted to him, saw the broken forms around the wreckage of the truck, he climbed back up the hill and put in a radio call to the carabinieri station in Tarvisio. His call was answered quickly, and soon the traffic was worsened by the arrival of two cars carrying six black-uniformed carabinieri. They left their cars parked on the shoulder of the highway and lurched down the slope towards the truck. When they found that the woman whose legs were pinned under the boards inside the truck was still alive, the carabinieri abandoned any interest they might have had in the traffic.

There followed a scene so confused that it might

4

have been comic, had it not been so grotesque. The piles of lumber pinning the woman's legs to the bottom of the truck were at least two metres high: they could easily be moved with a crane, but no crane could get down the slope. Men could shift them, surely, but to do so they would have to climb up and walk over them, adding to the weight.

The youngest of the officers crouched at the back of the truck, shivering in the bitter cold of the descending Alpine night. His regulation down parka lay tucked around the visible portion of the body of the woman pinned to the floor of the truck. Her legs disappeared at the thighs, straight into a solid pile of wood, as though the subject of a particularly whimsical Magritte.

He could see that she was young and blonde, but he could also see that she had grown visibly paler since his arrival. She lay on her side, cheek pressed down on the corrugated floor of the truck. Her eyes were closed, but she seemed still to breathe.

From behind him, he heard the sharp sound of something heavy falling on to the floor of the truck. The other five, ant-like, crawled up the sides of the pile, pulling, shoving at the neat packages of wooden beams, working them loose from the top. Each time they tossed one to the floor of the truck, they jumped down after it, picked it up, and heaved it out of the open back, passing the girl and young Monelli as they did.

Each time they walked past Monelli, they could see that the puddle of blood seeping out from under the boards was closer to his knees. Still they tore at

5

the beams, ripping their hands open on them, gone temporarily mad with the need to break the girl free. Even after Monelli pulled his jacket over the girl's face and got to his feet, two of them continued to rip boards from the pile and hurl them out into the growing darkness. They did this until their sergeant went to each of them in turn and placed his hands on their shoulders, telling their bodies that they could stop now. They grew calm then and returned to the routine investigation of the scene. By the time they finished that and called back down to Tarvisio for ambulances to carry the dead away, more snow had fallen, full night had come, and traffic was effectively tied up all the way back to the Austrian border.

Nothing more could be done until the following day, but the carabinieri were careful to post two guards, knowing the fascination the locus of death exerts over many people and afraid that evidence would be destroyed or stolen if the wreck were left unattended through the night.

As so often happens at that time of year, the next morning dawned rosy-fingered, and by ten the snow was no more than a memory. But the wrecked truck remained, as did the deep scars leading down to it. During the day, it was emptied, the wood stacked in low piles in an area well clear of the wreckage. As the carabinieri worked, grumbling at the weight, the splinters, and the mud that churned under their boots, a forensics team began a careful investigation of the truck's cab, dusting surfaces and slipping all papers and objects into clearly labelled and numbered plastic bags.

The driver's seat had been ripped from its frame by the force of the final impact; the two men working in the cab loosened it further and then peeled back its plastic and cloth cover, looking for something they did not find. Nor did they find anything in any way suspicious behind the plastic panelling of the cabin.

It was only in the back of the truck that anything at all unusual was found: eight plastic bags, the sort given by supermarkets, each holding a change of women's clothing and, in one case, a small prayer book printed in what one of the technicians identified as Romanian. All of the labels had been removed from the clothing in the bags, as turned out to be true of the clothing worn by the eight women killed in the crash.

The papers found in the truck were no more than what should have been there: the driver's passport and licence, insurance forms, customs papers, bills of lading, and an invoice giving the name of the lumberyard to which the wood was to be delivered. The driver's papers were Romanian, the customs papers were in order, and the shipment was on its way to a woodmill in Sacile, a small city about a hundred kilometres to the south.

Nothing more was to be learned from the wreckage of the truck, which was finally, with great difficulty and with enormous disruption of traffic, hauled up to the roadside by winches attached to three tow-trucks. There, it was lifted on to a flatbed truck and sent back to its owner in Romania. The wood was eventually delivered to the woodmill in Sacile, which refused to pay the extra charges imposed.

The strange death of the women was picked up by the Austrian and Italian press, where stories about them appeared in articles variously entitled, 'Der Todeslaster' and 'Il Camion della Morte'. Somehow, the Austrians had managed to get hold of three photos of the bodies lying in the snow and printed them with the story. Speculation was rife: economic refugees? illegal workers? The collapse of Communism had removed what would once have been the almost certain conclusion: spies. In the end, the mystery was never resolved, and the investigation died somewhere amidst the failure of the Romanian authorities to answer questions or return papers and the Italians' fading interest. The women's bodies, as well as that of the driver, were returned by plane to Bucharest, where they were buried under the earth of their native land and under the even greater weight of its bureaucracy.

Their story quickly disappeared from the press, driven off by the desecration of a Jewish cemetery in Milan and the murder of yet another judge. It did not disappear, however, before it was read by Professoressa Paola Falier, Assistant Professor of English Literature at the University of Ca'Pesaro in Venice and, not incidentally to this story, wife of Guido Brunetti, Commissario of Police in that city.

Chapter Three

Carlo Trevisan, Avvocato Carlo Trevisan, to give him the title he preferred to hear used when people spoke of him, was a man of very ordinary past, which in no way impinged upon the fact that he was a man of limitless future. A native of Trento, a city near the Italian border with Austria, he had gone to Padua to study law, which he did brilliantly, graduating with the highest honours and the united praise of his professors. From there, he accepted a position in a law office in Venice, where he soon became an expert on international law, one of the few men in the city to interest himself in such matters. After only five years, he left that firm and set up his own office, specializing in corporate and international law.

Italy is a country where many laws are passed one day, only to be repealed the next. Nor is it strange that, in a country where the point of even the simplest newspaper story is often impossible to decipher, there sometimes exists a measure of confusion as to the exact meaning of the law. The resulting fluidity of interpretation creates a climate most propitious to lawyers, who claim the ability to understand the law. Among these, then, Avvocato Carlo Trevisan.

Because he was both industrious and ambitious, Avvocato Trevisan prospered. Because he married well, the daughter of a banker, he was put in familial and familiar contact with many of the most successful and powerful industrialists and bankers of the Veneto. His practice expanded along with his waistline, until, the year he turned fifty, Avvocato Trevisan had seven lawyers working in his office, none of them a partner in the firm. He attended weekly Mass at Santa Maria del Giglio, had twice served with distinction on the City Council of Venice, and had two children, a boy and a girl, both bright and both beautiful.

On the Tuesday before the feast of La Madonna della Salute in late November, Avvocato Trevisan spent the afternoon in Padua, asked there by Francesco Urbani, a client of his who had recently decided to ask his wife of twenty-seven years for a separation. During the two hours the men spent together, Trevisan suggested that Urbani move certain monies out of the country, perhaps to Luxemburg, and that he immediately sell his share of the two factories in Verona which he held in silent partnership with another man. The proceeds from those transactions, Trevisan suggested, might well follow the others quickly out of the country.

After the meeting, which he had arranged to coincide with his next appointment, Trevisan met for a weekly dinner with a business associate. They had met in Venice the previous week, so tonight they met in Padua. Like all of their meetings, this one was marked by the cordiality that results from success and prosperity. Good food, good wine, and good news.

Trevisan's partner drove him to the railway station where, as he did every week, he caught the Intercity for Trieste, which would get him to Venice by 10.15. Though he held a ticket for the first-class section, which was at the back of the train, Trevisan walked through the almost empty carriages and took a seat in a second-class compartment: like all Venetians, he sat at the front of the train so as not to have to walk the length of the long platform when the train finally pulled into the Santa Lucia station.

He opened the calfskin briefcase on the seat opposite him and pulled from it a prospectus recently sent to him by the National Bank of Luxemburg, one offering interests as high as 18 per cent, though not for accounts in Italian lira. He slid a small calculator from its slot in the upper lid of the briefcase, uncapped his Montblanc, and began to make rough calculations on a sheet of paper.

The door of his compartment rolled back, and Trevisan turned away to take his ticket from his overcoat pocket and hand it to the conductor. But the person who stood there had come to collect something other than his ticket from Avvocato Carlo Trevisan.

The body was discovered by the conductor, Cristina Merli, while the train was crossing the *laguna* that separates Venice from Mestre. As she walked past the compartment in which the well-dressed gentleman lay slumped against the window, she first decided not to bother him by waking him to check his ticket, but then she remembered how often ticketless passengers, even well-dressed ones, would feign sleep on this short

11

trip across the *laguna*, hoping this way not to be disturbed as they stole their 1000-lira ride. Besides, if he had a ticket, he'd be glad to be awakened before the train pulled in, especially if he had to catch the No. 1 boat to Rialto, which left the *embarcadero* in front of the station exactly three minutes after the train arrived.

She rolled the door open and stepped into the small compartment. '*Buona sera, signore. Suo biglietto, per favore.*'

Later, when she talked about it, she thought she remembered the smell, remembered noticing it as soon as she slid back the door of the overheated compartment. She took two steps towards the sleeping man and raised her voice to repeat, '*Suo biglietto, per favore.*' So deeply asleep, he didn't hear her? Not possible: he must be without a ticket and now trying to avoid the inevitable fine. Over the course of her years on the trains, Cristina Merli had come almost to enjoy this moment: asking them for identification and then writing out the ticket, collecting the fine. So, too, did she delight in the variety of the excuses that were offered to her, all by now grown so familiar that she could recite them in her sleep: I must have lost it; the train was just pulling out, and I didn't want to miss it; my wife's in another compartment and she has the tickets.

Conscious of all of this, knowing she would now be delayed, right at the end of the long trip from Torino, she was sudden in her gestures, perhaps even harsh.

'Please, signore, wake up and show me your ticket,' she said, leaning down over him and shaking his shoulder. At the first touch of her hand, the man in the seat leaned slowly away from the window, toppled

12

over on to the seat, and slid to the floor. As he fell, his jacket slid open and she saw the red stains that covered the front of his shirt. The smell of urine and excrement rose up unmistakably from his body.

'Maria Vergine,' she gasped and backed very slowly out of the compartment. To her left, she saw two men coming towards her, passengers moving towards the door at the front of the train. 'I'm sorry, gentlemen, but that door at the front is blocked: you'll have to use the one behind you.' Used to this, they turned and walked back towards the rear of the carriage. She glanced out of the window and saw that the train was almost at the end of the causeway. Three, perhaps four minutes remained until the train drew to a stop in the station. When it did, the doors would open and the passengers would get out, taking with them whatever memories they might have of the trip and of people they had seen in the corridors of the long train. She heard the familiar clicks and bangs as the train was shunted to the proper track and the nose of the train slid under the roof of the station.

She had worked for the railway for fifteen years and had never known it to happen, but she did the only thing she could think of doing: she stepped into the next compartment and reached up to the handle of the emergency brake. She pulled at it and heard the tiny 'pop' as the tattered string broke apart, and then she waited, not without a distant, almost academic curiosity, to see what would happen.

Chapter Four

The wheels locked and the train slid to a halt; passengers were knocked to the floor of the corridors and into the laps of strangers sitting opposite them. Within seconds, windows were yanked down and heads popped out, searching up and down the track for whatever it was that had caused the train to grind to a stop. Cristina Merli lowered the window in the corridor, glad of the biting winter air, and stuck her head out, waiting to see who would come towards the train. It turned out to be two of the uniformed *polizia ferrovia* who came running up the platform. She leaned out from the window and waved at them. 'Here, over here.' Because she didn't want anyone except the police to hear what she had to tell them, she said nothing more until they were directly underneath her window.

When she told them, one of them broke away and ran back towards the station; the other moved towards the engine to tell the engineer what was going on. Slowly, with two false starts, the train began to crawl into the station, inching its way up the track until it came to a halt at its usual place on track 5. A few people stood on the platform, waiting for passengers to get down from the train or to climb aboard them-

14

selves for the late-night trip to Trieste. When the doors didn't open, they mulled together, asking one another what was wrong. One woman, assuming that this was yet another train strike, threw her hands into the air and her suitcase to the ground. As the passengers stood there, talking and growing irritated at the unexplained delay, yet another proof of the inefficiency of the railways, six police officers, each carrying a machine-gun, appeared at the front of the platform and walked along the train, positioning themselves at every second car. More heads appeared at the windows, men shouted down angrily, but no one listened to anything that was said. The doors of the train remained locked.

After long minutes of this, someone told the sergeant in charge of the officers that the train had a public-address system. The sergeant pulled himself up into the engine and began to explain to the passengers that a crime had been committed on the train and they were being held there in the station until the police could take their names and addresses.

When he finished speaking, the engineer unlocked the doors and the police swung themselves aboard. Unfortunately, no one had thought to explain anything to the people waiting on the platform, who consequently crowded on to the train, where they quickly became confused with the original passengers. Two men in the second carriage tried to push past the officer in the corridor, insisting that they had seen nothing, knew nothing, and were already late. He stopped them by raising his machine-gun across his chest in front of them, effectively blocking off the corridor and forcing them into a compartment, where they grumbled about police arrogance and their rights as citizens.

In the end, there proved to be only thirty-four people on the train, excluding those who had crowded on behind the police. After half an hour, the police got their names and addresses and asked if they had seen anything strange on the train. Two people remembered a black pedlar who got off at Vicenza; one said he'd seen a man with long hair and a beard coming out of the toilet before they pulled into Verona, and someone had seen a woman in a fur hat get off at Mestre, but aside from that, no one had noticed anything at all out of the ordinary.

Just as it began to look as though the train would be there all night and people were beginning to straggle off to telephone relatives in Trieste to tell them not to expect their arrival, an engine backed its way into the far end of the track and attached itself to the rear of the train, suddenly converting it into the front. Three blue-uniformed mechanics crawled under the train and detached the last carriage, the one in which the body still lay, from the rest of the train. A conductor ran along the platform, yelling '*In partenza, in partenza, siamo in partenza*', and passengers scrambled back up into the train. The conduttore slammed a door, then another one, and pulled himself up on to the train just as it started to move slowly out of the station. And Cristina Merli stood in the office of the Station Master, attempting to explain why she should not be subject to a fine of 1 million lire for having pulled the train's alarm.

Chapter Five

Guido Brunetti did not learn of the murder of Avvocato Carlo Trevisan until the following morning, and he learned of it in a most unpolicemanlike manner, from the shouting headlines of *Il Gazzettino*, the same newspaper that had twice applauded Avvocato Trevisan's tenure as city counsellor. 'Avvocato Assassinato sul Treno,' the headline cried, while *La Nuova*, ever drawn to melodrama, spoke of 'Il Treno della Morte'. Brunetti saw the headlines while on his way to work, stopped and bought both papers, and stood in the Ruga Orefici to read both articles while early-morning shoppers passed by him unnoticed. The article gave the barest facts: shot to death on the train, body found as it crossed the *laguna*, police conducting the usual investigation.

Brunetti looked up and allowed his eyes to wander sightlessly across the banked stalls of fruit and vegetables. The 'usual investigation'? Who had been on duty last night? Why hadn't he been called? And if he hadn't been called, which one of his colleagues had been?

He turned away from the news-stand and continued walking toward the Questura, calling to mind the various cases on which they were working at the moment,

17

trying to calculate who would be given this one. Brunetti was himself almost at the end of an investigation that had to do, in Venice's minor way, with the enormous spider web of bribery and corruption that had been radiating out from Milan for the last few years. Super highways had been built on the mainland, one to connect the city with the airport, and billions of lire had been spent to build them. It was not until after construction was completed that anyone had troubled to consider that the airport, one with fewer than a hundred daily flights, was already well served by road, public buses, taxis, and boats. It was only then that anyone thought to question the enormous expenditure of public monies on a road that no stretch of the imagination could view as being in any way necessary. Hence Brunetti's involvement and hence the warrants that had gone out for both the arrest and the freezing of the assets of the owner of the construction firm that had done the major portion of the work on the road and of the three members of the City Council who had fought most vociferously for his being awarded the contract.

Another commissario was busy with the Casino where, yet once again, the croupiers had found a way to beat the system and skim off a percentage. The other was involved with an on-going investigation of Mafia-controlled businesses in Mestre, an investigation that appeared to have no limits and, alas, no end.

And so it was no surprise for Brunetti to arrive at the Questura and be greeted by the guards at the front door with the news, 'He wants to see you.' If Vice-

Questore Patta wanted to see him this early, then perhaps Patta had been called last night and not one of the commissari. And if Patta was sufficiently interested in the death to be here this early, then Trevisan was more important or more powerfully connected than Brunetti had realized.

He went up to his own office and hung up his coat, then checked his desk. There was nothing on it that hadn't been there when he left the night before, which meant that any papers already generated by the case were down in Patta's office. He went down the back steps and into the Vice-Questore's outer office. Behind her desk, looking as though she were there only to meet the photographers from *Vogue*, sat Signorina Elettra Zorzi, today arrayed as were the lilies of the field, in a white crêpe-de-Chine dress that fell in diagonal, but decidedly provocative, folds across her bosom.

'*Buon giorno, commissario,*' she said, looking up from the magazine open on her desk and smiling.

'Trevisan?' Brunetti asked.

She nodded. 'He's been on the phone for the last ten minutes. The Mayor.'

'Who called whom?'

'The Mayor called him,' Signorina Elettra answered. 'Why, does it matter?'

'Yes, it probably means we have nothing to go on.'

'Why?'

'If he called the Mayor, it would mean he was sure enough about something to assure him that we had a suspect or would soon have a confession. That the

19

Mayor called him means Trevisan was important and they want it settled fast.'

Signorina Elettra closed her magazine and moved it to the side of the desk. When she had first started working for Patta, Brunetti remembered, she used to put them in the drawer when she wasn't reading them; now she didn't even bother to turn them face down.

'What time did he get here?' Brunetti asked.

'Eight-thirty.' Then, before Brunetti asked, she told him, 'I was already here, and I told him you'd been in and had gone out to see if you could talk to the Leonardis' maid.' He had spoken to the woman the afternoon before as part of his investigation of the builder, spoken to her and learned nothing.

'*Grazie*,' he said. Brunetti had more than once reflected upon the strangeness of the fact that a woman with Signorina Elettra's natural inclination towards the duplicitous should have chosen to work for the police.

She glanced down at her desk and saw that a red light on her phone had ceased to blink. 'He's finished talking,' she said.

Brunetti nodded and turned away. He knocked on Patta's door, waited for the shouted '*Avanti*', and went into the office.

Though the Vice-Questore had arrived early, he had apparently had ample time to perform his toilette: the scent of some pungent aftershave hung in the air, and Patta's handsome face glowed. His tie was wool, his suit silk; no slave to tradition, the Vice-Questore. 'Where have you been?' was Patta's greeting.

'At the Leonardis'. I thought I could talk to their maid.'

'And?'

'She knows nothing.'

'That doesn't matter,' Patta said, then gestured to the chair in front of his desk. 'Sit down, Brunetti.' When he was seated, Patta asked, 'Have you heard about this?'

It was not necessary to ask him what 'this' was. 'Yes,' Brunetti answered. 'What happened?'

'Someone shot him on the train from Torino last night. Twice, at very close range. Body shots. One must have severed an artery, there was so much blood.' If Patta said 'must have', that meant the autopsy hadn't been done yet, and he was only guessing.

'Where were you last night?' Patta asked, almost as if he wanted to eliminate Brunetti as a suspect before going any further.

'We went to dinner at a friend's house.'

'I was told they tried to reach you at home.'

'I was at a friend's house,' Brunetti repeated.

'Why don't you have an answering machine?'

'I have two children.'

'What's that supposed to mean?'

'That if I had an answering machine, I'd spend my time listening to messages from their friends.' Or that he'd spend it listening to his children's many prevarications as to their lateness or absence. It also meant that Brunetti saw it as his children's responsibility to take messages for their parents, but he didn't want to spend his time with Patta discussing the issue.

'They had to call me,' Patta said, making no attempt to disguise his indignation.

Brunetti suspected he was meant to apologize. He said nothing.

'I went to the railway station. The *polizia ferrovia* had made a mess of it, of course.' Patta looked down at his desk and pushed a few photos towards Brunetti.

Brunetti leaned forward, picked up the photos, and glanced at them while Patta continued to catalogue the many incompetencies of the *polizia ferrovia*. The first photo was taken from the door of the train compartment and showed the body of a man lying on his back between the facing seats. The angle made it impossible to see more than the back of the man's head, but the dark red splotches on the upturned dome of his paunch were unmistakable. The next photo showed the body from the other side of the compartment and must have been taken through the window of the carriage. In this one, Brunetti could see that the man's eyes were closed and that one of his hands was closed tightly around a pen. The other photos revealed little more, though they had been taken from inside the carriage. The man appeared to be sleeping; death had wiped his face free of all expression and left what seemed to be the sleep of the just.

'Was he robbed?' Brunetti asked, cutting into Patta's continuing complaint.

'What?'

'Was he robbed?'

'It seems not. His wallet was still in his pocket, and

22

his briefcase, as you can see, is still on the seat opposite where he was sitting.'

'Mafia?' Brunetti asked, the way one did, the way one had to.

Patta shrugged. 'He's a lawyer,' he answered, leaving it to Brunetti to infer if this made him more or less likely to merit execution by the Mafia.

'Wife?' Brunetti asked, expressing with the question the fact that he was both an Italian and a married man.

'Not likely. She's the Secretary of the Lions' Club,' Patta answered, and Brunetti, caught by the absurdity of his remark, involuntarily guffawed, but when he caught the look Patta shot him, he turned the noise into a cough, which turned into a real cough that left him red faced and teary eyed.

When he had recovered enough to breathe normally, Brunetti asked, 'Business partners? Anything there?'

'I don't know.' Patta tapped a finger on his desk, calling for Brunetti's attention. 'I've been looking over the case-load, and it seems like you're the one who's got the least to do.' One of the things that most endeared Patta to Brunetti was his unfailing felicity of phrase. 'I'd like to assign this case to you, but before I do, I want to be certain that you'll handle it in the proper fashion.'

This meant, Brunetti was certain, that Patta wanted to be sure he would defer to the social status implied by the secretaryship of the Lions' Club. Because he knew he wouldn't be there if Patta had not already decided to give him the case, Brunetti chose to ignore the admonition implicit in these words and, instead, asked, 'What about the people on the train?'

His talk with the Mayor must have impressed on Patta that speed was more important here than making a point with Brunetti, for he answered directly, 'The *polizia ferrovia* got the names and addresses of all the people who were on the train when it pulled into the station.' Brunetti raised his chin in an inquisitive gesture, and Patta went on, 'One or two of them said they saw people on the train. It's all in the file,' he said, tapping at a manila folder that lay in front of him.

'What judge has been assigned to this?' Brunetti asked. Once he knew this, Brunetti would know how much he'd have to defer to the Lions' Club.

'Vantuno,' Patta answered, naming a woman about Brunetti's own age, one with whom he had worked successfully in the past. A Sicilian, as was Patta, Judge Vantuno knew that there were complexities and nuances in the society of Venice that would be forever elusive to her, but she was confident enough in the local commissari to give them great liberty in the way they chose to conduct an investigation.

Brunetti nodded, unwilling to reveal even this minimal satisfaction to Patta.

'But I'll expect a daily report from you,' Patta went on. 'Trevisan was an important man. I've already had a call from the Mayor's office about it, and I make no secret that he wants this settled as quickly as possible.'

'Did he have any suggestions?' Brunetti asked.

Accustomed to impertinence from his inferior, Patta sat back in his chair and peered at Brunetti for a moment before asking, 'About what?', putting sharp emphasis on the second word to imply his disapproval of the question.

'About anything Trevisan might have been involved in,' Brunetti replied blandly. He was quite serious about this. The fact that a man was mayor did not exclude him from knowledge of the dirty secrets of his friends; in fact, the opposite was more likely to be the case.

'That is not a question I thought fit to ask the Mayor,' Patta answered.

'Then maybe I will,' Brunetti said evenly.

'Brunetti, don't go stirring up trouble with this.'

'I think that's already been done,' Brunetti said, dropping the photos back into the file. 'Will there be anything else, sir?'

Patta paused a moment before he answered. 'No, not now.' He pushed the file towards Brunetti. 'You can have this. And don't forget that I want a daily report.' When Brunetti made no acknowledgement of this, Patta added, 'Or give it to Lieutenant Scarpa,' and kept his eyes on Brunetti long enough to see what response he'd give to the name of Patta's universally despised assistant.

'Certainly, sir,' Brunetti said neutrally, took the folder, and got to his feet. 'Where have they taken Trevisan?'

'To the Ospedale Civile. I imagine the autopsy will be done this morning. And remember, he was a friend of the Mayor's.'

'Of course, sir,' Brunetti said and left the office.

Chapter Six

Signorina Elettra looked up from her magazine when Brunetti emerged from Patta's office and asked, '*Allora?*'

'Trevisan. And I'm to hurry because he was a friend of the Mayor's.'

'The wife's a tiger,' Signorina Elettra said, then added by way of encouragement, 'She'll give you trouble.'

'Is there anyone in this city you don't know?' Brunetti asked.

'This time I don't actually know her. But she used to be one of my sister's patients.'

'Barbara,' Brunetti said involuntarily, remembering where it was he had met her sister. 'The doctor.'

'The very same, commissario,' she said with a smile of real delight. 'I wondered how long it would take you to remember.'

When Signorina Elettra had first arrived, he remembered, he had thought her last name familiar; Zorzi wasn't at all a common name, but he would never have thought to associate the quick-witted, radiant – the other adjectives that presented themselves all suggested light and visibility – Elettra with the calm, understated doctor who numbered among her patients his father-in-law and now, it seemed, Signora Trevisan.

'Used to be?' Brunetti asked, leaving the question of Elettra's family to be considered at another time.

'Yes, until about a year ago. She and her daughter were both patients. But one day she went into Barbara's office and made some sort of a scene, demanding that Barbara tell her what she was treating her daughter for.'

Brunetti listened but asked nothing.

'The daughter was only fourteen, but when Barbara refused to tell her, Signora Trevisan insisted that Barbara had given her an abortion or sent her to the hospital to have one. She shouted at her and, in the end, she threw a magazine.'

'At your sister?'

'Yes.'

'What did she do?' Brunetti asked.

'Who?'

'Your sister?'

'She told her to get out of the office. Finally, after some more shouting, she did.'

'And then what?'

'The next day, Barbara sent her a registered letter with her medical records and told her to find another doctor.'

'And the daughter?'

'She never went back, either. But Barbara's seen her on the street, and the girl's explained that her mother has forbidden her to go back. Her mother took her to some private clinic.'

'What was the daughter there for?' Brunetti asked.

He watched Signorina Elettra weigh this one out. She quickly came to the conclusion that Brunetti would find out about it, anyway, and said, 'It was a venereal infection.'

'What sort?'

'I don't remember. You'll have to ask my sister.'

'Or Signora Trevisan.'

Elettra's response was immediate, and angry. 'If she learned what it was, she never learned it from Barbara.'

Brunetti believed her. 'So the daughter's about fifteen now?'

Elettra nodded. 'Yes, she must be.'

Brunetti thought for a moment. The law was vague here – when was it not? A doctor did not have to divulge information about a patient's health, but surely a doctor was at liberty to provide information about how a patient had behaved, and why, especially in a situation where it was not his or her own health that was at issue. Better that he speak to the doctor herself than ask Elettra to do it for him. 'Is your sister's *ambulatorio* still over near San Barnaba?'

'Yes. She'll be there this afternoon. Do you want me to tell her to expect you?'

'Does that mean you won't tell her I'm coming unless I ask you to, signorina?'

She glanced down at the keys of her computer, apparently found the answer she wanted there, and glanced back at Brunetti. 'It doesn't make any difference if she hears this from you or from me, commissario. She hasn't done anything wrong. So, no, I won't tell her.'

Moved by curiosity, he asked, 'And if it did make a difference? If she *had* done something wrong?'

'If it would help her, I'd warn her. Of course.'

'Even if it meant betraying a police secret, signorina?' he asked, then smiled to show he was only joking, although he wasn't.

She glanced at him, uncomprehending. 'Do you think police secrets would matter at all if something concerned my family?'

Chastened, he answered, 'No, signorina, I don't suppose they would.'

Signorina Elettra smiled, glad that she had again assisted the commissario towards understanding.

'Do you know anything else about the wife?' – he corrected himself – 'widow?'

'No, not personally. I've read about her in the paper, of course. She's always involved in Worthy Causes,' she said, making the capitals audible. 'You know, like collecting food to send to Somalia, that gets stolen and sent to Albania and sold. Or organizing those gala concerts at La Fenice that never seem to do anything but cover expenses and give the organizers a chance to get dressed up and show off to their friends. I'm surprised you don't know who she is.'

'I have a vague memory of having seen the name but no more than that. What about the husband?'

'International law, I think, and very good at it. I think I might have read something about a deal with Poland or Czechoslovakia – one of those places where they eat potatoes and dress badly – but I can't remember which.'

'What sort of deal?'

She shook her head, unable to remember.

'Could you find out?'

'If I went down to the *Gazzettino* offices and had a look, I suppose I could.'

'Do you have anything to do for the Vice-Questore?'

'I'll just make his lunch reservation, and then I'll go down to the *Gazzettino*. Would you like me to look for anything else?'

'Yes, about the wife, as well. Who is it who writes the society stuff these days?'

'Pitteri, I think.'

'Well, speak to him and see if there's anything he can tell you about either of them, the sort of thing he can't publish.'

'Which is always the sort of thing people most want to read.'

'So it seems,' Brunetti said.

'Anything else, sir?'

'No, thank you, signorina. Is Vianello here?'

'I haven't seen him yet.'

'When he comes in, would you send him up to me, please?'

'Certainly,' she answered and went back to her magazine. Brunetti glanced down to see what article she was reading – shoulder pads – and then went back up to his own office.

The file, as was always the case at the beginning of an investigation, contained little more than names and dates. Carlo Trevisan had been born in Trento fifty years ago, had been educated at the University of Padua, from which he took a degree in law and after which he established himself as a lawyer in Venice. Eighteen years ago, he married Franca Lotto, with whom he had two children, a daughter, Francesca, now fifteen, and a son, Claudio, seventeen.

Avvocato Trevisan had never interested himself in criminal law and had himself never been involved with the police in any way. Nor had he ever come under the scrutiny of the Guardia di Finanza, which suggested either a miracle or that the Avvocato's tax returns were always in order, this in itself another kind of miracle. The file contained the names of the people employed in Trevisan's law office and a copy of his passport application.

'*Lavata con Perlana,*' Brunetti said aloud as he laid the papers down on his desk, repeating the slogan of a liquid detergent that promised to get everything, anything, cleaner than clean. Who would be cleaner than Carlo Trevisan? More interestingly, who could have put two bullets in his gut and not bothered to take his wallet?

Brunetti pulled out his bottom drawer with the toe of his right foot, leaned back in his chair, and folded his feet on the open drawer. Whoever did it must have done it between Padua and Mestre: no one would have taken the chance of being caught on the same train when it pulled into the station at Venice. The train wasn't a local, so Mestre was the only stop between Padua and Venice. It was unlikely that someone getting off the train at Mestre would have drawn any special notice, but it was worth checking at the station. The conductors usually sat in the first compartment, so they would have to be questioned to see what they remembered. Check for the gun, of course; did the bullets match up with those used in any other crime? Guns were closely controlled, so it might be possible to trace the weapon. Why had Trevisan been in Padua? With whom? The wife, check the wife. Then check the neighbours and friends to see if what she said was true. The daughter – a venereal disease at the age of fourteen?

He leaned forward, pulled the drawer all the way out, and reached down for the telephone directory. He flipped it open and found the Zs. There were two listings for 'Zorzi, Barbara, Medico', one for her home and one for her office. He dialled the office number and got a machine, telling him that visiting hours began at four. He dialled the home number and heard the same voice telling him that the Dottoressa was *momentania-mente assente* and asking him to leave name, reason for his call, and the number at which he could be reached. His call would be returned *appena possibile*.

'Good morning, dottoressa,' he began after the beep. 'This is Commissario Guido Brunetti. I'm calling in regard to the death of Avvocato Carlo Trevisan. I've learned that his wife and daughter were . . .'

'*Buon giorno*, commissario,' the doctor's husky voice broke in. 'How may I help you?' Though it had been more than a year since they last met, she used the 'tu' form of address with him, making it clear to both of them by its use that the familiarity established then would be continued.

'Good morning, dottoressa,' he said. 'Do you always filter your calls?'

'Commissario, I have a woman who has called me every morning for the last three years, telling me I must make a house call. Each morning, she has different symptoms. Yes, I filter my calls.' Her voice was firm; but there was an undertone of humour.

'I didn't realize there were that many body parts,' Brunetti said.

'She plays interesting combinations,' Dottoressa Zorzi explained. 'How may I help you, commissario?'

'As I was explaining, I've learned that Signora Trevisan and her daughter were formerly patients of yours.' He paused there, waiting to see what the doctor would volunteer. Silence. 'You've heard about Avvocato Trevisan?'

'Yes.'

'I wanted to ask if you'd be willing to talk to me about them, his wife and daughter.'

'As people or as patients?' she asked, voice calm.

'Whichever you'd feel more comfortable in doing, dottoressa,' Brunetti answered.

'We could start with the first, and then if it seemed necessary, take up the second.'

'That's very kind of you, dottoressa. Could we do it today?'

'I have some house calls to make this morning, but I should be finished with them by eleven. Where would you like to meet?'

Since it was she who was doing the favour, Brunetti didn't feel comfortable asking her to come to the Questura.

'Where will you be at eleven, dottoressa?'

'One moment, please,' she said and set the phone down. In an instant, she was back. 'My patient lives near the *embarcadero* of San Marco,' she answered.

'Would you like to meet at Florian's, then?' he asked.

Her answer was not immediate and, remembering what he did of her politics, Brunetti half expected her to remark on the way he was choosing to spend the taxpayer's money.

'Florian's is fine, commissario,' she finally said.

'I look forward to it. And thank you again, dottoressa.'

'Eleven, then,' she said, and was gone.

He tossed the phone book into the drawer and slammed it closed with his foot. When he looked up, Vianello was coming into his office.

'You wanted to see me, sir?' the sergeant asked.

'Yes. Sit down. The Vice-Questore's given me Trevisan.'

Vianello nodded, suggesting that this was already old news at the Questura.

'How much have you heard?' Brunetti asked.

'Just what was in the papers and on the radio this morning. Found on the train last night, shot. No trace of a weapon and no suspect.'

Brunetti realized that, although he had read the official police file, he knew no more than that himself. He nodded Vianello towards a chair. 'You know anything about him?'

'Important,' Vianello began as he lowered himself into a chair, his size making it look immediately smaller. 'Used to be city councillor in charge of, if I remember correctly, sanitation. Married, a couple of children. Has a big office. Over by San Marco, I think.'

'Personal life?'

Vianello shook his head. 'I've never heard anything.'

'Wife?'

'I think I've read about her. Wants to save the rain forest. Or is that the Mayor's wife?'

'I think it is.'

'Then one of those things. Saving something. Africa, maybe.' Here Vianello snorted, whether at Signora Trevisan or at the likelihood of Africa's being saved, Brunetti wasn't sure.

'Can you think of anyone who might know something about him?' Brunetti asked.

'Family? Business partners? People who work in his office?' Vianello suggested. Seeing Brunetti's response, he added, 'Sorry I can't think of anything better. I don't remember anyone I know ever mentioning him.'

'I'll speak to his wife, but not before the afternoon. I'd like you to go to his office this morning and see what the general feeling is about his death.'

'You think they'll be there? The day after he's killed?'

'It will be interesting to find out if they are,' Brunetti said. 'Signorina Elettra said she heard something about his being involved in a business deal in Poland, or perhaps Czechoslovakia. See if anyone there knows anything about that. She thinks there was something in the paper, but she can't remember what it was. And ask about the usual things.' They had worked together for so long that Brunetti didn't have to specify what the usual things were: a disaffected employee, an angry business associate, a jealous husband, his own jealous wife. Vianello had the knack of getting people to talk. Especially if they were Venetians, the people he interviewed invariably warmed to this large, sweet-tempered man who gave every appearance of speaking Italian reluctantly, who was only too glad to lapse into their common dialect, a linguistic change that often carried its speakers along to unconscious revelation.

'Anything else, sir?'

'Yes. I'm going to be busy this morning, and I'll try to see the widow this afternoon, so I'd like you to send someone down to the station to talk to the conductor who found the body. Find out if the conductors on the train saw anything.' Before Vianello could protest, Brunetti said, 'I know, I know. If they had, they would have said something by now. But I want them to be asked about it, anyway.'

'Yes, sir.'

'And I'd like to see a list of the names and addresses of all the people who were on the train when it stopped, and transcripts of whatever they said when they were questioned.'

'Why didn't they rob him, sir?'

'If that was the reason, then someone could have come along the corridor and scared him away before he had time to search the body. Or else whoever did it wanted us to realize it wasn't a robbery.'

'That doesn't make much sense, does it?' Vianello asked. 'Wouldn't it be better for them to have us believe it was a robbery?'

'That depends on why they did it.'

Vianello considered this for a moment and then answered, 'Yes, I suppose so,' but he said it in a tone that suggested he wasn't fully convinced. Why would anyone want to give such an advantage to the police?

Not willing to spend the time pondering his own question, Vianello got to his feet, saying, 'I'll go over to his office now, sir, and see what I can learn. Will you be back here this afternoon?'

'Probably. It depends on what time I can see the widow. I'll leave word.'

'Good. Then I'll see you this afternoon,' Vianello said and left the office.

Brunetti turned back to the file, opened it, and read off the phone number listed for Trevisan's house. He dialled the number. It rang ten times before it was answered.

'*Pronto,*' a male voice said.

'Is this the home of Avvocato Trevisan?' Brunetti asked.

'Who's calling, please?'

'This is Commissario Guido Brunetti. I'd like to speak to Signora Trevisan, please.'

'My sister isn't able to come to the phone.'

Brunetti flipped back to the page in the file that listed Signora Trevisan's maiden name and said, 'Signor Lotto, I'm sorry to bother you at a time like this, even sorrier to bother your sister, but it is imperative that I speak to her as soon as possible.'

'I'm afraid that's impossible, commissario. My sister is under heavy sedation and can see no one. She's been destroyed by this.'

37

'I realize the pain she must be suffering, Signor Lotto, and I extend my most sincere condolences. But we need to speak to someone in the family before we begin our investigation.'

'What sort of information do you need?'

'We need to get a clearer idea of Avvocato Trevisan's life, of his business dealings, his associates. Until we have some idea of this, we'll have no idea of what might have motivated this crime.'

'I thought it was a robbery,' Lotto said.

'Nothing was taken from him.'

'But there's no other reason to kill my brother-in-law. The thief must have been scared away.'

'That's entirely possible, Signor Lotto, but we'd like to speak to your sister, if only to rule out other possibilities and thus allow ourselves to follow the idea of a robbery.'

'What other possibilities could there be?' Lotto asked angrily. 'I assure you, there was nothing in my brother-in-law's life that was in any way unusual.'

'I have no doubt of that's being true, Signor Lotto, but still I must speak to your sister.'

There was a long pause and then Lotto asked, 'When?'

'This afternoon,' Brunetti said and kept himself from adding, 'if possible'.

There was another long pause. 'Wait, please,' Lotto said and set the phone down. He was gone so long that Brunetti took a piece of paper from his drawer and began to write 'Czechoslovakia' on it, trying to remember how the word was spelled. He was on his sixth version when the phone was picked up again and Lotto said, 'If you come at four this afternoon, either I or my sister will speak with you.'

'Four o'clock,' Brunetti repeated and then gave a terse, 'I'll see you then,' before saying goodbye and hanging up. From long experience, he knew how unwise it was to seem grateful to any witness, no matter how sympathetic they might be.

He glanced down at his watch and saw that it was well past ten. He called the Ospedale Civile but, after speaking to five different people at three different extensions, got no information about the autopsy. He often thought that the only safe procedure a person could undergo at the Ospedale Civile was an autopsy: it was the only time when a patient ran no risk.

With that opinion of medical prowess in mind, he left his office to go and talk to Dottoressa Zorzi.

Chapter Seven

Brunetti turned right when he left the Questura, up towards the Bacino of San Marco and the Basilica. He was startled to find himself in full sunlight; earlier that morning, he had been so surprised by the news of Trevisan's murder that he had ignored the day given to the city, filled with the light of early winter and now, in mid-morning, so warm he regretted having worn his raincoat.

Few people were out, and those who were all seemed lifted almost to joy by the unexpected sun and warmth. Who would believe that, only yesterday, the city had been wrapped in fog and the vaporetti forced to use their radar for the short ride out to the Lido? Yet here he was, wishing for sunglasses and a lighter suit, and when he walked out to the waterside, he was momentarily blinded by the reflected light that came flashing up from the water. Opposite him, Brunetti could see the dome and tower of San Giorgio – yesterday they hadn't been there – looking as though they had somehow crept into the city during the night. How straight and fine the tower looked, unencumbered by the scaffolding that had imprisoned the tower of San Marco for the last few years, turning it into a pagoda and making Brunetti suspect that the city administration had gone and sold the city outright to the Japanese, who had begun this way to make themselves feel more at home.

He turned right and walked up towards the Piazza, and Brunetti found himself, to his own vast surprise, looking kindly upon the tourists who strolled past him, mouths agape and steps slowed by wonder. She could still knock them down, this old whore of a city, and Brunetti, her true son, protective of her in her age, felt a surge of mingled pride and delight and hoped that those people who walked by would see him and somehow know him for a Venetian and, in that, part heir to and part owner of all of this.

The pigeons, usually stupid and hateful, appeared almost charming to him as they bobbed up and down at the feet of their many admirers. Suddenly, for no reason, hundreds of them flocked up, swirled around, and settled back right where they had been, to continue with their bobbing and pecking. A stout woman stood with three of them on her shoulder, her face turned away in delight or horror, while her husband photographed her with a video recorder the size of a machine gun. A few metres away, someone opened a small bag of corn and threw it out in a wide circle, and again the pigeons swirled up and around, then settled to feed in the centre of the corn.

He went up the three low steps and through the etched-glass double doors of Florian's. Though he was ten minutes early, Brunetti looked through the small rooms on the right and then through those on the left, but he saw no sign of Dottoressa Zorzi.

When a white-jacketed waiter approached him, Brunetti asked for a table near one of the front windows. Part of him, this splendid day, wanted to sit with an attractive young woman by a window at Florian's, and another part of him wanted to be seen sitting with an attractive young woman by a window at Florian's. He pulled out one of the delicate, curve-backed chairs and took a seat, then turned it to allow himself a better sight of the Piazza.

As it had been for as long as Brunetti could remember, the façade of the Basilica was partially covered by wooden scaffolding. Had he once, as a child, had a clear view of the whole thing? Probably not.

'Good morning, commissario,' he heard from behind him, and he stood to shake hands with Dottoressa Barbara Zorzi. He recognized her instantly. Slender and straight, she greeted him with a warm handshake that was surprisingly strong. Her hair, he thought, was shorter than it had been last time, cut in a cap of tight dark curls that fitted close to her head. Her eyes were as dark as eyes could be: there was almost no difference between pupil and iris. The resemblance to Elettra was there, the same straight nose, full mouth, and round chin, but the element of ripeness that filled her sister had been toned down to a more sombre, tranquil beauty.

'Dottoressa, I'm glad you could spare the time,' he said, reaching out to help her off with her coat.

She smiled in response to this and placed a squat

brown leather bag on a chair near the window. He folded her coat and placed it on the back of the same chair and, looking at the bag, said, 'The doctor who used to come to see us when we were boys carried a bag just like that.'

'I suppose I should be more modern and carry a leather briefcase,' she said, 'but my mother gave me that as a present when I took my degree, and I've carried it ever since.'

The waiter came to the table, and they both ordered coffee. When he was gone, the doctor asked, 'How is it I can help you?'

Brunetti decided there was nothing to be gained in disguising how he came by the information and so began by saying, 'Your sister told me that Signora Trevisan used to be a patient of yours.'

'And her daughter,' the doctor added, reaching towards the brown bag, from which she took a crumpled package of cigarettes. While she was still groping around in the bottom of the bag for her lighter, a waiter appeared on her left and leaned forward to light her cigarette. '*Grazie*,' she said, turning her head towards the flame as if accustomed to this sort of service. Silently, the waiter moved away from their table.

She drew greedily at the cigarette, flipped the bag closed, and looked up at Brunetti. 'Am I to take it this is somehow related to his death?'

'At this point in our investigation,' Brunetti said, 'I'm not sure what is and what isn't related to his death.' She pursed her lips at this, and Brunetti realized how artificial and formal he had sounded. 'That's the truth, doctor. As of the moment, we have nothing, nothing aside from the physical evidence surrounding his death.'

'He was shot?'

'Yes. Twice. One bullet must have severed an artery, for he seems to have died very quickly.'

'Why do you want to know about his family?' she asked, not, he noticed, asking which member of the family he might be curious about.

'I want to know about his business, his friendships, his family, anything I can that will allow me to begin to understand what sort of a man he was.'

'You think that will help you learn who killed him?'

'It's the only way to learn why someone would want to kill him. After that, it's relatively easy to figure out who did.'

'You sound very optimistic.'

'No, I'm not,' Brunetti said, shaking his head. 'Not at all, and I won't be until I can begin to understand him.'

'And you think that by learning about his wife and daughter, you will?'

'Yes.'

The waiter reappeared at their left and set two cups of espresso and a silver sugar bowl down on the table between them. Each of them spooned two sugars into their small cups and stirred them round, allowing this ceremony to serve as a natural pause in the conversation.

After she sipped at the coffee and replaced the cup in her saucer, the doctor said, 'Signora Trevisan brought her daughter, who was then about fourteen, to see me a little more than a year ago. It was obvious that the girl didn't want her mother to know what was wrong with her. Signora Trevisan insisted she come into the examining room with her daughter, but I kept her out.' She flicked ash from her cigarette, smiled, and added, 'Not without difficulty.' She sipped again at her coffee; Brunetti said nothing to hasten her.

'The girl was suffering from a flare-up of genital herpes. I asked her the usual questions: whether her partner was using a prophylactic, whether she had other sexual partners, how long she had had the symptoms. With herpes, it's usually the first outbreak of the symptoms that's the worst, so I wanted to know if this was the first. Knowing that would help me assess the seriousness of the infection.' She stopped talking and crushed her cigarette into the ashtray on the table. When that was done, she took the ashtray and, without explanation, leaned aside to move it to the next table.

'And was it the first outbreak?'

'She said at first that it was, but it seemed to me that she was lying. I spent a long time explaining to her why I had to know, that I couldn't prescribe the right medicines unless I knew how serious the infection was. It took a while, but she finally told me that this was the second outbreak and that the first one had been much worse.'

'Why hadn't she gone to see you?'

'They were on vacation when it happened, and she was afraid, if she went to a different doctor, he'd tell her parents what was wrong with her.'

'How serious was that outbreak?'

'Fever, chills, genital pain.'

'What did she do?'

'She told her mother she had cramps and went to bed for two days.'

'And the mother?'

'What about her?'

'Did she believe it?'

'Apparently so.'

'And this time?'

'She told her mother that she had very bad cramps again and wanted to see me. I've been her doctor for about seven years, since she was a little girl.'

'Why did the mother come with her?'

She looked down into her empty coffee cup as she answered, 'Signora Trevisan has always been overly protective of her. When Francesca was smaller, her mother would call me if she had the least sign of fever. Some winters, she'd call me at least twice a month and ask me to go to the house to see her.'

'Did you?'

'In the beginning – I was new in my practice – I did, but then I gradually learned who would call only when they were really very sick and who would call . . . well, who would call for less than that.'

'Did Signora Trevisan call you for her own illnesses?'

'No, never. She'd come to the office.'

'For what?'

'That doesn't seem relevant to me, commissario,' she said, surprising him by the use of his title. He left it.

'What were the girl's answers to the other questions?'

'She said that her partner did not use prophylactics.

He said it would interfere with their pleasure.' She gave a crooked grimace, as if displeased to hear herself repeating such a self-serving cliché.

' "Partner", singular?'

'Yes, she said there was only one.'

'Did she tell you who he was?'

'I didn't ask. It's none of my business.'

'Did you believe her? That there was only one?'

'I saw no reason not to. As I told you, I've known her since she was a child. It seemed, from what I know of her, that she was telling me the truth.'

'And the magazine her mother threw at you?' Brunetti asked.

She glanced across at him, clearly surprised. 'Ah, my sister, when she tells a story, she tells it all, doesn't she?' But there seemed to be no real anger in her voice, only the grudging admiration that a lifetime with Elettra, Brunetti was sure, would command.

'That came later,' she began. 'When we came out of the examining room, Signora Trevisan demanded to know what was wrong with Francesca. I said it was a minor infection and would clear up soon. She seemed content with that, and they left the office.'

'How'd she find out?' Brunetti asked.

'The medicine. Zovirax, it's specific for herpes. There's no other reason she'd be taking it. Signora Trevisan has a friend who's a pharmacist, and she asked him – I'm sure she did it very, very casually – what the medicine was for. He told her. It isn't used for anything else, or very rarely. The next day, she was back in my office, without Francesca, and she made some offensive remarks.' She stopped.

'What sort of remarks?'

'She accused me of having arranged an abortion for Francesca. I told her to get out of the *ambulatorio*, and that was when she picked up the magazine and threw it at me. Two of my patients, elderly men, took her by the arms and put her out of the office. I haven't seen her since then.'

'And the girl?'

'As I told you, I've seen her once or twice on the street, but she's no longer my patient. I had a request from another doctor to verify my diagnosis, which I did. I'd already sent both of their records back to Signora Trevisan.'

'Have you any idea where or how she might have got the idea you arranged an abortion?'

'No, none. I couldn't do it without her parents' consent, anyway.'

Brunetti's own daughter, Chiara, was the same age as Francesca had been: fourteen. He wondered how he or his wife would respond to news that she had a venereal infection. He shied away from the thought with something he realized was horror.

'Why are you reluctant to discuss Signora Trevisan's medical history?'

'I told you, because I don't think it's relevant.'

'And I've told you that anything might be relevant,' he said, trying to soften his tone, perhaps succeeding.

'If I told you she had a bad back?'

'If that were the case, then you wouldn't have hesitated to tell me in the first place.'

She said nothing for a moment and then shook her head. 'No. She was my patient, so I can't discuss anything I know.'

'Can't or won't?' Brunetti asked, all attempt at humour gone from his voice.

Her look was direct and even. 'Can't,' she repeated and then broke away her glance to look down at her watch. This time, it was Snoopy, he noticed. 'I've got one more house call to make before lunch.'

Brunetti knew this was a decision that could not be opposed. 'Thank you for your time and for what you've told me,' he said, meaning it. On a more personal note, he added, 'I'm surprised I didn't realize you and Elettra were sisters before this.'

'Well, she's five years younger than I am.'

'I wasn't thinking about appearance,' he said. In response to the inquisitive tilt of her chin, he added, 'Your character. It's very similar.'

Her smile was swift and broad. 'Many people have told us that.'

'Yes, I imagine they would,' Brunetti said.

For a moment, she said nothing, but then she laughed with real delight. Still laughing, she pushed back her chair and reached for her coat. He helped her with it, glanced at the sum on the bill, and dropped some money on to the table. She picked up her brown bag, and together they went out into the Piazza, there to discover it had grown even warmer.

'Most of my patients are sure this means it will be a

terrible winter,' she said, waving her arm to encompass both the Piazza and the light that filled it. They walked down the three low steps and started across the Piazza.

'If it were unnaturally cold, what would they say then?' Brunetti asked.

'Oh, they'd say the same thing, that it's a sure sign of a bad winter,' she answered casually, not at all troubled by the contradiction. Venetians both, they understood.

'We are a pessimistic people, aren't we?' Brunetti asked.

'We once had an empire. Now all we have,' she said, repeating the same gesture, again encompassing the Basilica, the *campanile* and, below it, Sansovino's Loggetta, 'all we have is this Disneyland. I think that's sufficient cause for pessimism.'

Brunetti nodded but said nothing. She hadn't persuaded him. The moments came rarely, but for him the city's glory still lived.

They parted at the foot of the *campanile*, she to see a patient who lived in Campo della Guerra and he to walk towards Rialto and, from there, home for lunch.

Chapter Eight

The shops were still open when he reached his neighbourhood, so he went into the corner grocery store and bought four glass bottles of mineral water. In a weak moment of ecological appeasement, Brunetti had agreed to take part in his family's boycott of plastic bottles, and so he had, like the rest of them – he had to give them that – developed the habit of stopping at the store each time he passed to pick up a few bottles. He sometimes wondered if the rest of them bathed in the stuff while he wasn't there, with such rapidity did it disappear.

At the top of the fifth flight, he set the bag of bottles down on the final step and fished out his keys. From inside, he heard the radio news, no doubt bringing an eager public up to date on the Trevisan murder. He pushed open the door, set the bottles down inside, and closed the door behind him. From the kitchen, he heard a voice intone, '. . . denies all knowledge of the charges made against him and points to twenty years of faithful service to the ex-Christian Democratic Party as proof of his commitment to justice. From his cell in the Regina Coeli Prison, however, Renato Mustacci, confessed Mafia killer, still maintains that he was following the Senator's orders when he and two other men shot and killed Judge Filippo Preside and his wife, Elvira, in Palermo in May of last year.'

The solemn voice of the announcer was replaced by a song about soap powder, over which he could hear Paola talking aloud to herself, often her preferred audience. 'Filthy, lying pig. Filthy lying DC pig and all like him. "Commitment to justice. Commitment to justice." ' There followed one of the more scurrilous epithets to which his wife was given, strangely enough, only when she spoke to herself.

She heard him coming down the hall and turned to him. 'Did you hear that, Guido? Did you hear that? All three of the killers have said he sent them to kill the judge, and he talks about his commitment to justice. They ought to take him out and hang him. But he's a Member of Parliament, so they can't touch him. Lock the whole lot of them up. Just put Parliament, every one of them, in prison and save us all a lot of time and trouble.'

Brunetti walked across the kitchen and stooped down to put the bottles in the low cabinet beside the refrigerator. There was only one other bottle there, though he had carried five up the day before. 'What's for lunch?' he asked.

She took a small step backwards and shot an accusing finger at his heart. 'The Republic's collapsing, and all he can think about is food,' she said, this time addressing the invisible listener who had, for more than twenty years, been a silent participant in their marriage.

'Guido, these villains will destroy us all. Perhaps they already have. And you want to know what's for lunch.'

Brunetti stopped himself from remarking that someone wearing cashmere from Burlington Arcade made not the best revolutionary and, instead, said, 'Feed me, Paola, and then I'll go back to my own commitment to justice.'

That was enough to remind her of Trevisan and, as Brunetti knew she would, Paola eagerly abandoned her philosophical fulminations for a bit of gossip. She turned off the radio and asked, 'Has he given it to you?'

Brunetti nodded as he pushed himself up from his knees. 'He observed that I had nothing much to do at the moment. The Mayor has already called, so I leave it to you to imagine the state he's in.' There was no need to provide explication of 'it' or 'he'.

As Brunetti knew she would be, Paola was diverted from considerations of political justice and rectitude. 'The story I read said nothing more than that he had been shot. On the train from Torino.'

'He had a ticket from Padua. We're trying to find out what he was doing there.'

'A woman?'

'Could be. Too early yet to say anything. What's for lunch?'

'Pasta fagioli and then cotoletta.'

'Salad?'

'Guido,' she asked with pursed lips and upraised eyes, 'when haven't we had salad with cutlets?'

Instead of answering her question, he asked, 'Is there any more of that good Dolcetto?'

'I don't know. We had a bottle of it last week, didn't we?'

He muttered something and knelt back down in front of the cabinet. Behind the bottles of mineral water were three bottles of wine, all white. Getting to his feet again, he asked, 'Where's Chiara?'

'In her room. Why?'

'I want her to do me a favour.'

Paola glanced at her watch. 'It's a quarter to one, Guido. The stores will be closed.'

'Not if she goes up to Do Mori. They're open until one.'

'And you're going to ask her to go up there, just to get you a bottle of Dolcetto?'

'Three,' he said, leaving the kitchen and going down the hall towards Chiara's room. He knocked at the door and, from behind him, heard the radio turned on.

'*Avanti, Papà,*' she called out.

He opened the door and walked in. The bed, across which Chiara sprawled, had a white ruffled canopy running above it. Her shoes lay on the floor, next to her school bag and jacket. The shutters were open, and light swept into the room, illuminating the bears and other stuffed animals which shared the bed with her. She brushed a handful of dark blonde hair back from her face, looked up at him, and gave him a smile that competed with the light.

'*Ciao, dolcezza,*' he said as he came in.

'You're home early, Papà.'

54

'No, right on time. You been reading?'

She nodded, glancing back at her book.

'Chiara, would you do me a favour?'

She lowered the book and peered at him over the top of the pages.

'Would you, Chiara?'

'Where?' she asked.

'Just down to Do Mori.'

'What are we out of?' she asked.

'Dolcetto.'

'Oh, Papà, why can't you drink something else with lunch?'

'Because I want Dolcetto, sweetie.'

'I'll go if you'll come with me.'

'But then I might as well go by myself.'

'If you want to do that, then just go, Papà.'

'I don't want to go, Chiara. That's why I'm asking you to go for me.'

'But why should I go?'

'Because I work hard to support you all.'

'Mamma works, too.'

'Yes, but my money pays for the house and everything we buy for it.'

She set her book face down on the bed. 'Mamma says that's capitalistic blackmail and I don't have to listen to you when you do it.'

'Chiara,' he said, speaking very softly, 'your mother is a troublemaker, a malcontent, and an agitator.'

'Then how come you always tell me I have to do what she says?'

He took a very deep breath. Seeing that, Chiara slid

55

to the edge of the bed and fished for her shoes with her toes. 'How many bottles do you want?' she asked truculently.

'Three.'

She bent down and tied her shoes. Brunetti reached out a hand and caressed her head, but she pulled herself to one side to avoid him. When her shoes were tied, she stood and snatched her jacket up from the floor. She walked past him, saying nothing, and started down the hall. 'Ask your mother for the money,' he called to her and went down the hall to the bathroom. While he was washing his hands, he heard the front door slam.

Back in the kitchen, Paola was busy setting the table, but only for three. 'Where's Raffi?' Brunetti asked.

'He's got an oral exam this afternoon, so he's spending the day in the library.'

'What's he going to eat?'

'He'll get some sandwiches somewhere.'

'If he's got an exam, he should have a good meal first.'

She looked across the room at him and shook her head.

'What?' he asked.

'Nothing.'

'No, tell me. What are you shaking your head for?'

'I wonder, at times, how it was I married such an ordinary man.'

'Ordinary?' Of all the insults Paola had hurled at him over the years, this one somehow seemed the worst. 'Ordinary?' he repeated.

She hesitated for a moment, then launched herself

into an explanation. 'First you try to blackmail your daughter into going out to buy wine she doesn't drink, and then you worry that your son doesn't eat. Not that he doesn't study, but that he doesn't eat.'

'What should I worry about if not that?'

'That he doesn't study,' Paola shot back.

'He hasn't done anything but study for the last year, that and moon about the house, thinking about Sara.'

'What's Sara got to do with it?'

What did any of this, Brunetti wondered, have to do with it.

'What did Chiara say?' he asked.

'That she offered to go if you'd go with her, but you refused.'

'If I had wanted to go, I would have gone myself.'

'You're always saying you don't have enough time to spend with the children, and when you get the chance, you don't want to.'

'Going to a bar to buy a bottle of wine isn't exactly how I want to spend time with my children.'

'What is, sitting around the table and explaining to them the way money gives people power?'

'Paola,' he said, enunciating all three of the syllables slowly, 'I have no idea what any of this is about, but I'm fairly sure it doesn't have anything to do with sending Chiara to the store.'

She shrugged and turned back to the large pot that was boiling on the stove.

'What is it, Paola?' he asked, staying where he was but reaching out to her with his voice.

She shrugged again.

57

'Tell me, Paola. Please.'

She kept her back to him and spoke in a soft voice. 'I'm beginning to feel old, Guido. Raffi's got a girl-friend, and Chiara's almost a woman. I'll be fifty soon.' He marvelled at her maths but said nothing. 'I know it's stupid, but I find it depressing, as if my life were all used up, the best part gone.' Good lord, and she called him ordinary?

He waited, but it seemed she had finished.

She took the lid off the pot and was, for a moment, enveloped in the cloud of steam that spilled up from it. She took a long wooden spoon and stirred at whatever was in the pot, managing to look anything but witchlike as she did it. Brunetti tried, with very little success, to strip his mind clear of the love and familiarity of more than twenty years and look at her objectively. He saw a tall, slender woman in her early forties with tawny blonde hair that spilled down to her shoulders. She turned and shot him a glance, and he saw the long nose and dark eyes, the broad mouth which had, for decades, delighted him.

'Does that mean I get to trade you in?' he risked.

She fought the smile for an instant but then gave in to it.

'Am I being a fool?' she asked.

He was about to tell her that, if she was, it was no more than he was accustomed to when the door burst open and Chiara launched herself back into the apartment.

'Papà,' she shouted from down the hall, 'you didn't tell me.'

'Tell you what, Chiara?'

'About Francesca's father. That somebody killed him.'

'You know her?' Brunetti asked.

She came down the hall, cloth bag hanging from one hand. Obviously, curiosity about the murder had driven her anger with Brunetti from her mind. 'Sure. We went to school together. Are you going to look for whoever did it?'

'I'm going to help,' he said, unwilling to open himself to what he knew would turn into unrelenting questioning. 'Did you know her very well?'

'Oh, no,' she said, surprising him by not claiming to have been her best friend and, as such, somehow privy to whatever he might learn. 'She hung around with that Pedrocci girl, you know, the one who had all those cats at home. She smelled, so no one would be her friend. Except Francesca.'

'Did Francesca have other friends?' Paola asked, interested herself now and hence willingly complicit in her husband's attempt to pry information from their own child. 'I don't think I ever met her.'

'Oh, no, she never came back here with me. Anyone who wanted to play with her had to go back to her house. Her mamma insisted on that.'

'Did the girl with all the cats go?'

'Oh, yes. Her father's a judge, so Signora Trevisan didn't mind that she smelled.' Brunetti was struck by how clearly Chiara saw the world. He had no idea in which direction Chiara would travel, but he had no doubt that she would go far.

'What's she like, Signora Trevisan?' Paola asked and then shot a glance toward Brunetti, who nodded. It had been gracefully done. He pulled out a chair and silently took a place at the table.

'Mamma, why don't you let Papà ask these questions since he's the one who wants to know about her?' Without waiting for her mother's lie, Chiara walked across the kitchen and folded herself into Brunetti's lap, placing the now forgotten, or forgiven, bottles on the table in front of them. 'What do you want to know about her, Papà?' Well, at least she hadn't called him Commissario.

'Anything you can remember, Chiara,' he answered. 'Maybe you could tell me why everyone had to go and play at their house.'

'Francesca wasn't sure, but once, about five years ago, she said she thought it was because her parents were afraid that someone would kidnap her.' Even before Brunetti or Paola could comment on the absurdity of this, Chiara continued, 'I know, that's stupid. But that's what she said. Maybe she was just making it up to make herself sound important. No one paid any attention to her, anyway, so she stopped saying it.' She turned her attention to Paola and asked, 'When's lunch, Mamma? I'm starved, and if I don't eat soon, I'll faint,' whereupon she did just that, collapsing and sliding down towards the floor, only to be saved by Brunetti, who instinctively wrapped both arms around her and pulled her back towards him.

'Fake,' he whispered in her ear and began to tickle her, holding her prisoner with one arm while he poked

60

and prodded her side, running his fingers up and down her ribs.

Chiara shrieked and waved her arms in the air, gasping with shock and delight. 'No, Papà. No, let me go. Let me . . .' The rest was lost in high peals of laughter.

Order was restored before lunch, but only just. By tacit adult agreement, they asked Chiara no more questions about Signora Trevisan and her daughter. Throughout the meal, much to Paola's disapproval, Brunetti continued to reach an occasional, sudden hand out to Chiara, in her usual place beside him. Each motion brought on new peals of gleeful fear and left Paola wishing she had sufficient authority to send a commissario of police to his room without lunch.

Chapter Nine

A well-fed Brunetti left the house directly after lunch and walked back to the Questura, stopping along the way for a coffee in the hopes that it would pull him out of the sleepiness induced by good food and the continuing warmth of the day. Back in his office, he pulled off his coat and hung it up, then went over to his desk to see what had arrived during his absence. As he hoped, the autopsy report was there, not the official one but one that must have been typed by Signorina Elettra from notes dictated over the phone.

The pistol that killed Trevisan was of small calibre, a .22 target pistol, not a heavy weapon. As had been surmised before, one of the bullets had severed the artery leading from Trevisan's heart, so death had been virtually instantaneous. The other had lodged in his stomach. It would appear, from the entrance wounds, that whoever shot him had been standing no more than a metre from him and, from the angle, it would seem that Trevisan had been sitting when he was shot, his killer standing above him and to his right.

Trevisan had eaten a full meal shortly before he was killed, had drunk a moderate amount of alcohol, certainly not enough to fuddle his senses in any way.

A bit overweight, perhaps, Trevisan appeared to have been in good health for a man of his age. There were no signs of his ever having had a serious illness, though his appendix had been removed, and he had had a vasectomy. The pathologist saw no reason why he would not have lived, barring serious illness or accident, at least another twenty years.

'Two decades stolen,' Brunetti said under his breath when he read that and thought of the vast expanse of things a man could do with twenty years of life: watch a child mature, even watch a grandchild grow; achieve success in business; write a poem. And Trevisan would now never have the chance to do any of these things, to do anything at all. One of the most savage elements in murder, Brunetti had always believed, was the way it mercilessly cut off possibility and stopped the victim from ever again achieving anything. He had been raised a Catholic, so he was also aware that, to many people, the greatest horror lay in the fact that the victim was prevented the chance to repent. He remembered the passage in the *Inferno* where Dante speaks to Francesca da Rimini and hears her tell him how she was 'torn unshriven to my doom'. Though he did not believe, he was not untouched by the magic of belief, and so he realized what a fearful prospect this would be for many men.

Sergeant Vianello knocked on the door and came in, one of the Questura's plain blue folders in his right hand. 'This man was clean,' he said without introduction and placed the folder on Brunetti's desk. 'As far as we're concerned, he might as well never have existed.

The only record any of us has for him is his passport, which he renewed – ' Vianello began and then opened the folder to check the date. 'Four years ago. Aside from that, nothing.'

In itself, this was not surprising: many people managed to go through their entire lives without ever coming to the attention of the police until they became the occasional victims of random violence: drunk drivers, robbery and assault, the panic of a burglar. Few of them, however, were ever the victims of what appeared so strongly to be a professional murder.

'I have an appointment to speak to his widow this afternoon,' Brunetti said. 'At four.'

Vianello nodded. 'There's nothing on the immediate family, either.'

'Strange, wouldn't you say?'

Vianello considered this and answered, 'It's normal enough that people, even a whole family, might never come to our attention.'

'Then why does it feel so strange?' Brunetti asked.

'Because the pistol was a .22 calibre?' They both knew it was the gun used by many professional killers.

'Any chance of tracing it?'

'Beyond the type, not much,' Vianello said. 'I've sent a copy of the information on the bullets to Rome and Geneva.' They both also knew how unlikely this was to produce any useful information.

'At the railway station?'

Vianello repeated what the officers had learned the night before. 'Doesn't help much, does it, dottore?'

Brunetti shook his head, then asked, 'What about his office?'

'By the time I got there, most of them had left for lunch. I spoke to one secretary, who was actually in tears, and to the lawyer who seemed to have taken charge,' Vianello said, paused a moment, and added, 'who was not.'

'In tears?' Brunetti asked, looking up and looking interested.

'Yes. Not in tears. In fact, he seemed relatively undisturbed by Trevisan's death.'

'What about the circumstances?'

'That it was murder?'

'Yes.'

'That seemed to unsettle him. I got the impression that he didn't much care for Trevisan, but that the fact he was murdered shocked him.'

'What did he say?'

'Nothing, really,' Vianello answered and then explained. 'It was all in what he didn't say, all those things we say when someone dies, even if we didn't like them: that it was a tremendous loss, that he felt great sympathy for the family, that no one could replace him.' He and Brunetti had heard these responses for years, so often that they were no longer surprised when they realized that the speaker was lying. What remained surprising, however, was for someone not to bother to say these things at all.

'Anything else?' Brunetti asked.

'No. The secretary said the entire staff would be at work tomorrow — they'd been told they didn't have to go back this afternoon, out of respect – so I'll go back and talk to them then.' Before Brunetti could ask, Vianello said, 'I called Nadia and told her to ask around. She didn't know him, but she thinks he might once have handled – this is at least five years ago – the will of that man who had the shoe store on Via Garibaldi. She's going to call the widow. And she said she'd ask in the neighbourhood.'

Brunetti nodded at this. Though Vianello's wife was not on the payroll, she was often an excellent source of the kind of information that was never entered in official files. 'I'd like to do a financial check on him,' Brunetti said. 'The usual things: bank accounts, tax returns, property. And see if you can get an idea of the law practice, how much it brings in a year.' Though these were routine questions, Vianello made note of them.

'Should I ask Elettra to see what she can find?' Vianello asked.

This question always conjured up in Brunetti the image of Signorina Elettra, swathed in heavy robes and wearing a turban – the turban was always brocade, with heavy encrustations of opulent stones pinned to the front – peering into the screen of her computer, from which rose a thin column of smoke. Brunetti had no idea how she did it, but she invariably managed to ferret out financial, and often personal, information about victims and suspects which surprised even their families and business associates. Brunetti was of the opinion that no one could elude her and sometimes wondered – or was it worried? – that she would use her not inconsiderable powers to have a look into the private lives of the people with whom and for whom she worked.

'Yes, see what she can come up with. I'd also like a list of his clients.'

'All of them?'

'Yes.'

Vianello nodded and made another note, though he knew how difficult this would be: it was almost impossible to get lawyers to name their clients. The only people who gave the police more trouble on this front were whores.

'Anything else, sir?'

'No. I'll see the widow in,' he began, looking at his watch, 'a half-hour. If she tells me anything that we can use, I'll come back here; otherwise, I'll see you tomorrow morning.'

Taking this as leave to go, Vianello put his notebook back in his pocket, got to his feet, and went back down to the second floor.

Brunetti left the Questura five minutes later and started up towards Riva degli Schiavoni, where he got on to the No. 1 vaporetto. He got off at Santa Maria del Giglio, made a left at the Hotel Ala, crossed two bridges, cut to his left, down a small *calle* that led to the Grand Canal, and stopped at the last door on the left. He rang the bell marked 'Trevisan', and when the door clicked open, walked up to the third floor.

At the top of the stairs, a door stood open, and in it stood a grey-haired man with a substantial stomach expertly disguised by the expensive cut of his suit. As

Brunetti reached the top of the stairs, the man asked, without extending his hand, 'Commissario Brunetti?'

'Yes. Signor Lotto?'

The man nodded but still did not extend his hand. 'Come in, then. My sister is waiting for you.' Though Brunetti was three minutes early, the man managed to make it sound like Brunetti had kept the widow waiting.

The entrance hall was lined on both sides with mirrors and gave the illusion that the small area was crowded with many duplicates of Brunetti and Signora Trevisan's brother. The floor was patterned with gleaming squares of alternating black and white marble, inducing in Brunetti the feeling that he and his reflection were moving about on a chess board and thus forcing him to view the other man as an opponent.

'I appreciate Signora Trevisan's agreeing to see me,' Brunetti said.

'I told her not to,' her brother said brusquely. 'She shouldn't see anyone. This is terrible.' The look he gave Brunetti made him wonder if the man was referring to Trevisan's murder or Brunetti's presence in the house of mourning.

Cutting in front of Brunetti, the other man led him down another corridor and into a small room off to the left. It was difficult to tell what purpose the room was meant to serve: there were no books, no television, and the only chairs in the room were straight-backed and stood in the four corners. Two windows on one wall were covered with dark green drapes. In the centre stood a round table and on it a vase of dried flowers. Nothing more and no clue as to purpose or function.

'You can wait here,' Lotto said and left the room. Brunetti stood still for a moment, then walked over to one of the windows and pulled back the drape. Beyond him lay the Grand Canal, sunlight playing on its surface, and off to the left Palazzo Dario, the golden tiles of the mosaic that covered its façade catching the light that shot up from the water below, only to shatter it into fragments and sprinkle it back on the waters of the canal. Boats floated by; minutes went with them.

He heard the door behind him open, and he turned to greet the widow Trevisan. Instead, a young girl with dark hair that fell to her shoulders came into the room, saw Brunetti standing by the window, pulled back, and left as quickly as she had entered, pulling the door closed behind her. A few minutes after this, the door was opened again, but this time it was a woman in her early forties who came into the room. She wore a simple black woollen dress and shoes with heels that raised her almost to Brunetti's height. Her face was the same shape as the girl's, her hair also shoulder length and the same dark brown, though the woman's colour showed signs of assistance. Her eyes, wide-spaced like her brother's, were bright with intelligence and what Brunetti thought was curiosity rather than unshed tears.

She came across the room to Brunetti and extended her hand. 'Commissario Brunetti?'

'Yes, signora. I'm sorry we have to meet in circumstances such as these. I'm very grateful you consented to speak to me.'

'I want to do anything that will help you find Carlo's murderer.' Her voice was soft, the accent slightly brushed with the swallowed aspirants of Florence.

She looked around her, as if noticing the room for the first time. 'Why did Ubaldo put you in here?' she asked, then added, turning towards the door, 'Come with me.'

Brunetti followed her out into the corridor, where she turned right and opened another door. He followed her into a much larger room, this one with three windows that looked back up towards Campo San Maurizio and which appeared to be an office or a library. She led him towards two deep armchairs and took her place in one, indicating the second with her hand.

Brunetti sat, started to cross his legs, but realized the chair was too low to make that comfortable. He propped both elbows on the arms of the chair and joined his hands across his stomach.

'What is it you'd like me to tell you, commissario?' Signora Trevisan asked.

'I'd like you to tell me if, during the last few weeks, months perhaps, your husband seemed in any way uncomfortable or nervous or if his behaviour had changed in any way that seemed peculiar to you.'

She waited to see if there was anything else to the question, and when there seemed not to be, she paused for a moment, considering. Finally, she answered, 'No, I can't think of anything. Carlo was always very much caught up in his work. What with the political changes of the last few years, the opening up of new markets, he's been especially busy. But, no, during the last few

70

months he hasn't been nervous in any special way, not more than his work would normally warrant.'

'Did he ever speak to you about any case he was working on, or perhaps a client, which gave him particular trouble or caused him undue concern?'

'No, not really.'

Brunetti waited.

'He had one new client,' she finally said. 'A Dane who was trying to open an import business – cheese and butter, I think – who found himself caught up in the new EC regulations. Carlo was trying to find a way for him to transport his products through France, rather than through Germany. Or perhaps it was the other way. He was very busy with this, but I can't say that he was upset about it.'

'And at work? What were his relations with his employees like? Peaceful? Friendly?'

She joined her hands together in her lap and looked down at them. 'I think so. He certainly never mentioned having trouble with any of his staff. If he had, I'm sure he would have told me.'

'Is it true that the firm was entirely his, that the other lawyers were all salaried employees?'

'Excuse me?' she asked, giving him a puzzled glance. 'I'm afraid I don't understand the question.'

'Did your husband share the proceeds of his law practice with the other lawyers or did they work for him, as salaried employees?'

She looked up from her hands and glanced across at Brunetti. 'I'm afraid I can't answer that question,

Dottor Brunetti. I know almost nothing about Carlo's business. You'd have to speak to his accountant.'

'And who is that, signora?'

'Ubaldo.'

'Your brother?'

'Yes.'

'I see,' Brunetti replied. After a short pause, he continued, 'I'd like to ask you some questions about your personal life, signora.'

'Our personal life?' she repeated, as though she had never heard of such a thing. When he didn't answer this, she nodded, signalling him to begin.

'Could you tell me how long you and your husband were married?'

'Nineteen years.'

'How many children do you have, signora?'

'Two. Claudio is seventeen, and Francesca is fifteen.'

'Are they in school in Venice, signora?'

'She looked up at him sharply when he asked this. 'Why do you want to know that?'

'My own daughter, Chiara, is fourteen, so perhaps they know one another,' he answered and smiled to show what an innocent question it had been.

'Claudio is in school in Switzerland, but Francesca is here. With us. I mean,' she corrected, rubbing a hand across her forehead, 'with me.'

'Would you say yours was a happy marriage, signora?'

'Yes,' she answered immediately, far faster than Brunetti would have answered the same question, though he would have given the same response. She did not, however, elaborate.

'Could you tell me if your husband had any particularly close friends or business associates?'

She looked up at this question, then as quickly down again at her hands. 'Our closest friends are the Nogares, Mirto and Graziella. He's an architect who lives in Campo Sant' Angelo. They're Francesca's godparents. I don't know about his business associates: you'll have to ask Ubaldo.'

'Other friends, signora?'

'Why do you need to know all this?' she said, voice rising sharply.

'I'd like to learn more about your husband, signora.'

'Why?' The question leaped from her, almost as if beyond her volition.

'Until I understand what sort of man he was, I can't understand why this happened.'

'A robbery?' she asked, voice just short of sarcasm.

'It wasn't robbery, signora. Whoever killed him intended to do it.'

'No one could have a reason to want to kill Carlo,' she insisted. Brunetti, having heard this same thing more times than he cared to remember, said nothing.

Suddenly Signora Trevisan got to her feet. 'Do you have any more questions? If not, I would like to be with my daughter.'

Brunetti got up from the chair and put out his hand. 'Again, signora, I appreciate your having spoken to me. I realize what a painful time this must be for you and your family, and I hope you find the courage that will help you through it.' Even as he spoke the words, they sounded formulaic in his ears, the sort of thing that

73

got said in the absence of perceived grief, which was the case here.

'Thank you, commissario,' she said, giving his hand a quick shake and walking towards the door. She held it open for him, then walked along the corridor with him towards the front door of the apartment. There was no sign of the other members of the family.

At the door, Brunetti nodded to the widow as he left the apartment and heard the door close softly behind him as he started down the steps. It seemed strange to him that a woman could be married to a man for almost twenty years and know nothing about his business dealings. Stranger still, when her own brother was his accountant. What did they discuss at family dinners – soccer? Everyone Brunetti knew hated lawyers. Brunetti hated lawyers. He could not, consequently, believe that a lawyer, let alone a famous and successful one, had no enemies. Tomorrow he could discuss this with Lotto and see if he proved to be any more forthcoming than his sister.

Chapter Ten

While Brunetti had been inside the Trevisan apartment, the sky had clouded over, and the shimmering warmth of the day had fled. He glanced at his watch and saw that it was not yet six, and so, if he chose, he could still go back to the Questura. Instead, he turned back towards the Accademia Bridge, crossed it, and headed up towards home. Halfway there, he stopped in a bar and asked for a small glass of white wine. He picked up one of the small pretzels on the bar, took a bite, but tossed the rest into an ashtray. The wine was as bad as the pretzel, so he left that, too, and continued towards home.

He tried to recall the expression on Francesca Trevisan's face when she had so suddenly appeared at the door, but he could remember no more than eyes flashing wide at the sight of him there. The eyes had been dry and had registered nothing more than surprise; she resembled her mother in absence of grief, as well as in feature. Had she been expecting someone else?

How would Chiara respond if he were to be killed? And Paola, would she be so easily capable of answering questions, were a policeman to come to ask about their personal life? Surely, Paola would not be able to say, as had Signora Trevisan, that she knew nothing about her husband's, her late husband's, professional life. It snagged in Brunetti's mind, this protestation of ignorance, and he couldn't let it go, nor could he believe it.

When he let himself into the apartment, the radar of years told him that it was empty. He went down to the kitchen, where he found the table littered with newspapers and what seemed to be Chiara's homework, papers covered with numbers and mathematical signs that made no sense at all to Brunetti. He picked up a sheet of paper and studied it, saw the neat, right-slanting hand of his younger child in a long series of numbers and signs that he thought might be, if memory served, a quadratic equation. Was this calculus? Trigonometry? It had been so long ago, and Brunetti had been so unsuited to mathematics that he could recall almost nothing of it, though surely he had gone through four years of it.

He put the papers aside and turned his attention to the newspapers, where Trevisan's murder competed for attention with yet another senator and yet another bribe. Years had passed since Judge Di Pietro handed down the first formal accusation, and still villains ruled the land. All, or what seemed like all, of the major political figures who had ruled the country since Brunetti was a child had been named in accusation, named again on different charges, and had even begun to name one another, and yet not one of them had been tried and sentenced, though the coffers of the state had been sucked dry. They'd had their snouts in the public trough for decades, yet nothing seemed strong enough – not public rage, not an upwelling of national disgust – to sweep them from power. He turned a page and saw photos of the two worst, the hunchback and the balding pig, and he flipped the paper closed with tired loathing. Nothing would change. Brunetti knew not a little about these scandals, knew where a lot of money had gone and who was likely next to be named, and the one thing he knew with absolute certainty was that nothing would change. Lampedusa had it right – things had to seem to change so that things could remain the same. There'd be elections; there'd be new faces and new promises, but all that would happen would be that different trotters would go into the trough, and new accounts would be opened in those discreet private banks across the border in Switzerland.

Brunetti knew this mood and almost feared it, this recurring certainty of the futility of everything he did. Why bother to put the boy who broke into a house in gaol when the man who stole billions from the health system was named ambassador to the country to which he had been sending the money for years? And what justice imposed a fine on the person who failed to pay the tax on the radio in his car when the manufacturer of that same car could admit to having paid billions of lire to the leaders of trade unions to see that they would prevent their members asking for pay rises, could admit it and remain free? Why arrest anyone for murder, or why bother to look for the person who murdered Trevisan, when the man who had for decades been the highest politician in the country stood accused of having ordered the murders of the few honest judges who had the courage to investigate the Mafia?

This bleak reverie was interrupted by Chiara's arrival. She slammed the apartment door and came in with a great deal of noise and a large pile of books. Brunetti watched as she went down to her room and emerged a few moments later without the books.

'Hello, angel,' he called down the hall. 'Would you like something to eat?' When wouldn't she, he asked himself.

'*Ciao*, Papà,' she called out and came down the hall, struggling to extricate herself from the sleeves of her coat and managing, instead, only to pull one of them completely inside out and trap her hand in it. As he watched, she tore her other hand free and reached to pull at the sleeve. He glanced away and, when he looked back, the coat lay in a heap on the floor, and Chiara was bending to pick it up.

She came into the kitchen and tilted her face up to him, expecting a kiss, which he gave her.

She went over and opened the refrigerator, stooped down to see into it, reached into the back and pulled out a paper-wrapped wedge of cheese. She stood, took a knife from a drawer, and cut herself a thick slice.

'Want some bread?' he asked, pulling a bag of rolls down from the top of the refrigerator. She nodded, and they did a trade, he getting a thick wedge of cheese in exchange for two of the rolls.

'Papà,' she began, 'how much do policemen get paid an hour?'

'I don't know exactly, Chiara. They get a salary, but

sometimes they have to work more hours a week than people who work in offices do.'

'You mean if there's a lot of crime, or they have to follow someone?'

'*Sì.*' He nodded toward the cheese, and she cut him another piece, handing it to him silently.

'Or if they spend time questioning people, suspects and things like that?' she asked, clearly not going to give this up.

'*Sì,*' he repeated, wondering what she was getting at. She finished her second roll and put her hand into the bag for another.

'Mamma's going to kill you if you eat all the bread,' he said, a threat rendered almost sweet by years of repetition.

'But how much do you think it would work out to an hour, Papà?' she asked, ignoring him, as she sliced the roll in two.

He decided to invent, knowing that, whatever sum he named, he was going to end up being asked for it. 'I'd say it isn't more than about 20,000 lire an hour.' Then, because he knew he was meant to, he asked, 'Why?'

'Well, I knew you'd be interested to know about Francesca's father, so I asked some questions about him today, and I thought that, since I was doing the police's work, they should pay me for my time.' It was only when he saw signs of venality in his children that Brunetti regretted Venice's thousand-year-old trading heritage.

He didn't answer her, so Chiara was forced to stop eating and look at him. 'Well, what do you think?'

He gave it some thought and then answered, 'I think it would depend on what you found out, Chiara. It's not as if we'd be paying you a salary, regardless of what you did, as we do with the real police. You'd be a sort of private contractor, working freelance, and we'd pay you in relation to the value of what you brought us.'

She considered this for a moment and appeared to see the sense of it. 'All right. I'll tell you what I found out, and then you tell me how much you think it's worth.'

Not without admiration, Brunetti noted the skill with which she had evaded the critical question of whether he would be willing to pay for the information in the first place and had simply arrived at the point where the deal was already cut and only details remained to be worked out. Well, all right.

'Tell me.'

All business now, Chiara finished the last of the third roll, wiped her hands on a kitchen towel, and sat at the table, hands folded in front of her. 'I had to talk to four different people before I really learned anything,' she began, as serious as if she were giving testimony in court. Or on television.

'Who were they?'

'One was a girl at the school where Francesca is now; one was a teacher at my school, and a girl there, too, and the other was one of the girls we used to go to grammar school with.'

'You managed all of this today, Chiara?'

'Oh, sure. I had to take the afternoon off, to go see Luciana, and then go over to Francesca's school to talk to that girl, but I talked to the teacher and the girl at my school before I left.'

'You took the afternoon off?' Brunetti asked, but merely out of curiosity.

'Sure, the kids do it all the time. All you have to do is give them a note from one of your parents, saying you're sick or have to go somewhere, and no one ever asks questions.'

'Do you do this often, Chiara?'

'Oh, no, Papà, only when I have to.'

'Who wrote the note?'

'Oh, it was Mamma's turn. Besides, her signature's much easier to do than yours.' As she spoke, she picked up the pieces of homework lying on the table and arranged them into a neat stack, then placed them to the side and glanced up at him, eager to continue with important things.

He pulled out a chair and sat facing her. 'And what did these people tell you, Chiara?'

'The first thing I learned was that Francesca had told this other girl the kidnapping story, too, and I think I remember that she told a bunch of us the same story when we were in grammar school, but that was five years ago.'

'How many years did you go to school with her, Chiara?'

'We did all of elementary school together. But then her family moved, and she went to the Vivaldi middle school. I see her occasionally, but we weren't friends or anything like that.'

'Was this girl she told the story to a good friend of hers?'

He watched Chiara draw her lips together at the question, and he said, 'Perhaps you'd better tell me all this in your own way.' She smiled.

'This girl I spoke to at my school knew her from middle school, and she said that Francesca told her that her parents had warned her always to be very careful who she spoke to and never to go anywhere with someone she didn't know. That's pretty much the same thing she told us about when we were at school with her.'

She glanced across at him, looking for approval, and he smiled at her, though this wasn't much more than what she had told them at lunch.

'I already knew this, so I figured I better go talk to someone at the school where she is now. That's why I had to take the afternoon off, so I'd be sure to find her.' He nodded. 'This girl told me that Francesca had a boyfriend. No, Papà, a real one. They're lovers and all.'

'Did she say who the boyfriend was?'

'No, she said Francesca wouldn't ever tell her his name, but she said he was older, in his twenties. Francesca said she wanted to run away with him, but he wouldn't do it, not till she was older.'

'Did the girl say why Francesca wanted to run away?'

'Well, not in so many words, but she had the feeling

it was her mother, that she and Francesca fought a lot, and that was why Francesca wanted to run away.'

'What about her father?'

'Oh, Francesca liked him a lot, said he was very good to her, only she never saw him much because he was always so busy.'

'Francesca has a brother, hasn't she?'

'Yes, Claudio, but he's away in school in Switzerland. That's why I talked to the teacher. She used to teach in the middle school where he went, before he went to Switzerland, and I thought I could get her to tell me something about him.'

'And did you?'

'Oh, sure. I told her I was Francesca's best friend and how worried Francesca was that Claudio was going to be upset about their father's death, being in Switzerland and all. I said I knew him, too; I even let her believe I had a crush on him.' She paused here and shook her head. 'Yuck, everybody, but everybody, says Claudio is a real creep, but she believed me.'

'What did you ask her?'

'I said Francesca wanted to know if the teacher could suggest how she should behave with Claudio.' When she saw Brunetti's surprise, Chiara added, 'Yes, I know it's stupid, and no one would ever ask that, but you know how teachers are, always wanting to tell you what to do with your life and how you should behave.'

'Did the teacher believe you?'

'Of course,' Chiara responded seriously.

Half joking, Brunetti said, 'You must be a good liar.'

'I am. Very good. Mamma's always believed it's

83

something we should learn to do well.' She didn't bother to look at Brunetti when she said this and continued, 'The teacher said that Francesca should bear in mind – that was her expression, "bear in mind", – that Claudio had always been fonder of his father than his mother, so this time would be very difficult for him.' She twisted up her face in disgust. 'Big deal, huh? I went halfway across the city to get that. And it took her a half-hour to tell me.'

'What did the other people tell you?'

'Luciana – I had to go all the way down to Castello to see her – she told me that Francesca really hates her mother, said that she was always pushing her father around, telling him what to do. She doesn't like her uncle much, either, says he thinks he's the boss of the family.'

'Pushing him around in what way?'

'She didn't know. But that's what Francesca told her, that her father always did what her mother said.' Before Brunetti could make a joke of this, Chiara added, 'It's not like with you and Mamma. She always tells you what to do, but you just agree with her and then do what you want to, anyway.' She glanced up at the clock on the wall and asked, 'Where do you think Mamma is? It's almost seven. What'll we do for dinner?' The second question, clearly, was the one with which Chiara was most concerned.

'Probably kept at the university, telling some student what to do with his life.' Before Chiara could decide whether to laugh or not, Brunetti suggested, 'If that's all the detecting you have to report to me, why don't

'Favero? The man who committed suicide?'

'Suicide?' della Corte asked. 'With four milligrams
Roipnal in his blood?'

Brunetti was immediately alert. 'What's the connec-
 with Trevisan?' he asked.

We don't know. But we ran a trace on all the
bers we found in his address book. That is, on all
umbers that were listed without names. Trevisan's
ne of them.'

ve you got the records yet?' Neither of them had
ify that Brunetti meant the record of all of the
ade from Favero's phone.

re's no record that he called either Trevisan's
r his home, at least not from his own phones.'
 why would he have the number?' Brunetti

 exactly what we were wondering.' Della
ne was dry.

many other numbers were listed without

One is the phone in a bar in Mestre. One is
one in Padua railway station. And the rest

 you mean, they don't exist?'
 don't exist as possible numbers anywhere

 checking it for other cities, other

t. Either they've got too many digits or
espond to any numbers in this country.'

we start getting dinner ready? That way, Mamma can
come home and find dinner ready for a change.'

'But how much is it worth?' Chiara wheedled.

Brunetti considered this for a moment. 'I'd guess
about thirty thousand,' he finally answered. Since it was
to come out of his pocket, that's all it would be, though
the information she'd given him about Signora Trevisan's pushing her husband around, should it prove true
and should it apply to his professional life, might be
worth inestimably more than that.

Chapter Eleven

The following day, the *Gazzettino* carried a front page article about the suicide of Rino Favero, one of the most successful accountants in the Veneto Region. Favero, it was reported, had chosen to drive his Rover into the two-car garage beneath his house, close the door of the garage, and leave the engine running, himself quietly stretched across the front seat. It was further stated that Favero's name was about to be revealed in the expanding scandal that was currently playing itself out in the corridors of the Ministry of Health. Though, by now, all of Italy was familiar with the accusation that the former Minister of Health had accepted immense bribes from various pharmaceutical companies and in return had allowed them to raise the prices of the medicines they manufactured, it was not common knowledge that Favero had been the accountant who handled the private finances of the president of the largest of these firms. Those who did know assumed that he had decided to imitate so many of the men named in this ever-spreading web of corruption; had chosen to preserve his honour by removing himself from accusation, guilt, and possible punishment. Few

seemed to question the proposition that hor
preserved in this manner.

The Padua police did not concern them
such speculation as to motive, for the a
formed on Favero's body revealed that, at
his death, his blood contained a suffic
of barbiturate to make driving, let alon
his garage and closing the door, imp
possible that he had taken the pills a
the garage. Why, then, was no bottle
in the car, and why were no barbit
found in the house? Subsequent m
ation of Favero's pockets revealed
contained the least trace of barb
information, however, was giver
Favero's death remained, at lea
sciousness, a suicide.

Three days after Favero's de
it five days after Trevisan's m
his office to hear the phone

'Brunetti,' he answered, l
hand and unbuttoning his

'Commissario Brunetti
of the Padua police.' B
vaguely, and with the se
about della Corte in
favour.

'Good morning,
'You can tell me
up in your investig
train.'

'They've got to be.'

'No indication of country code?'

'Two look like they're in Eastern Europe, and two could be in either Ecuador or Thailand, and don't ask me how the guys who told me know this. They're still working on the others,' della Corte answered. 'And he never called any of those numbers from either of his phones, either the foreign ones or the ones here in the Veneto.'

'But he had them,' Brunetti said.

'Yes, he had them.'

'He could easily call from a public phone,' Brunetti suggested.

'I know, I know.'

'What about other international calls? Any country he called often?'

'He called a lot of countries often.'

'International clients?' Brunetti asked.

'Some of the calls were to clients, yes. But a lot of them don't correspond to anyone he worked for.'

'What countries?' Brunetti asked.

'Austria, the Netherlands, and the Dominican Republic,' della Corte began, then added, 'Wait and I'll get the list.' The phone clunked down, Brunetti heard the rustle of papers, and then della Corte's voice returned. 'And Poland, Romania, and Bulgaria.'

'How often did he call?'

'Some of them twice a week.'

'The same number or numbers?'

'Often, but not always.'

'You trace them?'

'The Austrian number is listed as a travel agency in Vienna.'

'And the others?'

'Commissario, I don't know how familiar you are with Eastern Europe, but they don't even have phone books, let alone an operator who can tell you who a number belongs to.'

'The police?'

Della Corte let out a snort of contempt.

'Have you called the numbers?' Brunetti asked.

'Yes. No one answers.'

'None of them?'

'None of them.'

'What about the phone in the railway station and the bar?' Brunetti asked.

As an answer, he got another of those snorts, but then della Corte explained. 'I was lucky to get permission to trace the numbers.' Della Corte paused a long time, and Brunetti waited for the request he knew was coming. 'I thought that, as you're so much closer, you might be able to get someone to keep an eye on the phone in the bar.'

'Where is it?' Brunetti asked, taking a pen from his desk but being very careful not to promise anything.

'Does that mean you'll send someone?'

'I'll try,' Brunetti answered, the best he could do. 'Where is it?'

'All I have is a name and address. I don't know Mestre well enough to know where it is.' As far as Brunetti was concerned, Mestre was not a city worth knowing well enough to know where anything was.

'It's called Bar Pinetta. Via Fagare, number 16. You know where it is?' della Corte asked.

'Via Fagare's somewhere around the railway station, I think. But I've never heard of the bar.' Having agreed, sort of, to help with this, Brunetti thought he could ask for some information in return. 'Have you got any idea how they might be connected?'

'You know about the pharmaceuticals?' della Corte asked.

'Who doesn't?' Brunetti asked by way of answer. 'You think they might both be mixed up in that?'

Instead of answering directly, della Corte said, 'It's a possibility. But we want to start by checking all of his clients. He worked for a lot of people in the Veneto.'

'The right kind of people?'

'The very best kind of people. In the last couple of years, he'd begun to call himself a "consultant" instead of just an accountant.'

'Was he good?'

'He's said to have been the best.'

'Good enough to figure out the tax form then,' Brunetti suggested, hoping with the joke to create more fellow feeling with della Corte. All Italians, he knew, were united in their loathing of the tax office, but this year, with a tax form that numbered thirty-two pages and which the Minister of Finance had confessed himself unable to understand or complete, that loathing had reached new intensity.

Della Corte's muttered obscenity, though it certainly made clear his feelings about the tax office, did not speak over much of fellow feeling. 'Yes, it seems he was good enough even for that. I tell you, his list of clients would make most accountants sick with envy.'

'Did it include Medi-tech?' Brunetti asked, naming the largest of the companies embroiled in the current price-fixing scandal.

'No. It looks like he didn't have anything to do with their work for the Ministry. And his work for the Minister appears to have been entirely private, that is, on his personal income.'

'He wasn't involved in the scandal?' Brunetti asked, finding this even more interesting.

'Not that we can see.'

'Any other possible motive for . . .' Brunetti paused for a moment, then found the right word, 'For his death?'

Della Corte paused a moment before answering. 'We haven't turned up anything. He was married, thirty-seven years, apparently happily. Four children, all of them university graduates, and none of them, from what we can see, any cause of trouble.'

'Murder, then?'

'Most probably.'

'You going to give it to the press?'

'No, not until we have something else to tell them or unless one of them finds out about the coroner's report,' answered della Corte, making it sound like he would be able to prevent that from happening for some time.

'And when they find out?' Brunetti was leery of the press and its many violences upon the truth.

'I'll worry about that when it happens,' della Corte

said brusquely. 'Will you let me know if you find out anything about that bar?'

'Certainly. Can I call you at the Questura?'

Della Corte gave him the direct number to his office. 'And, Brunetti, if you find anything, don't give the information to anyone else who might answer my phone, all right?'

'Of course,' Brunetti agreed, though he found the request strange.

'And I'll call you if Trevisan's name comes up again. See if you can find out any way they might have been connected. A phone number isn't all that much.'

Brunetti agreed, though it was something, and as far as Trevisan's death was concerned, it was a good deal more than they had.

Della Corte's goodbye was abrupt, as if he had been called away to more important things.

Brunetti replaced the phone and sat back in his chair, trying to think of a connection that could link the Venetian lawyer to the accountant from Padua. Both men would have travelled in the same social and professional circles, so it was not at all to be wondered at if they knew one another or if one's address book listed the other's number. How odd, though, for it to be listed without a name, and what odd company for it to keep, two public phones and numbers in some foreign country. Odder still was the fact that the number should appear in the address book of a man who was murdered during the same week as Trevisan.

Chapter Twelve

Brunetti called down to Signorina Elettra to ask if SIP had yet responded to his request that they supply a record of all of Trevisan's phone calls for the last six months, only to learn that she had placed their report on his desk the previous day. He hung up and began to sort through the papers on the top of his desk, shoving aside personnel reports he had postponed completing for the last two weeks and a letter from a colleague with whom he had worked in Naples, too depressing to be reread or answered.

The phone records were there, a manila folder that contained what turned out to be fifteen sheets of computer print-out. He cast his eye down the first page and saw that only long-distance calls were noted, both from Trevisan's office and from his home. Each column began with the numerical city code or, where it applied, country code and then listed the number called, the time of the call, and its duration. In a separate column to the right were listed the names of the cities and countries to which those codes corresponded. Quickly, he paged through the report and saw that it listed only outgoing calls made from the phones and bore no listing of those received. Perhaps no request had been made, or perhaps SIP took longer to trace those, or perhaps, just as likely, some new bureaucratic nightmare had been invented for the processing of such a request, and the information would be delayed.

Brunetti ran his eyes down the column of cities on the right. No pattern appeared on the first pages, but by the fourth, he could see that Trevisan – or whoever had been calling from Trevisan's phones, as he was careful to remind himself – called three numbers in Bulgaria with some regularity, at least two or three times a month. The same was true of numbers in Hungary and Poland. He remembered that the first country had been named by della Corte, though the others had not been. Interspersed with these were calls to the Netherlands and England, these perhaps explained by the nature of Trevisan's law practice. The Dominican Republic appeared nowhere on the list, and the calls to Austria and the Netherlands, the other countries della Corte had mentioned, seemed not to have been made with any great frequency.

Brunetti had no idea now much of a lawyer's business would be handled by phone, so he had no idea if the list he was reading represented an inordinate number of phone calls.

He called down to the switchboard and asked to be connected to the number della Corte had given him. When the other policeman answered, Brunetti identified himself and asked to be given the numbers in Padua and Mestre that had been listed in Favero's address book.

After della Corte read them out to him, Brunetti

said, 'I've got a list of Trevisan's calls here, but only the long distance, so the Mestre number won't appear. You want to wait while I check it for the Padua number?'

'Ask me if I want to die in the arms of a sixteen-year-old,' della Corte said. 'You'll get the same answer.'

Taking that for a yes, Brunetti ran his eye down the list, pausing wherever he saw the 049 prefix of Padua. The first three pages revealed nothing, but then on the fifth, and again on the ninth, he saw the number. It disappeared for a time, and then appeared on the fourteenth page, called three times in the same week.

Della Corte's answer when Brunetti told him this was a low, two-syllable hum. 'I think I better get some-one to cover that phone in Padua.'

'And I'll get someone to go and have a look at the bar,' Brunetti said, interested now, eager to know what the bar was like, who frequented it, but most eager to get his hands on a list of Trevisan's local calls and see if the bar's number appeared on it.

Brunetti's long years and grim experience as a policeman had destroyed whatever belief he might ever have had in coincidence. A number that was known to two men who had been murdered within a few days of one another was not some random fact, some statistical curiosity to be commented on and then forgotten. The number in Padua had significance, though Brunetti had no idea what it was, and he was suddenly sure that the number of the bar in Mestre was going to appear on the list of Trevisan's local calls.

Promising to let della Corte know as soon as he learned anything about the phone in Mestre, he depressed the bar on the receiver and dialled Vianello's extension. When the sergeant answered, Brunetti asked him to come up to his office.

A few minutes later, Vianello came in. 'Trevisan?' he asked, meeting Brunetti's gaze with one of frank curiosity.

'Yes. I've just had a call from the police in Padua, about Rino Favero.'

'The accountant, the one who worked for the Minister of Health?' Vianello asked. When Brunetti nodded, Vianello burst out, speaking with real passion, 'They should all do it.'

Brunetti looked up, momentarily startled.

'Do what?' he asked.

'Kill themselves, the whole filthy lot of them.' As suddenly as he had erupted, Vianello subsided and sat in the chair in front of Brunetti's desk.

'What brought that on?' Brunetti asked.

Instead of answering, Vianello shrugged, waving one hand in the air in front of him.

Brunetti waited.

'It was the editorial in the *Corriere* this morning,' Vianello finally answered.

'Saying what?'

'That we should have pity on these poor men, driven to take their own lives by the shame and suffering imposed on them, that the judges should let them out of prison, return them to their wives and families. I forget the rest of it; just reading that much made me sick.' Brunetti remained silent, so Vianello continued. 'If someone who snatches a purse gets put in gaol, we

97

don't read editorials, at least not in the *Corriere*, begging that they be released or that we all feel sorry for them. And God knows how much these pigs have stolen. Your taxes. Mine. Billions, thousands of billions.' Suddenly conscious of how high his voice was rising, Vianello repeated the wave of his hand, brushing away his anger, and asked, in a far more moderate voice, 'What about Favero?'

'It wasn't suicide,' Brunetti said.

Vianello's look was frankly surprised. 'What happened?' he asked, his explosion apparently forgotten.

'He had so much barbiturate in him there was no way he could have driven.'

'How much?' Vianello asked.

'Four milligrams,' but before Vianello could tell him this was hardly a heavy dosage, he added, 'of Roipnol.' Vianello knew as well as did Brunetti that four milligrams would put either one of them to sleep for the next day and a half.

'What's the connection with Trevisan?' Vianello asked.

Like Brunetti, Vianello had long since lost his faith in coincidence, so he listened with fixed attention to the story of the phone number known to both of the dead men.

'The Padua railway station?' Vianello asked. 'Via Fagare?'

'Yes, it's a bar called Pinetta's. You know it?'

Vianello looked off to the side for a moment and then nodded. 'I think so, if it's the place I'm thinking of. Off to the left of the railway station?'

'I don't know,' Brunetti answered. 'I know it's near the railway station, but I've never heard of it.'

'Yes, I think it's this place. Pinetta's?'

Brunetti nodded, waiting for Vianello to say more.

'If it's the one I'm thinking of, it's pretty bad. Lots of North Africans, those 'vous compras' you see all over the place.' Vianello paused for a moment, and Brunetti prepared himself to hear some sort of slighting remark about these unlicensed vendors who crowded the streets of Venice, selling their imitation Gucci bags and African carvings. But Vianello surprised him by saying, instead, 'Poor devils.'

Brunetti had long since abandoned the hope of ever hearing anything like political consistency from his fellow citizens, but still he wasn't prepared for Vianello's sympathy for these immigrant street vendors, usually the most despised of the hundreds of thousands of people flooding into Italy in hopes of dining on the crumbs that fell under the table of the country's wealth. Yet here was Vianello, a man who not only voted for the Lega Nord but who argued strongly that Italy should be divided in half just north of Rome – in his wilder moments, he was known to call for the building of a wall to keep out the barbarians, the Africans, for they were all Africans south of Rome – here was Vianello calling these same Africans 'poor devils' and apparently meaning it.

Though the remark puzzled Brunetti, he didn't want to spend time talking about it now. So he asked, instead, 'Have we got someone who can go in there at night?'

'And do what?' Vianello asked, just as glad as Brunetti to avoid the other topic.

'Have a couple of drinks. Talk to people. See who uses the phone. Or answers it.'

'Someone who doesn't look like a cop, you mean?' Brunetti nodded.

'Pucetti?' Vianello suggested.

Brunetti shook his head. 'Too young.'

'And probably too clean,' Vianello added immediately.

'You make it sound like a nice place, Pinetta's.'

'It's the kind of place where I'd prefer to be wearing my gun,' Vianello said. Then, after a moment's reflection, he added, too casually, 'Sounds like the place for Topa,' mentioning a sergeant who had retired six months before, after thirty years with the police. Topa's real name was Romano, but no one had called him that for more than five decades, not since he was a child, small and round-bodied, looking just like the little baby mouse his nickname suggested. Even after he got his full growth and became so thick-chested that his uniform jackets had to be specially made, the name remained, wildly incongruous but no less unchangeable. No one ever laughed at Topa for having a nickname with a feminine ending. A number of people, during his thirty years of service, had tried to harm him, but no one had ever dared laugh at his nickname.

When Brunetti said nothing, Vianello glanced quickly up at him and then as quickly down. 'I know how you feel about him, commissario.' And then, before Brunetti had time to comment, 'He wouldn't even be working, at least not officially. He'd just be doing you a favour.'

'By going into Pinetta's?'

Vianello nodded.

'I don't like it,' Brunetti said.

Vianello continued. 'He'd just be a retired man, going into a bar for a drink, perhaps for a game of cards.' In the face of Brunetti's continuing silence, Vianello added, 'A retired policeman can go into a bar and have a game of cards if he wants to, can't he?'

'That's the thing I don't know,' Brunetti said.

'What?'

'Whether he'd want to.' Neither of them, it was clear, wanted to mention or saw any sense in bringing up the reasons for Topa's early retirement. A year ago, Topa had arrested the twenty-three-year-old son of a city councillor for molesting an eight-year-old school-girl. The arrest took place late at night, at the young man's home, and when the suspect arrived at the Questura, his left arm and his nose were broken. Topa insisted that the young man had attacked him in an attempt to escape; the young man maintained that Topa had stopped on the way to the Questura, pulled him into an alley, and beaten him.

The man at the desk when they arrived at the Questura that night tried, with no success, to describe the look that Topa gave the suspect when he began to tell this story. The young man never repeated it, and no official complaint was ever launched. But a week later word filtered down from Vice-Questore Patta's office that it was time for the sergeant to retire, and he did, losing out on a part of his pension by doing so. The young man was sentenced to two years of house arrest. Topa, who had one grandchild, a girl of seven, was never heard to speak of the arrest, his retirement, or the events surrounding it.

Refusing to acknowledge Brunetti's glance, Vianello asked, 'Should I call him?'

Brunetti hesitated for a moment and then said, with singular lack of good grace, 'All right.'

Vianello knew better than to smile. 'He's not back from work until eight. I'll call him then.'

'Work?' Brunetti asked, though he knew he shouldn't. The law forbade retired officers from working: if they did, they forfeited their pensions.

'Work,' Vianello repeated but said no more. He got to his feet. 'Will there be anything else, sir?' Brunetti remembered that Topa had been Vianello's partner for more than seven years and that the sergeant had wanted to quit when Topa was forced into retirement, persuaded away from that idea only by Brunetti's fierce opposition. Topa had never seemed to Brunetti the sort of man over whom a high moral position could be taken.

'No, nothing else. On your way down, would you ask Signorina Elettra to get on to the people at SIP and see if she can get the list of Trevisan's local calls from them?'

'Pinetta's isn't the sort of place an international lawyer would call,' Vianello said.

It didn't sound like the sort of place a successful accountant would call, either, but Brunetti chose not to volunteer this. 'The records will tell us,' he said blandly.

Vianello waited, but when Brunetti said nothing further, he went down to his office, leaving Brunetti to speculate on the reasons wealthy and successful men might have for making calls to public telephones, especially in a place as squalid as Pinetta's.

Chapter Thirteen

Dinner that night for the three of them was enlivened – Brunetti could think of no kinder word – by a heated confrontation between Chiara and her mother which blew up when Chiara told her father that, after school, she had gone back to do her maths homework at the home of the girl who was Francesca Trevisan's best friend.

Before Chiara could say any more than that, Paola slammed her hand down on the table. 'I will not live in the same house as a spy,' she shouted at her daughter.

'I'm not a spy,' Chiara answered sharply. 'I'm working for the police.' Then, turning to Brunetti, she asked, 'Aren't I, Papà?'

Ignoring her, Brunetti reached across the table and picked up the nearly empty bottle of Pinot noir.

'Well, aren't I?' Chiara insisted.

'It doesn't matter', her mother began, 'if you're working for the police or not. You can't go around trying to get information from your friends.'

'But Papà's always getting information from his friends, too. Does that mean he's a spy?'

Brunetti sipped at his wine and peered across the

top of his glass at his wife, curious how she would answer this.

Paola looked at him but spoke to Chiara. 'It's not that he gets information from his friends, it's that when he does it, they know who he is and why he's doing it.'

'Well, my friends know who I am and they ought to be able to figure out why I'm doing it,' Chiara insisted, her cheeks slowly suffusing with red.

'It's not the same thing, and you know it,' Paola answered.

Chiara muttered something that, to Brunetti, sounded like, 'Is so,' but her head was lowered over her empty plate, and so he wasn't sure.

Paola turned to Brunetti. 'Guido, would you please try to explain the difference to your daughter?' As ever, in the heat of argument, Paola, like some sort of negligent rodent, had sloughed off all claim to motherhood and abandoned the young thing to its father.

'Your mother's right,' he said. 'When I question people, they know I'm a policeman, and so they tell me things in knowledge of that fact. And they know that they can be held liable for what they say, so that allows them the chance to be cautious, if they want to be.'

'But don't you ever trick anyone?' Chiara asked. 'Or try to?' she added before he could answer.

'I'm sure I've done both,' he admitted. 'But remember, nothing that anyone says to you has any legal weight. They can always deny they said it, and then it would just be your word against theirs.'

'But why would I lie?'

'Why would they?' Brunetti returned.

'Who cares if what people say is legally binding or not?' Paola asked, jumping back into the fray. 'We're not talking about what's legally binding; we're talking about betrayal. And, if the people at this table will permit me the use of the word,' she said, looking at the two of them in turn, 'honour.'

Chiara, Brunetti observed, got one of those, 'Oh, here she goes again' looks on her face and turned to him for moral support, but he gave her none.

'Honour?' Chiara asked.

'Yes, honour,' Paola said, suddenly calm, but no less dangerous for that. 'You can't get information from your friends. You can't take what they say and make use of it against them.'

Chiara interrupted her here. 'But nothing Susanna said can be used against her.'

Paola closed her eyes for a moment, then picked up a piece of bread and began to crumble it into small pieces, something she often did when she was upset. 'Chiara, it doesn't matter what use ever gets made or doesn't get made of anything she told you. What cannot be done,' she began and then repeated the entire phrase, 'what cannot be done is to lead our friends on to say things to us when we are alone with them and then turn around and repeat that information or make some use of it that they didn't know we had in mind when they were talking to us. That's to betray a confidence.'

'You make it sound like a crime,' Chiara said.

'It's worse than a crime,' Paola shot back. 'It's wrong.'

'And crime isn't?' Brunetti asked from the sidelines.

106

She pounced. 'Guido, unless I invented them, we had three plumbers in the house last week, for two days. Can you produce a *ricevuto fiscale* for that work? Do you have some proof that the money we paid them will be reported to the government and taxes be paid on it?' When he said nothing, she insisted, 'Do you?' His silence continued. 'That's a crime, Guido, a crime, but I defy you or anyone in this stinking government of pigs and thieves we have to tell me that it's wrong.'

He reached for the bottle but it was empty.

'You want more?' Paola asked, and he knew she wasn't talking about the wine. He didn't particularly, but Paola was up on her soapbox now, and long experience told him that there was no getting her down until she had finished. He regretted only that he had finished the wine.

From the corner of his eye, he saw Chiara get out of her chair and go over to the cabinet. In a moment she was back with two small glasses and a bottle of grappa, which she slid silently across the table towards him. Her mother could call her whatever she pleased – traitor, spy, monster – to him, the child was an angel.

He saw Paola give Chiara a long look and was glad to see her eyes soften, however momentarily. He poured himself a small glass of grappa, sipped at it and sighed.

Paola reached across the table and picked up the bottle. She poured herself some and took a sip. The truce was held.

'Chiara,' Paola said, 'I don't mean to yell at you about this.'

'But you just did,' her ever-literal daughter replied.

'I know I did, and I'm sorry.' Paola took another sip. 'You know I feel strongly about this.'

'You get it from those books, don't you?' Chiara asked simply, managing to suggest that her mother's career as a professor of English Literature had somehow exerted a pernicious influence on her moral development.

Both of her parents sought sarcasm or disdain in her tone, but neither was there, nothing more than the desire for information.

'I suppose I do,' Paola admitted. 'They knew about honour, the people who wrote those books, and it was important to them.' She paused here and considered what she had just said. 'But it wasn't important just to them, the writers; their whole society thought some things were important: honour, a person's good name, one's word.'

'I think those things are important, Mamma,' Chiara said, sounding, as she spoke, far younger than she was.

'I know you do. And I do, and Raffi does, and your father does, too. But our world doesn't, not any more.'

'Is that why you like those books so much, Mamma?'

Paola smiled and, Brunetti thought, clambered down from her soapbox before she answered. 'I suppose so, *cara*. Besides, knowing about them gives me a job at the university.'

Brunetti's pragmatism had been butting itself against the various forms of Paola's idealism for more than two decades, so he believed that she looked to 'those books' for considerably more than a job.

'Do you have much homework tonight, Chiara?'

Brunetti asked, knowing that he could ask her later, or tomorrow morning, to tell him whatever she had learned from Francesca's friend. Seeing this as the dismissal it was, Chiara said that she had and went back to her own room to begin it, leaving her parents alone to continue to discuss, if they chose, honour.

'I didn't know she'd take my offer so seriously, Paola, and go out and start asking people questions,' Brunetti said by way of explanation and, at least partly, apology.

'I don't mind her getting the information,' Paola said. 'But I don't like the way she got it.' She took another sip of her grappa. 'Do you think she understood what I was trying to say?'

'I think she understands everything we say,' Brunetti answered. 'I'm not sure she agrees with a lot of it, but she certainly understands.' Then, going back to what she had said earlier, he asked, 'What other examples did you have of things that are criminal but not wrong?'

She rolled her small glass between her palms. 'I think that's too easy,' she said, 'especially given the insane laws in this country. The harder one to figure out is the things that are wrong but not criminal.'

'Like what?' he asked.

'Like letting your children watch television,' she said with a laugh, apparently tired of the subject.

'No, tell me, Paola,' he said, interested now. 'I'd like you to give me an example.'

Before she spoke, she pinged a fingernail against the glass bottle of mineral water that stood on the table. 'I know you're tired of hearing me say this, Guido, but I think plastic bottles are wrong, but they're certainly not criminal. Though', she quickly added, 'I think they will be within a few years. If we have any sense, that is.'

'I was hoping for a larger example,' Brunetti said.

She thought for a while and then answered. 'If we were to have raised the children to believe that my family's wealth gave them special privileges, that would be wrong.'

It surprised Brunetti that Paola would use this example: over the years, she had seldom alluded to her parents' wealth save, at those times when political discussion escalated into argument, to point to it as an example of social injustice.

They exchanged a look, but before Brunetti could say anything, Paola continued, 'I'm not sure it's all that much larger an issue, but I think if I were to speak slightingly of you, it would be wrong.'

'You always speak slightingly of me,' Brunetti said, forcing himself to smile.

'No, Guido, I speak slightingly *to* you. That's different. I would never say any of those things *about* you.'

'Because that's dishonourable?'

'Precisely,' she said, smiling.

'But it's not dishonourable to say them *to* me?'

'Of course not, especially if they're true. Because that's between us, Guido, and that doesn't belong, in any sense, to the world.'

He reached over and took back the grappa bottle. 'It seems to me it's getting harder and harder to tell the difference,' he said.

'Between what?'

'The criminal and the wrong.'

'Why do you think that is, Guido?'

'I'm not sure. Perhaps because, as you said before, we don't believe in the old things any more, and we haven't found anything new, anything else, to believe in.'

She nodded, considering this.

'And all the old rules have been broken,' he continued. 'For fifty years, ever since the end of the war, all we've ever been is lied to. By the government, the Church, the political parties, by industry and business and the military.'

'And the police?' she asked.

'Yes,' he agreed with no hesitation whatsoever. 'And the police.'

'But you want to stay with them?' she asked.

He shrugged and poured some more grappa. She waited. Finally he said, 'Someone's got to try.'

Paola leaned across the table and placed the palm of her hand against his cheek, tilting his face towards her. 'If I ever try to lecture you about honour again, Guido, hit me with a bottle, all right?'

He turned his head and kissed her palm. 'Not until you let me buy some plastic ones.'

Two hours later, as Brunetti sat yawning over Procopius' *Secret History*, the phone rang.

'Brunetti,' he answered and glanced down at his watch.

'Commissario, this is Alvise. He said to call you.'

'Who said to call me, Officer Alvise?' Brunetti asked,

fishing a used vaporetto ticket from his pocket and sticking it in the page to keep his place. Calls with Alvise had a tendency to be either long or confusing. Or both.

'The sergeant, sir.'

'Which sergeant, Officer Alvise?' Brunetti closed his book and set it aside.

'Sergeant Topa, sir.'

Alert now, Brunetti asked, 'Why did he tell you to call me?'

'Because he wants to talk to you.'

'Why didn't he call me himself, officer? My name is in the phone book.'

'Because he can't, sir.'

'And why can't he?'

'Because the rules say he can't.'

'What rules?' Brunetti asked, his growing impatience audible in his tone.

'The rules down here, sir.'

'Down here, where, officer?'

'At the Questura, sir. I'm on night duty.'

'What is Sergeant Topa doing there, officer?'

'He's been arrested, sir. The Mestre boys picked him up, but then they found out who he was, well, found out what he was. Or what he used to be. I mean a sergeant. Then they sent him back here, but they told him he could come in by himself. They called to tell us he was coming, but they let him get here by himself.'

'So Sergeant Topa has arrested himself?'

Alvise considered this for a moment and then answered, 'It would seem that way, sir. I don't know

112

how to fill out the report, where it says, "arresting officer".'

Brunetti held the phone away from his ear for a moment then brought it back and asked, 'What has he been arrested for?'

'He got into a fight, sir.'

'Where?' Brunetti asked, though he knew the answer even before he asked.

'In Mestre.'

'Who did he have the fight with?'

'Some foreigner.'

'And where's the foreigner?'

'He got away, sir. They had a fight, but then the foreigner got away.'

'How do you know he was a foreigner?'

'Sergeant Topa told me. He said the man had an accent.'

'If the foreigner ran away, who's filing the complaint against Sergeant Topa, officer?'

'I figured that's why the boys in Mestre sent him back to us, sir. They must have thought we'd know what to do.'

'Did the people in Mestre tell you to make out an arrest report?'

'Well, no, sir,' Alvise said after a particularly long pause. 'They told Topa to come back here and make a report about what happened. The only form I saw on the desk was an arrest report, so I thought I should use that.'

'Why didn't you let him call me, officer?'

'Oh, he'd already called his wife, and I know they're just supposed to get one phone call.'

'That's on television, officer, on American television,' Brunetti said, straining towards patience. 'Where is Sergeant Topa now?'

'He's gone out to get a coffee.'

'While you fill out the arrest report?'

'Yes, sir. It didn't seem right to have him here while I did that.'

'When Sergeant Topa gets back – he is coming back, isn't he?'

'Oh yes, sir, I told him to come back. That is, I asked him to, and he said he would.'

'When he comes back, tell him to wait. I'm on my way down there.' Knowing himself able to endure no more, Brunetti hung up without waiting for Alvise's reply.

Twenty minutes later, having told Paola that he had to go to the Questura to straighten something out, he arrived and went directly up to the uniformed officers' room. Alvise sat at a desk, and across from him sat Sergeant Topa, looking no different from the way he had looked a year ago when he left the Questura.

The former sergeant was short, barrel-shaped; the light from the overhead fixture gleamed on his almost bald head. He had tipped his chair back on its rear legs and sat with his arms folded over his chest. He looked up when Brunetti came in, studied him for a moment with dark eyes hidden under thick white eyebrows, and let his chair fall to the floor with a heavy thud. He got to his feet and held out his hand to Brunetti, no longer the sergeant and hence able to shake hands as an equal with the commissario, and, at that gesture, Brunetti found himself suffused with the dislike he had always felt for the sergeant, a man in whom violence boiled below the surface in much the same way that fresh-poured polenta waited the chance to burn the mouth of anyone who tried to eat it.

'Good evening, sergeant,' Brunetti said, shaking his hand.

'Commissario,' he answered but no more than that.

Alvise stood and glanced back and forth between the other men, but he said nothing.

'Perhaps we could go up to my office to talk,' Brunetti suggested.

'Yes,' Topa agreed.

Brunetti switched on the light when they went in, didn't bother to remove his coat, hoping that way to make it clear that he didn't have much time to spend on this, and went to sit behind his desk.

Topa sat in a chair to the left of the desk.

'Well?' Brunetti asked.

'Vianello called and asked me to go and have a look at this place, Pinetta's. I'd heard about it, but I'd never gone in. Didn't like what I heard about it.'

'What had you heard?'

'Lots of blacks. And Slavs. They're worse, Slavs.' Brunetti, who tended to agree with this notion, said nothing.

Seeing that he was not going to be prodded into telling his story, Topa abandoned his comments on national and racial differences and continued. 'I went in and had a glass of wine. A couple of guys were playing cards at a table, so I went and looked over their shoulders. No one seemed to mind. I had some more wine and started to talk to another man at the bar. One of the card-players left, so I took his place and played a few hands. I lost about 10,000 lire, and then the man who was playing came back, so I stopped playing and went back to the bar and had another glass of wine.' It sounded to Brunetti that Topa could have had a more exciting evening staying home and watching television.

'What about the fight, sergeant?'

'I'm getting to that. After another quarter-hour or so, one of the other men left the table, and they asked me if I wanted to play some more. I told them I didn't, so the man at the bar with me went and played a few hands. Then the man who had left came back and had a drink at the bar. We started to talk, and he asked me if I wanted a woman.

'I told him I didn't have to buy it, that there was plenty going around for free, and then he said that I'd never be able to get any of what he could get me.'

'What was that?'

'He said he could get me girls, young girls. I told him I wasn't interested in that, preferred women, and then he said something insulting.'

'What did he say?'

'He said he didn't think I was interested in women, either, and I told him I preferred women, real women, to what he had in mind. And then he started to laugh and shouted something, in Slav, I think, to

116

some of the men who were playing cards. They laughed. That's when I hit him.'

'We asked you to go there to try to get information, not to start a fight,' Brunetti said, making no attempt to disguise his irritation.

'I won't have people laugh at me,' Topa said, voice mounting into the tight, angry tone that Brunetti remembered.

'Do you think he meant it?'

'Who?'

'The man in the bar. Who offered you girls.'

'I don't know. Could have. He didn't look like a pimp, but with Slavs it's hard to tell.'

'Would you know him if you saw him again?'

'He's got a broken nose, so he ought to be easy to spot.'

'Are you sure?' Brunetti asked.

'About what?'

'The nose.'

'Of course I'm sure,' Topa said, holding up his right hand. 'I felt the cartilage break.'

'Would you recognize him or a picture of him?'

'Yes.'

'All right, sergeant. It's too late to do anything about this now. Come back in the morning and take a look at the photos, see if you spot him.'

'I thought Alvise wanted to arrest me.'

Brunetti waved his hand in front of his face, as if brushing at a fly. 'Forget about it.'

'Nobody talks to me like that guy did,' Topa said, voice truculent.

'In the morning, sergeant.' Brunetti told him.

Topa shot him a glance, one that reminded Brunetti about the story of his last arrest, got to his feet, and left Brunetti's office, leaving the door open behind him. Brunetti waited a full ten minutes before he left his office. Outside, it had begun to rain, the first icy drizzle of winter, but its chill drift against his face was a welcome relief after the heat of his dislike for Topa's company.

Chapter Fourteen

Two days later, but not before Brunetti had been forced to request an order for the files from Judge Vantuno, the Venice office of SIP provided the police with a list of the local calls made from Trevisan's home and office during the six months prior to his death. As Brunetti had expected, some calls had been made to Pinetta's bar, though no pattern was evident. He checked the list of long-distance calls for the dates of the calls to the Padua railway station, but there was no correspondence between the dates or times of those calls and the ones to the bar in Mestre.

He placed both lists side by side on his desk and stared down at them. Unlike the long-distance calls, the local calls had the address of the phone, as well as the name of the person in whose name it was listed, in a long column that ran down the right of the more than thirty pages of numbers. He started to read down the column of names and addresses but gave it up after a few minutes.

He took the paper, left his office, and went down the steps to Signorina Elettra's open cubicle. The table that stood in front of the window appeared to be a new one, but the same hand-blown Venini glass vase stood on it, today filled with nothing more elegant, though nothing could hope to be more happy, than a massive bouquet of black-eyed Susans.

In complement to them, Signorina Elettra today wore a scarf the secret of whose colour had been stolen from canaries. 'Good morning, commissario,' she said as he came in, breaking into a smile quite as happy as that the flowers wore.

'Good morning, signorina,' he said. 'I have a question for you,' he began, using the plural, and with a friendly nod indicating that the other half was her computer.

'That?' she asked, looking at the SIP print-out in his hand.

'Yes. It's the list of Trevisan's calls. Finally,' he added, unable to disguise the anger he felt at having wasted so much time waiting for official channels to divulge the information.

'Oh, you should have let me know that you wanted them in a hurry, commissario.'

'A friend at SIP?' he asked, no longer surprised by the extent of Signorina Elettra's web.

'Giorgio,' she said and left it at that.

Brunetti began, 'Do you think he could . . . ?'

She smiled and held out her hand.

He passed the papers to her. 'I need to have them arranged in order of the frequency he called them.'

She looked down and made a note on the pad on her desk. She smiled, suggesting child's play. 'Anything else?'

'Yes, I'd like to know how many of them are phones in public places: bars, restaurants, even phone booths.'

She smiled again; more of the same. 'Is that all?'

'No. I'd like to know which one is the number of the person who killed him.' If he expected her to make a note of this, he was disappointed. 'But I don't suppose you can get that.' Brunetti added this last with a smile, to show her he wasn't serious.

'I don't think we can, sir, but perhaps it's in among these,' she suggested, flourishing the papers. Probably was, Brunetti thought.

'How long will that take?' he asked, meaning how many days.

Signorina Elettra glanced down at her watch and then flipped to the end of the papers to see how many pages there were. 'If Giorgio is in the office today, I should have it by the afternoon.'

'How?' Brunetti blurted out before he had time to phrase a more nonchalant question.

'I've had a modem installed on the Vice-Questore's phone,' she said, pointing to a metal box that sat on the desk a few centimetres from the phone. Wires, Brunetti saw, led from the box to her computer. 'All Giorgio has got to do is bring up the information, program it to arrange the calls by frequency, and then send it directly through to my printer.' She paused a moment. 'It'll arrive listed by frequency, and then they'll give the date and time of the call. Would you like to know how long each call lasted?' She held her pen above her pad and waited for his answer.

'Yes. And do you think he could get a list of calls from the public phone in the bar in Mestre?'

She nodded but said nothing, busy writing.

'By this afternoon?' Brunetti asked.

'If Giorgio is there, certainly.'

When Brunetti left her office, she was lifting her phone, no doubt to contact Giorgio and, together with him and through that rectangular thing attached to her computer, leap over whatever obstacles SIP might attempt to place in front of the information in its files as well as over any laws regarding what might be available without a court order.

Back in his office, he wrote his brief report to Patta and took the trouble to sketch in his plans for the next few days. Much of the former was frustration, and the latter was made up of equal measures of invention and optimism, but he thought it would be enough to content Patta for awhile. That done, he took the phone and called Ubaldo Lotto and asked to see him that afternoon, explaining that he needed information about Trevisan's legal practice. After some initial hesitation and insisting that he knew nothing about the legal practice, only the financial dealings, Lotto reluctantly agreed and told Brunetti to come to his office at 5.30.

That office, which turned out to be in the same building and on the same floor as Trevisan's legal studio, was on Via XXII Marzo, above the Banca Commerciale d'Italia, about as good a business address as one could hope to have in Venice. Brunetti presented himself there a few minutes before 5.30 and was shown into an office so conspicuous in its evidence of industry as to be almost predictable, the sort of place a bright young television director might select as the set for a scene that dealt with a bright young accountant. In an open area half the size of a tennis court sat eight separate desks, each holding a computer terminal and screen, each work area surrounded by waist-high folding screens covered in light green linen. Five young men and three young women sat at the terminals; Brunetti found it interesting that none of them bothered to glance at him when he walked past their desks, following in the footsteps of the male receptionist who had let him into the office.

This young man stopped before a door, knocked twice, and then, without waiting for an answer, opened the door and held it open for Brunetti. When he entered, Brunetti noticed Lotto standing at the doors of a high cabinet placed against the far wall, leaning forward and reaching into it. Brunetti heard the door close behind him and glanced back over his shoulder to see if the young man had come into the room with him. He had not. When he turned back, Lotto stood a bit back from the cabinet, a bottle of sweet vermouth in his right hand, two short glasses cupped in his left.

'Would you like a drink, commissario?' he asked. 'I usually have one at about this time.'

'Thank you,' said Brunetti, who loathed sweet drinks. 'That would be very welcome.' He smiled and Lotto waved him to the other side of the office, where two chairs stood on opposite sides of a low, thin-legged table.

Lotto poured two generous drinks and brought them

across the room. Brunetti took one, thanked him, but waited until his host had put the bottle down on the table between them and taken his own seat before he raised his glass, smiled his friendliest smile, and said, '*Cin cin.*' The sweet liquid slithered over his tongue and down his throat, leaving a thick slime behind it. The alcohol was overwhelmed by the cloying sweetness: it was like drinking aftershave sweetened with apricot nectar.

Though all that could be seen from the windows of the room were those of the buildings across the street, Brunetti said, 'Compliments on your office. It's very elegant.'

Lotto waved his glass in the air in front of him, pushing back the compliment. 'Thank you, dottore. We try to give an appearance that will assure our clients that their affairs are safe with us and that we understand how to take care of them.'

'That must be very difficult,' Brunetti suggested.

A shadow crossed Lotto's face but disappeared immediately, taking part of his smile with it. 'I'm afraid I don't understand you, commissario.'

Brunetti tried to look shamefaced, a man not at home with language who had expressed himself, yet once again, badly. 'I mean with the new laws, Signor Lotto. It must be very difficult to understand them or how they apply. Ever since the new government changed the rules, my own accountant has admitted he isn't sure what he has to do or even how to fill out the forms.' He sipped at his drink, but he took a very small sip, one might even have called it a humble little sip,

124

and went on, 'Of course, my finances are hardly so complicated that they would create any confusion, but I imagine that you must have many clients whose finances deserve the attention of an expert.' Another little sip. 'I don't understand these things, of course,' he began and permitted himself a glance at Lotto, who appeared to be listening attentively. 'That's why I asked to see you, to see if you could give me any information you might think important about Avvocato Trevisan's finances. You were his accountant, weren't you? And his business manager?'

'Yes,' Lotto answered briefly, then asked, voice neutral, 'What sort of information?'

Brunetti smiled and made an open-handed gesture, as if trying to throw his fingers away. 'That's what I don't understand and why I came to see you. Since Avvocato Trevisan trusted you with his finances, I thought you might be able to tell us if there were any of his clients who might have been – I'm not sure of the right word to use here – might have been displeased with Signor Trevisan.'

' "Displeased", commissario?'

Brunetti glanced down at his knees, a man caught again in the web of his own ineptitude with language, surely a man Lotto could safely believe to be equally inept as a policeman.

Lotto broke the expanding silence. 'I'm afraid I still don't understand,' he said, pleasing Brunetti with the too-heavy sincerity of his confusion, for it suggested Lotto believed himself in the company of man unaccustomed to subtlety or complexity.

'Well, Signor Lotto, since we don't have a motive for this killing . . .' Brunetti began.

'Not robbery?' Lotto interrupted, raising his eyebrows in surprise as he spoke.

'Nothing was taken, sir.'

'Couldn't the thief have been disturbed? Surprise?'

Brunetti gave this suggestion the consideration it would deserve if no one had ever mentioned it, as he so clearly wanted Lotto to believe no one had.

'I suppose that's possible,' Brunetti said, speaking as to an equal. He nodded to himself, mulling over this new possibility. Then, with dog-like persistence, he returned to his first idea. 'But if that wasn't the case? If what we're dealing with here is a deliberate murder, then the motive might lie in his professional life.' Brunetti wondered if Lotto would try to cut off the heavy-treaded progress of his thought before it arrived at the next likely possibility, that the motive might lie in Trevisan's personal life.

'Are you suggesting that a client might have done this?' Lotto asked, voice rich with incredulity: clearly this policeman could never hope to understand the sort of clients a man like Trevisan dealt with.

'I know how unlikely that is,' Brunetti said and smiled, he hoped, nervously. 'But it is possible that Signor Trevisan, in his capacity as lawyer, might have come into possession of information that it would be dangerous for him to have.'

'About one of his clients? Are you suggesting this, commissario?' The shock Lotto pumped into his voice was an indication of how certain he was of his ability to dominate this policeman.

'Yes.'

'Impossible.'

Brunetti gave another small smile. 'I realize it is hard to believe, but still we need to see, if only to help us exclude this possibility, a list of Signor Trevisan's clients, and I thought that you, as his business manager, might be able to provide us with one.'

'And are you going to drag them into this?' Lotto asked, making sure that Brunetti heard his tone of precipitant indignation.

'I assure you that we will do everything in our power to see that they never realize we are in possession of their names.'

'And if you were not to be given these names?'

'We would be forced to ask for a court order.'

Lotto finished his drink and set the empty glass on the table to his left. 'I suppose I could have one prepared for you.' His reluctance was audible. He was, after all, dealing with the police. 'But I want you to bear in mind that these are not the sort of people who are usually subject to police investigation.'

In ordinary circumstances, Brunetti would have remarked that, for the last few years, the police had been investigating little except 'people like these', but he chose to keep his own counsel and, instead, answered, 'I appreciate this, Signor Lotto.'

The accountant cleared his throat. 'Is that all?'

'Yes,' Brunetti said, swirling the remaining liquid around in his glass, watching it as it slid up the sides and then back down again. 'There was one other thing, but it hardly bears mention.' The viscous liquid slid from side to side in Brunetti's glass.

'Yes?' Lotto asked, not really interested now that the main purpose of this policeman's visit was disposed of.

'Rino Favero,' Brunetti said, letting the name drop into the room as lightly as a butterfly leaps, plashless, into streams of air.

'What?' Lotto said with astonishment too strong to be contained. Content, Brunetti blinked in his most bovine manner and looked again at the liquid in his glass. Lotto changed his question to a neutral, 'Who?'

'Favero. Rino. He was an accountant. In Padua, I think. I wondered if you knew him, Signor Lotto.'

'I might have heard the name. Why do you ask?'

'He died recently. By his own hand.' To Brunetti that seemed just like the sort of euphemism a man in his social station would be expected to use in reference to the suicide of someone in Favero's. He paused, waiting to see how strong Lotto's curiosity would be.

'Why do you ask?'

'I thought that, if you knew him, it would be a difficult moment for you, losing two friends so closely together.'

'No, I didn't know him. Not personally, at least.'

Brunetti shook his head. 'A sad thing.'

'Yes,' Lotto agreed dismissively and got to his feet. 'Will there be anything else, commissario?'

Brunetti stood, looked around awkwardly for somewhere to put his unfinished drink, allowed Lotto to take it from him and place it beside the other glass on the table. 'No. Just that list of clients.'

'Tomorrow. Or the day after,' Lotto said, starting for the door.

Brunetti suspected it would be the latter, but he didn't allow that to stop him from extending his hand and his effusive thanks to the accountant for his time and co-operation.

Lotto saw Brunetti to the door of the office, shook his hand again, and then closed the door behind him. In the corridor, Brunetti paused for a moment and studied the discreet bronze plaque that stood to the right of the door across the hall: 'C. Trevisan Avvocato'. Brunetti had no doubt that the same atmosphere of efficient industry would prevail behind that door, as well, though he was now also convinced that the two offices were linked together by far more than their physical location, just as he was now certain they were both somehow linked to Rino Favero.

Chapter Fifteen

The following morning, Brunetti found on his desk, faxed to him by Capitano della Corte at the Padua police, a copy of the file on Rino Favero, whose death was still being reported, at least to the press and public, as a suicide. It told him little more about Favero's death than della Corte had told him on the phone; what Brunetti found interesting was what it revealed about Favero's apparent position in the society and the world of financial affairs in Padua, a sleepy, rich town about a half-hour to the west of Venice.

Favero specialized in corporate law, was the head of an office of seven accountants which enjoyed the highest reputation, not only in Padua but in the entire province. His clients included many of the major businessmen and industrialists of this factory-dense province as well as the chairmen of three different departments of the university, one of the best in Italy. Brunetti recognized the names of many of the companies whose finances Favero examined as well as the names of many of his private clients. There was no discernible pattern: chemicals, leather goods, travel and employment agencies, the Department of Political Science: Brunetti could see no way to connect them.

Nervous and eager for action, or even a change of location, he thought of going out to Padua to speak to della Corte, but after a moment's reflection decided to call him, instead. That thought brought to mind della Corte's admonition that he not speak to anyone else about Favero, a warning that suggested there was more to be known about Favero – perhaps about the Padua police, as well – than della Corte had at first been willing to reveal.

'Della Corte,' the captain answered on the first ring.

'Good morning, capitano, it's Brunetti. In Venice.'

'Good morning, commissario.'

'I called to ask if anything's new there,' Brunetti said.

'Yes.'

'About Favero?'

'Yes,' della Corte answered briefly and then added, 'It seems you and I have some friends in common, dottore.'

'We do?' Brunetti asked, surprised by the remark.

'After speaking to you yesterday, I called around to some people I know.'

Brunetti said nothing.

'I mentioned your name,' della Corte said. 'In passing.'

Brunetti doubted that. 'What people?' he asked.

'Riccardo Fosco, for one. In Milano.'

'Ah, and how is he?' Brunetti asked, though his real curiosity concerned the reason della Corte would have called an investigative reporter to ask about Brunetti, for he was sure the call to Fosco had not been made in passing.

'He said a number of things about you,' della Corte began. 'All good.'

As little as two years ago, if Brunetti had learned that a policeman felt it necessary to call a reporter to learn if another policeman could be trusted, he would have been shocked, but now all he felt was grinding despair that they were reduced to this. 'How is Riccardo?' he asked blandly.

'Fine, fine. He asked to be remembered to you.'

'Did he get married?'

'Yes, last year.'

'Are you part of the hunt?' Brunetti asked, referring to Fosco's friends on the police who, years after the shooting, still hoped to find the persons responsible for the attack that had partially crippled him.

'Yes, but we never hear anything. You?' della Corte asked, pleasing Brunetti by assuming that he, too, would still be looking for some trace, even though the trail was more than five years old.

'Not a thing. Did you call Riccardo for anything else?'

'I wanted to know if he could tell me anything about Favero, something we might be interested in knowing but might not be able to find out.'

'And did he?' Brunetti asked.

'No, nothing.'

Following a sudden hunch, Brunetti asked, 'Did you call him from your office?'

The noise della Corte made might have been a laugh. 'No.' Brunetti said nothing, and there ensued

Chapter Sixteen

unetti walked down the steps of Mestre railway
tion at ten minutes to ten that night and turned to
left, having located Via Fagare on the map in the
nt of the Venice phone book. The usual cluster of
s was parked illegally in front of the station, and
t traffic flowed by in both directions. He crossed
road and started up to the left. At the second street,
turned right, walking towards the centre of the city.
th sides of the street were lined with the metal
tters of small shops, pulled down now like portcul-
s in the face of the possible invasions of the night.
Occasionally puffs of wind swirled papers and leaves
lazy circles at his feet; the unaccustomed reverber-
of traffic disturbed him, as it always did when he
out of Venice and exposed to it. Everyone com-
ed about Venice's climate, humid and unforgiving,
o Brunetti the numbing sound of traffic was far
, and when to that was added the terrible smell
he marvelled that people could live in its midst
ccept it as part of the ordinary business of life.
et, each year, more and more Venetians left the
d moved here, to this, forced out by the general
of business and the sky-rocketing rents. He

a long silence, at the end of which della Corte said,
'Do you have a direct line to your office?'

Brunetti gave him the number.

'I'll call you back in ten minutes.'

While he waited for della Corte to call, Brunetti
toyed with the idea of calling Fosco to find out about
the other policeman, but he didn't want to tie up his
line, and he assumed that della Corte's having mentioned the journalist was sufficient recommendation.

A quarter of an hour later, della Corte called. As he
listened, Brunetti could hear the sound of traffic, horns,
and motors roaring over della Corte's voice.

'I'm assuming your line is safe,' della Corte said by
way of explanation that his own was not. Brunetti
resisted the impulse to ask what the line was safe from.

'What's wrong there?' Brunetti asked.

'We've changed the cause of death. It's now suicide.
Officially.'

'What do you mean?'

'The autopsy report now reads two milligrams.'

'Now?' Brunetti asked.

'Now,' della Corte repeated.

'So Favero would have been able to drive?' Brunetti
asked.

'Yes, and pull his car into the garage and close the
door and, in short, commit suicide.' Della Corte's voice
was tight with anger. 'I can't find a judge who will
issue an order to proceed with a murder investigation
or to exhume the body for a second autopsy.'

'How did you get the original report you called me
about?'

'I spoke to the doctor who did the autopsy; he's one of the assistants at the hospital.'

'And?' Brunetti asked.

'When the official lab report came back – he had done a blood exam immediately after the autopsy, but he sent the samples up to the lab to have them confirmed – it said that the level of barbiturate was much lower than what he had found.'

'Did he check his notes? What about the samples?'

'Both are gone.'

'Gone?'

Della Corte didn't bother to answer.

'Where were they?'

'In the pathology lab.'

'What usually happens to them?'

'After the official autopsy report is issued, they're kept for a year and then destroyed.'

'And this time?'

'When the official report came down, he went to check his notes, to see if he'd been wrong. And then he called me.' Della Corte paused for a moment and then continued. 'That was two days ago. Since then he's called to tell me his original results must have been mistaken.'

'Someone got to him?'

'Of course,' della Corte answered sharply.

'Have you said anything?'

'No. I didn't like what I heard when he told me about the notes, the second time I talked to him. So I agreed with him that these things happen and pretended to be angry with him that he had made the

mistake, warned him to be more careful the n[...] he did an autopsy.'

'Did he believe you?'

Della Corte's shrug came right down the li[...] knows?'

'And so?' Brunetti asked.

'So I called Fosco to find out about you[...] heard strange noises on the line and in[...] wondered if his own phone was tapped, bu[...] noises clarified themselves into the clinks[...] that said della Corte was feeding more coi[...] machine.

'Commissario,' della Corte said, 'I don't[...] more change. Can we meet to talk about t[...]

'Of course. Unofficially?'

'Absolutely.'

'Where?' Brunetti asked.

'Split the distance?' della Corte suggeste[...]

'Pinetta's bar?'

'Tonight at ten?'

'How will I know you?' Brunetti asked[...] Corte wouldn't be a cop who looked lik[...]

'I'm bald. How will I know you?'

'I look like a cop.'

could understand that it happened, that economic moves could drive people from their city. But to exchange it for this? Surely, a sordid boon.

After another few minutes, a neon sign came into view at the end of the next block. The letters, running vertically from the top of the building to a distance about a man's height above the pavement, spelled out 'B r ine ta'. Keeping his hands in the pockets of his overcoat, he turned his shoulders sideways and slipped into the bar without having to open the door any wider.

The owner of the bar, apparently, had seen too many American films, for it tried to resemble the sort of place where Victor Mature had pushed his weight around. The wall behind the bar was mirrored, though so much dust and smoke had accumulated on it that no image could any longer be reflected with accuracy. Instead of the many rows of bottles so familiar in Italian bars, here there was only one row, all bourbon and Scotch. Instead of the straight counter and espresso machine, this bar curved in a horseshoe, at the centre of which stood a bartender with a once-white apron tied tight around his waist.

Tables stood to both sides of the bar: those on the left held trios or quartets of card-playing men; those on the right held mixed duets who were clearly engaged in other games of chance. All of the walls held blown-up photos of American film stars, many of whom seemed to take a dim view of what circumstance had doomed them to observe.

Four men and two women stood at the bar. The

first man, short and stocky, held both hands protectively around his drink and stared down into it. The second, taller and slighter, stood with his back to the bar, turning his head slowly from side to side as he studied, first the card-players, then the other bidders. The third was bald, obviously della Corte. The last man, thin to the point of emaciation, stood with one of the women on either side of him, turning his head nervously back and forth between them as they spoke to him in turn. He glanced up at Brunetti when he came in, and the women, seeing him look towards the door, turned to study Brunetti. The look in the eyes of the Three Fates as they snipped the thread of a man's life could be no bleaker.

Brunetti went up to della Corte, a thin man with a heavily lined face and a thick moustache, and slapped him on the shoulder. Speaking in thick Veneziano and far more loudly than was necessary, he said, '*Ciao*, Bepe, *come stai*? Sorry I'm late, but my bitch of a wife . . .' He let his voice trail off and waved his hand in the air in an angry gesture directed at all bitches, all wives. He turned to the bartender and said, voice even louder, '*Amico mio*, give me a whisky', then, turning to della Corte, he asked, 'What are you drinking, Bepe? Have another one.' He was careful, when he turned towards the bartender, to turn his whole body, not just his head, and to be sure to turn it too far. To steady himself, he put one hand on the bar and muttered, 'Bitch,' again.

When the whisky came, he picked up the tall glass and tossed the drink down in one gulp, slammed the glass loudly down on the bar, and wiped his mouth with the back of his hand. A second drink appeared in front of him, but before he could pick it up, he saw della Corte's hand reach out and take it.

'*Cin cin*, Guido,' della Corte said, lifting the glass and tilting it towards Brunetti in a gesture filled with old friendship. 'I'm glad you got away from her.' He sipped at the drink, sipped again. 'Are you going to come hunting with us this weekend?'

He and della Corte hadn't prepared a script for this meeting, but Brunetti assumed one topic was as good as another for two middle-aged drunks at a cheap bar in Mestre. He answered that he wanted to go, but his bitch of a wife wanted him to stay home that weekend because it was their anniversary, and she expected him to take her out to dinner. Why did they have a stove in the house if she wasn't going to use it to cook his dinner? After a few minutes of this, one of the couples got up from their table and left the bar. Della Corte, ordering two more drinks, pulled Brunetti by the sleeve over towards the empty table and helped him sit down in one of the chairs. After the drinks came, Brunetti propped his chin up on one palm and asked in a low voice, 'Have you been here long?'

'About a half-hour,' della Corte answered, his voice no longer thickened either by alcohol or the heavy Veneto accent he had used when speaking at the bar.

'And?' Brunetti asked.

'The man at the bar, the one with the women,' della Corte said and paused to sip at his drink. 'Every so often men come into the bar and talk to him. Twice, one of the women with him has gone to sit at the bar and have a drink with the man. Once, one of them left with the man, then came back alone about twenty minutes later.'

'Fast work,' Brunetti said, and della Corte nodded again, then took another sip of his drink.

'From the look of him,' della Corte continued, 'I'd say he's on heroin.' He glanced over at the bar and grinned broadly when one of the women caught his eye.

'You sure?' Brunetti asked.

'I worked drugs for six years. I've seen hundreds like him.'

'Anything else in Padua?' Brunetti asked. During their conversation, they showed little apparent interest in the other people in the bar, but each of them was memorizing faces and keeping careful watch of what went on.

Della Corte shook his head. 'I've stopped talking about it, but I sent one of the men I trust down to the lab to see if anything else is missing.'

'And?'

'Whoever did it was very careful. All of the notes and samples for the autopsies done that day are missing.'

'How many were there?'

'Three.'

'In Padua?' Brunetti asked, unable to hide his surprise.

'Two old people died in the hospital after eating spoiled meat. Salmonella. The pathologist's notes and the samples from their autopsies were missing, too.'

we start getting dinner ready? That way, Mamma can come home and find dinner ready for a change.'

'But how much is it worth?' Chiara wheedled.

Brunetti considered this for a moment. 'I'd guess about thirty thousand,' he finally answered. Since it was to come out of his pocket, that's all it would be, though the information she'd given him about Signora Trevisan's pushing her husband around, should it prove true and should it apply to his professional life, might be worth inestimably more than that.

Chapter Eleven

The following day, the *Gazzettino* carried a front page article about the suicide of Rino Favero, one of the most successful accountants in the Veneto Region. Favero, it was reported, had chosen to drive his Rover into the two-car garage beneath his house, close the door of the garage, and leave the engine running, himself quietly stretched across the front seat. It was further stated that Favero's name was about to be revealed in the expanding scandal that was currently playing itself out in the corridors of the Ministry of Health. Though, by now, all of Italy was familiar with the accusation that the former Minister of Health had accepted immense bribes from various pharmaceutical companies and in return had allowed them to raise the prices of the medicines they manufactured, it was not common knowledge that Favero had been the accountant who handled the private finances of the president of the largest of these firms. Those who did know assumed that he had decided to imitate so many of the men named in this ever-spreading web of corruption; had chosen to preserve his honour by removing himself from accusation, guilt, and possible punishment. Few seemed to question the proposition that honour was preserved in this manner.

The Padua police did not concern themselves with such speculation as to motive, for the autopsy performed on Favero's body revealed that, at the time of his death, his blood contained a sufficient quantity of barbiturate to make driving, let alone driving into his garage and closing the door, impossible. It was possible that he had taken the pills after pulling into the garage. Why, then, was no bottle or package found in the car, and why were no barbiturates of any sort found in the house? Subsequent microscopic examination of Favero's pockets revealed that none of them contained the least trace of barbiturate. None of this information, however, was given to the press, and so Favero's death remained, at least in the popular consciousness, a suicide.

Three days after Favero's death, which would make it five days after Trevisan's murder, Brunetti arrived at his office to hear the phone ringing.

'Brunetti,' he answered, holding the phone with one hand and unbuttoning his raincoat with the other.

'Commissario Brunetti, this is Capitano della Corte of the Padua police.' Brunetti recognized the name, vaguely, and with the sense that whatever he had heard about della Corte in the past had been to the man's favour.

'Good morning, captain, what can I do for you?'

'You can tell me if Rino Favero's name has come up in your investigation of the murder you had on the train.'

'Favero? The man who committed suicide?'

'Suicide?' della Corte asked. 'With four milligrams of Roipnal in his blood?'

Brunetti was immediately alert. 'What's the connection with Trevisan?' he asked.

'We don't know. But we ran a trace on all the numbers we found in his address book. That is, on all the numbers that were listed without names. Trevisan's was one of them.'

'Have you got the records yet?' Neither of them had to clarify that Brunetti meant the record of all of the calls made from Favero's phone.

'There's no record that he called either Trevisan's office or his home, at least not from his own phones.'

'Then why would he have the number?' Brunetti asked.

'That's exactly what we were wondering.' Della Corte's tone was dry.

'How many other numbers were listed without names?'

'Eight. One is the phone in a bar in Mestre. One is a public phone in Padua railway station. And the rest don't exist.'

'What do you mean, they don't exist?'

'That they don't exist as possible numbers anywhere in the Veneto.'

'Are you checking it for other cities, other provinces?'

'We did that. Either they've got too many digits or they don't correspond to any numbers in this country.'

'Foreign?'

a long silence, at the end of which della Corte said, 'Do you have a direct line to your office?'

Brunetti gave him the number.

'I'll call you back in ten minutes.'

While he waited for della Corte to call, Brunetti toyed with the idea of calling Fosco to find out about the other policeman, but he didn't want to tie up his line, and he assumed that della Corte's having mentioned the journalist was sufficient recommendation.

A quarter of an hour later, della Corte called. As he listened, Brunetti could hear the sound of traffic, horns, and motors roaring over della Corte's voice.

'I'm assuming your line is safe,' della Corte said by way of explanation that his own was not. Brunetti resisted the impulse to ask what the line was safe from.

'What's wrong there?' Brunetti asked.

'We've changed the cause of death. It's now suicide. Officially.'

'What do you mean?'

'The autopsy report now reads two milligrams.'

'Now?' Brunetti asked.

'Now,' della Corte repeated.

'So Favero would have been able to drive?' Brunetti asked.

'Yes, and pull his car into the garage and close the door and, in short, commit suicide.' Della Corte's voice was tight with anger. 'I can't find a judge who will issue an order to proceed with a murder investigation or to exhume the body for a second autopsy.'

'How did you get the original report you called me about?'

'I spoke to the doctor who did the autopsy; he's one of the assistants at the hospital.'

'And?' Brunetti asked.

'When the official lab report came back – he had done a blood exam immediately after the autopsy, but he sent the samples up to the lab to have them confirmed – it said that the level of barbiturate was much lower than what he had found.'

'Did he check his notes? What about the samples?'

'Both are gone.'

'Gone?'

Della Corte didn't bother to answer.

'Where were they?'

'In the pathology lab.'

'What usually happens to them?'

'After the official autopsy report is issued, they're kept for a year and then destroyed.'

'And this time?'

'When the official report came down, he went to check his notes, to see if he'd been wrong. And then he called me.' Della Corte paused for a moment and then continued. 'That was two days ago. Since then he's called to tell me his original results must have been mistaken.'

'Someone got to him?'

'Of course,' della Corte answered sharply.

'Have you said anything?'

'No. I didn't like what I heard when he told me about the notes, the second time I talked to him. So I agreed with him that these things happen and pretended to be angry with him that he had made the mistake, warned him to be more careful the next time he did an autopsy.'

'Did he believe you?'

Della Corte's shrug came right down the line. 'Who knows?'

'And so?' Brunetti asked.

'So I called Fosco to find out about you.' Brunetti heard strange noises on the line and immediately wondered if his own phone was tapped, but then the noises clarified themselves into the clinks and beeps that said della Corte was feeding more coins into the machine.

'Commissario,' della Corte said, 'I don't have much more change. Can we meet to talk about this?'

'Of course. Unofficially?'

'Absolutely.'

'Where?' Brunetti asked.

'Split the distance?' della Corte suggested. 'Mestre?'

'Pinetta's bar?'

'Tonight at ten?'

'How will I know you?' Brunetti asked, hoping della Corte wouldn't be a cop who looked like a cop.

'I'm bald. How will I know you?'

'I look like a cop.'

Chapter Sixteen

Brunetti walked down the steps of Mestre railway station at ten minutes to ten that night and turned to his left, having located Via Fagare on the map in the front of the Venice phone book. The usual cluster of cars was parked illegally in front of the station, and light traffic flowed by in both directions. He crossed the road and started up to the left. At the second street, he turned right, walking towards the centre of the city. Both sides of the street were lined with the metal shutters of small shops, pulled down now like portcullises in the face of the possible invasions of the night.

Occasionally puffs of wind swirled papers and leaves into lazy circles at his feet; the unaccustomed reverberation of traffic disturbed him, as it always did when he was out of Venice and exposed to it. Everyone complained about Venice's climate, humid and unforgiving, but to Brunetti the numbing sound of traffic was far worse, and when to that was added the terrible smell of it, he marvelled that people could live in its midst and accept it as part of the ordinary business of life. And yet, each year, more and more Venetians left the city and moved here, to this, forced out by the general decline of business and the sky-rocketing rents. He

could understand that it happened, that economic moves could drive people from their city. But to exchange it for this? Surely, a sordid boon.

After another few minutes, a neon sign came into view at the end of the next block. The letters, running vertically from the top of the building to a distance about a man's height above the pavement, spelled out 'B r ine ta'. Keeping his hands in the pockets of his overcoat, he turned his shoulders sideways and slipped into the bar without having to open the door any wider.

The owner of the bar, apparently, had seen too many American films, for it tried to resemble the sort of place where Victor Mature had pushed his weight around. The wall behind the bar was mirrored, though so much dust and smoke had accumulated on it that no image could any longer be reflected with accuracy. Instead of the many rows of bottles so familiar in Italian bars, here there was only one row, all bourbon and Scotch. Instead of the straight counter and espresso machine, this bar curved in a horseshoe, at the centre of which stood a bartender with a once-white apron tied tight around his waist.

Tables stood to both sides of the bar: those on the left held trios or quartets of card-playing men; those on the right held mixed duets who were clearly engaged in other games of chance. All of the walls held blown-up photos of American film stars, many of whom seemed to take a dim view of what circumstance had doomed them to observe.

Four men and two women stood at the bar. The

first man, short and stocky, held both hands protectively around his drink and stared down into it. The second, taller and slighter, stood with his back to the bar, turning his head slowly from side to side as he studied, first the card-players, then the other bidders. The third was bald, obviously della Corte. The last man, thin to the point of emaciation, stood with one of the women on either side of him, turning his head nervously back and forth between them as they spoke to him in turn. He glanced up at Brunetti when he came in, and the women, seeing him look towards the door, turned to study Brunetti. The look in the eyes of the Three Fates as they snipped the thread of a man's life could be no bleaker.

Brunetti went up to della Corte, a thin man with a heavily lined face and a thick moustache, and slapped him on the shoulder. Speaking in thick Veneziano and far more loudly than was necessary, he said, '*Ciao*, Bepe, *come stai*? Sorry I'm late, but my bitch of a wife . . .' He let his voice trail off and waved his hand in the air in an angry gesture directed at all bitches, all wives. He turned to the bartender and said, voice even louder, '*Amico mio*, give me a whisky', then, turning to della Corte, he asked, 'What are you drinking, Bepe? Have another one.' He was careful, when he turned towards the bartender, to turn his whole body, not just his head, and to be sure to turn it too far. To steady himself, he put one hand on the bar and muttered, 'Bitch,' again.

When the whisky came, he picked up the tall glass and tossed the drink down in one gulp, slammed the glass loudly down on the bar, and wiped his mouth

with the back of his hand. A second drink appeared in front of him, but before he could pick it up, he saw della Corte's hand reach out and take it.

'*Cin cin*, Guido,' della Corte said, lifting the glass and tilting it towards Brunetti in a gesture filled with old friendship. 'I'm glad you got away from her.' He sipped at the drink, sipped again. 'Are you going to come hunting with us this weekend?'

He and della Corte hadn't prepared a script for this meeting, but Brunetti assumed one topic was as good as another for two middle-aged drunks at a cheap bar in Mestre. He answered that he wanted to go, but his bitch of a wife wanted him to stay home that weekend because it was their anniversary, and she expected him to take her out to dinner. Why did they have a stove in the house if she wasn't going to use it to cook his dinner? After a few minutes of this, one of the couples got up from their table and left the bar. Della Corte, ordering two more drinks, pulled Brunetti by the sleeve over towards the empty table and helped him sit down in one of the chairs. After the drinks came, Brunetti propped his chin up on one palm and asked in a low voice, 'Have you been here long?'

'About a half-hour,' della Corte answered, his voice no longer thickened either by alcohol or the heavy Veneto accent he had used when speaking at the bar.

'And?' Brunetti asked.

'The man at the bar, the one with the women,' della Corte said and paused to sip at his drink. 'Every so often men come into the bar and talk to him. Twice, one of the women with him has gone to sit at the bar

and have a drink with the man. Once, one of them left with the man, then came back alone about twenty minutes later.'

'Fast work,' Brunetti said, and della Corte nodded again, then took another sip of his drink.

'From the look of him,' della Corte continued, 'I'd say he's on heroin.' He glanced over at the bar and grinned broadly when one of the women caught his eye.

'You sure?' Brunetti asked.

'I worked drugs for six years. I've seen hundreds like him.'

'Anything else in Padua?' Brunetti asked. During their conversation, they showed little apparent interest in the other people in the bar, but each of them was memorizing faces and keeping careful watch of what went on.

Della Corte shook his head. 'I've stopped talking about it, but I sent one of the men I trust down to the lab to see if anything else is missing.'

'And?'

'Whoever did it was very careful. All of the notes and samples for the autopsies done that day are missing.'

'How many were there?'

'Three.'

'In Padua?' Brunetti asked, unable to hide his surprise.

'Two old people died in the hospital after eating spoiled meat. Salmonella. The pathologist's notes and the samples from their autopsies were missing, too.'

Brunetti nodded. 'Who could do it?' he asked the captain. 'Or who would want to have it done?'

'Whoever gave him the barbiturates, I'd say.'

Brunetti nodded.

The bartender made a sweep around the tables. Brunetti pulled his head up from his hand and signalled to him to bring two more drinks, though his second sat in front of him, almost untouched.

'With what people in the lab are paid, a couple of hundred thousand lire will buy a lot of co-operation,' della Corte said.

Two men came into the bar together, talking and laughing in loud voices, loud in the way men tend to make their voices when it's important that strangers notice them.

'Anything on Trevisan?' della Corte asked.

Brunetti shook his head from side to side with the ponderous solemnity drunks give to trivial things.

'And so?' della Corte asked.

'I guess one of us is going to have to sample the merchandise,' Brunetti said as the bartender approached their table. He looked up, smiled at the bartender, nodded at him to set their drinks down on the table, and waved him closer. When he did, Brunetti looked up at him and said, 'Drinks for the *signorine*,' waving an unsteady hand in the direction of the two women who stood at the bar, still on either side of the man.

The bartender nodded, went back behind the bar, and poured out two glasses of bubbling white wine. Brunetti was sure it was the worst sort of rotgut Prosecco and equally certain his bill would say it was

French champagne. The bartender moved down the bar to the place where the man and the two women were standing, leaned forward, placed the glasses on the bar, and said something to the man, who glanced in Brunetti's direction. The man turned and said something to the woman on his left, a short, dark woman with a broad mouth and reddish hair that cascaded down her shoulders. She looked at the man, then at the drinks, then across the room towards where Brunetti sat at the table. He smiled in her direction, half rose from his chair, and bowed clumsily towards her.

'Are you out of your mind?' della Corte asked, smiling broadly and reaching forward to pick up his drink.

Instead of answering, Brunetti waved towards the three at the bar and kicked back the empty chair that stood to his left. He smiled towards the woman and pointed at the chair beside him. The redheaded woman detached herself from her friends, picked up her glass of wine, and started across the room in the direction of Brunetti's table. Seeing her approach, Brunetti smiled at her again and asked della Corte in a soft voice, 'Did you come by car?'

The captain nodded.

'Good. When she comes over, leave. Wait for me in your car and follow us when we leave here.'

Just as the woman reached the table, della Corte pushed back his chair and got to his feet, almost bumping into the woman and seeming surprised at her arrival. He looked at her for a moment, then said,

'Good evening, signorina. Please have a seat,' slipping back into his broad Veneto accent and smiling broadly.

The woman gathered her skirt under her and sat beside Brunetti. She smiled at him, and he saw that, under the caked make-up, she was pretty: even teeth, dark eyes, and a short, happy nose. '*Buona sera*,' she said, almost whispering. 'Thanks for the champagne.'

Della Corte leaned across the table towards Brunetti and extended his hand. 'I've got to be going, Guido. I'll give you a call next week.'

Brunetti ignored his outstretched hand, all of his attention directed at the woman. Della Corte turned towards the men at the bar, smiled, shrugged, and left, closing the door behind him.

'*Ti chiami Guido?*' the woman asked, using the informal 'tu' and, by that, making clear just what all this was about.

'Yes, Guido Bassetti. What's your name, sweetheart?'

'Mara,' she said and laughed as though she'd said something clever. 'What do you do, Guido?' Underneath her words, Brunetti could detect two things: some sort of a foreign accent, definitely a Latin language, though he couldn't tell whether it was Spanish or Portuguese; even more audible was the bold double meaning of her question, which landed heavily on the last word.

'I'm a plumber,' Brunetti said, making himself sound very proud of it. As he spoke, he made a vulgar gesture which made it clear he had understood the suggestion in her question.

'Oh, how interesting,' Mara said and laughed again, but couldn't think of anything else to say.

Brunetti saw that a good deal of liquor still remained in his second drink, and his third was untouched. He drank some of the second, pushed it aside, and picked up the third glass.

'You're a very pretty girl, Mara,' he said, making no attempt to disguise the fact that this was entirely irrelevant to the business at hand. She didn't seem to care.

'Is that your friend at the bar?' Brunetti asked, nodding his chin towards the place where the man still stood, though the other woman was gone now.

'Yes,' Mara answered.

'You live near here?' Brunetti asked, a man no longer interested in wasting time.

'Yes.'

'Can we go there?'

'Yes.' She smiled again, and he watched her force warmth and interest into her eyes.

He allowed all the good humour to flow out of him. 'How much?'

'A hundred thousand,' she answered with the alacrity of a woman who had heard this question too many times.

Brunetti laughed, took another sip of his drink, and got to his feet, careful to push his chair back so quickly that it fell over behind him. 'You're crazy, little Mara. I've got a wife at home. She'll give it to me for nothing.'

She shrugged and glanced at her watch. It was eleven, and no one had come into the bar in the last twenty minutes. He could see her calculating time and opportunity.

'Fifty,' she said, apparently willing to save time and energy.

Brunetti put his drink, still unfinished, down on the table and reached for her arm. 'All right, little Mara, let me show you what a real man can do for you.'

She offered no resistance and got to her feet. Brunetti, pulling at her arm, went over to the bar. 'How much do I owe you?' he asked the bartender.

With no hesitation, the bartender answered, 'Sixty-three thousand lire.'

'Are you crazy?' Brunetti asked angrily. 'For three drinks, and lousy whisky, too?'

'And two for your friend, and champagne for the ladies,' the bartender said.

'Ladies,' Brunetti repeated sarcastically, but he reached into his pocket and pulled out his wallet. He took a fifty, a ten, and three 1000-lire notes and tossed them on to the counter. Before he could put his wallet back, Mara reached up and grabbed at his arm.

'You can give the money to my friend,' she said, gesturing with her chin to the thin man at the bar, who looked at Brunetti without smiling. Brunetti looked around him, face flushed with confusion, a man seeking someone to help him understand this. No one did. He took a 50,000-lire note from his wallet and tossed it on to the counter, not looking at the man, who didn't bother to glance at the money. Then, in an attempt to restore his damaged pride, Brunetti grabbed the woman's arm and pulled her towards the door. She paused only long enough to take a fake leopard-skin jacket from a hook by the door, and then she went out into the street with Brunetti, who slammed the door violently behind them.

Outside, Mara turned to the left and started to walk away from Brunetti. She took quick steps, but they were shortened by the tightness of her skirt and the height of her heels, so Brunetti had no trouble in keeping up with her. At the first corner, she turned to the left and then, three doors down, stopped in front of a doorway. Her key was ready in her hand. She opened the door and stepped inside, not bothering to look back for Brunetti, who paused for a moment at the door, just long enough to see a car turn into the narrow street. It blinked its lights twice, and he followed the woman inside the building.

At the top of a single flight of stairs, she opened the door on the right, again leaving it open behind her for Brunetti. When he walked in, he saw that the room contained a low divan, covered with a brightly striped bedspread, a desk and two chairs, and one window, closed and shuttered. She switched on a light, a naked, low-watt bulb that hung from the ceiling at the end of a short piece of wire.

Without turning to him, Mara took off her jacket and hung it carefully over the back of one of the chairs. She sat on the edge of the bed, bent down and unstrapped her shoes. Brunetti heard her sigh with relief as she kicked them off. Still not looking at him, she stood, unbuttoned her skirt, removed it, and folded it carefully over the jacket. Beneath it, she wore

nothing. She sat, then lay, on the divan, still not bothering to look at him.

'It's extra if you want to touch my breasts,' she said,
then turned to one side to straighten out the cover,
which was bunched up under her shoulder.

Brunetti walked across the room and sat on the other
chair, not the one holding her clothing. 'Where are
you from, Mara?' he asked in his normal voice, speaking
Italian, not dialect.

She looked up at him, surprised either by the question or by the completely normal conversational tone
in which it was asked. 'Look, Mr Plumber,' she said,
voice tired rather than sharp, 'you didn't come here to
talk, and neither did I, so let's do this and I can get
back to work, all right?' She turned fully on to her back
and opened her legs wide.

Brunetti looked away. 'Where do you come from,
Mara?' he asked again.

She pulled her legs together and put them over the
side of the bed, sitting up to face him. 'Look, you, if
you want to fuck, then let's do it, all right? I haven't
got all night to sit here and talk. And it's none of your
god-damned business where I come from.'

'Brazil?' he asked, taking a stab at the accent.

She made an angry, disgusted noise, pushed herself
to her feet, and reached for her skirt. She held it low
and stepped into it, pulled it up, and yanked angrily at
the zip. With one foot, she began to feel under the
bed for her shoes, which she had shoved under there
after she took them off. She sat back down on the edge
of the bed and began to strap her shoes back on.

'He can be arrested, you know,' Brunetti said in the same calm tone. 'He let me give him the money. That's good for at least a couple of months inside.'

The bands that held her shoes to her ankles were both securely buckled, but she didn't look up at Brunetti, nor did she make any move to get up from the bed. She sat with her head lowered, listening.

'I don't think you'd want that to happen to him, would you?' Brunetti asked.

She gave a disgusted, unbelieving snort.

'Then think about what he'd be likely to do when he got out, Mara. You didn't spot me. He's bound to blame you for that.'

She looked up at him and put out her hand. 'Let me see some identification.'

Brunetti gave it to her.

'What do you want?' she said when she handed the warrant card back to him.

'I'd like you to tell me where you come from.'

'Why, so you can send me back?' she asked, meeting his eyes.

'I'm not from the immigration police, Mara. I don't care whether you're here legally or illegally.'

'Then what do you want?' she asked, voice sparked with anger.

'I told you. I want to know where you're from.'

She hesitated only a moment, examining the question for peril and, seeing none, answered him. 'São Paulo.' He was right; the faint accent was Brazilian.

'How long have you been here?'

'Two years,' she said.

'Working as a prostitute?' he asked, trying to pronounce the word as definition, not condemnation.

'Yes.'

'Have you always worked for that man?'

She looked up at him. 'I won't tell you his name,' she said.

'I don't want to know his name, Mara. I want to know if you've always worked for him.'

She said something, but her voice was so low he couldn't hear her.

'Excuse me?' he said.

'No.'

'Always in that bar?'

'No.'

'Where did you work before?'

'Somewhere else,' she said evasively.

'How long have you worked in the bar?'

'Since September.'

'Why?'

'Why what?'

'Why did you move to the bar?'

'The cold weather. I'm not used to it, and I got sick last winter, working outside. So he told me I could work in the bar this winter.'

'I see,' Brunetti said. 'How many other girls are there?'

'In the bar?'

'Yes.'

'Three.'

'And on the street?'

'I don't know how many there are. Four? Six? I don't know.'

'Are any of the others Brazilian?'

'Two of them are.'

'And the rest, where are they from?'

'I don't know.'

'What about the telephone?'

'What?' she asked, looking up at him, eyes narrowed in what might be honest confusion.

'The telephone. In the bar. Who gets calls there? Does he?'

The question clearly puzzled her. 'I don't know,' she said. 'Everybody uses the phone.'

'But who gets calls on it?'

She thought for a moment. 'I don't know.'

'Does he?' Brunetti insisted.

She shrugged, tried to glance away, but Brunetti snapped his fingers in her face, and she looked back at him.

'Does he get calls?'

'Sometimes,' she said, then glanced down at her watch and up at him. 'You should be finished by now.'

He glanced at his own watch; fifteen minutes had passed.

'How much time does he let you take?'

'Usually a quarter of an hour. He lets the old ones take longer if they're regulars. But if I'm not back soon, he'll ask questions, make me tell him why it took so long.'

From the way she spoke, it was evident to Brunetti that any question the man asked, the woman would answer. For a moment, he debated whether it would be better to let the man realize the police were asking questions about him. He studied the woman's lowered face, trying to determine how old she was. Twenty-five? Twenty?

'All right,' he said, getting to his feet.

At his sudden motion, she flinched away and looked up at him. 'That's all?' she asked.

'Yes, that's all.'

'No quickie?'

'What?' he asked, lost.

'A quickie. Usually, when the cops pull us in for questioning, that's what we have to do.' Her voice was neutral, nonjudgemental, tired.

'No, nothing like that,' he said, moving towards the door.

Behind him, she got to her feet and stuffed one arm, then the other, into the sleeves of her jacket. He held the door open while she left the room and then followed her out into the hall. She turned and locked the door, started down the single flight of steps. She shoved open the front door of the building, turned to the right, and was gone, back in the direction of the bar. Brunetti turned the opposite way and walked to the end of the street, crossed it, and stood under a street light until, a moment later, della Corte's black car pulled up beside him.

Chapter Seventeen

'Well?' della Corte asked as Brunetti slid into the front seat of the car. Brunetti liked the fact that there was no suggestion of a leer in the question.

'She's Brazilian, works for the man who was with her in the bar. She says he's received calls on the phone.'

'And?' della Corte asked, slipping the car into gear and heading slowly back towards the railway station.

'And that's all,' Brunetti answered. 'That's all she told me, but I think we can infer a lot more from that.'

'Such as?'

'Such as she's illegal, has no residence permit, and so doesn't have much of a say in what she does for a living.'

'She might do it because she likes it,' della Corte suggested.

'You ever know a whore who did?' Brunetti asked.

Ignoring the question, della Corte turned a corner and slowed to a stop in front of the train station. He set the brake but left the motor running. 'Now what?'

'I think we've got to get the man with her arrested. At least that way we can find out who he is. And maybe talk to the woman again while we've got him.'

'You think she'll talk?'

Brunetti shrugged. 'Maybe, if she's not afraid that she'll be sent back to Brazil if she does.'

'How likely is that?'

'Depends on who talks to her.'

'A woman?' della Corte asked.

'Probably be better.'

'You got one?'

'We've got a psychiatrist who does consulting for us every once in a while. I could try to get Mara to talk to her.'

'Mara?' della Corte asked.

'That's what she told me. I'd like to think she was allowed to keep at least that much, her own name.'

'When will you move on the man?'

'As soon as possible.'

'Any idea of how you'll do it?'

'Easiest way is to pick him up the next time he has one of Mara's clients put the money on the bar for him.'

'How long can you keep him on that?'

'Depends on what we find out about him, if he has a record or if there are any warrants out against him.' Brunetti thought for a moment. 'If you're right about the heroin, a couple of hours ought to be enough.'

Della Corte's smile was not pretty. 'I'm right about the heroin.' When Brunetti said nothing, della Corte asked, 'Until then?'

'I'm working on a few things. I want to learn more about Trevisan's family and whatever I can about his practice.'

'Anything in particular?'

'No, not really. Just a couple of things that make me uncomfortable, little things that don't add up.' That was all Brunetti was prepared to say, and so he asked, 'And you?'

'We'll do the same with Favero, but there's an awful lot to check, at least as far as his business is concerned.' Della Corte paused a moment and then added, 'I had no idea these guys earned so much.'

'Accountants?'

'Yes. Hundreds of millions a year, it seems. And that's just his declared income, so you can imagine how much more he's making under the table.' Brunetti had but to recall some of the names on the list of Favero's clients, and he too could imagine the extent of his earnings, both declared and undeclared.

He opened the door and got out of the car, then came around to della Corte's side. 'I'll send some of our men out here tomorrow night. If he and Mara are working the bar, it ought to be easy to bring them in.'

'Both?' della Corte asked.

'Yes. She might be more willing to talk after she spends a night in a cell.'

'I thought you wanted her to talk to a psychiatrist,' della Corte said.

'I do. But I want her to have had a taste of gaol before she does. Fear tends to make people more talkative, particularly women.'

'Cold-hearted bastard, aren't you?' della Corte asked, not without respect.

Brunetti shrugged. 'She might have information

about a murder. The more scared and confused she is, the more likely she is to tell us what she knows.'

Della Corte smiled and released the brake. 'For a minute, I thought you were going to start telling me about the whore with the heart of gold.'

Brunetti pushed himself back from the car and started towards the station. He took a few steps and then turned back towards della Corte, who was rolling up the window as the car pulled slowly away. 'No one has a heart of gold,' he said, but della Corte drove away without giving any sign that he had heard.

Next morning, Signorina Elettra greeted Brunetti by telling him that she'd managed to find the story about Trevisan in the *Gazzettino* but that it was an entirely innocuous account of a joint venture in tourism which he had organized between the chambers of commerce of Venice and Prague. Signora Trevisan's life, at least according to the society columnist of that newspaper, was equally bland.

Though Brunetti had expected something like this, the news disappointed him. He asked Signorina Elettra to see if Giorgio – Brunetti surprised himself by speaking of Giorgio as though he were an old friend – could get a list of the calls made from and to the phone in Pinetta's bar. When he had done that, he contented himself with reading through his mail and then made a few phone calls in response to one of the letters.

He called Vianello and arranged to have three men go to Pinetta's that night and arrest Mara and her pimp.

Then he had no choice but to address himself to the papers on his desk, though he found it difficult to pay attention to what he read: statistics from the Ministry of the Interior gave staffing projections for the next five years, discussed the cost of a computer link with Interpol, and gave the specifications and performance records on a new type of pistol. Brunetti tossed the papers down on his desk in disgust. The Questore had recently received a memorandum from the Minister of the Interior, informing him that the national police budget for the next year was going to be cut by at least 15 per cent, perhaps 20, and that no increase in funding was foreseeable in the near future. Yet these fools in Rome kept sending him projects and plans, as if there were money to spend, just as if it hadn't all been stolen or sent to secret accounts in Switzerland.

He pulled out the paper on which were written the specifications for the pistols that would never be bought, flipped it over, and began to list the people he wanted to speak to: Trevisan's widow and her brother, her daughter Francesca, and someone who could give him accurate information about both Trevisan's legal practice and his personal life.

In a second column, he listed those things that grated at his mind: Francesca's story – or was it boast? – that someone might try to kidnap her; Lotto's reluctance to provide a list of Trevisan's clients; Lotto's surprise at the mention of Favero's name.

And overriding all of this, he realized, were the phone numbers and the phone calls to so many places, still without pattern, still without explainable cause.

As he reached into his bottom drawer for the phone book, he thought how helpful it would be to emulate Favero and keep a notebook with frequently called numbers. But this was a number he had never called, never before wanting to call in the favour he was owed.

Three years ago, his friend Danilo, the pharmacist, had called him early in the evening and asked him to come to his apartment, where he found the young man with one eye swollen almost shut, looking as though he'd been in a brawl. There had, indeed, been violence, but it had been entirely one-sided, for Danilo had made no attempt to resist the young man who pushed his way into the pharmacy just as he was closing up for the night. Nor had he offered any opposition when the young man pried open the cabinet where the narcotic drugs were kept and pulled out seven ampoules of morphine. But Danilo did recognize him and, as the young man was leaving, said only, 'Roberto, you shouldn't be doing this,' which was enough to provoke the man into giving Danilo an angry shove, sending the pharmacist crashing sideways against the angle of a display cabinet.

Roberto, as not only Danilo and Brunetti but most of the police of the city knew, was the only son of Mario Beniamin, Chief Judge of the criminal court of Venice. Until that night, his addiction had never led him to violence, for he made do with false prescriptions and with what he managed to exchange for articles stolen from the homes of family and friends. But with his attack on the pharmacist, however unintentional it had been, Roberto had joined the criminals of the city.

After speaking to Danilo, Brunetti went to the Judge's home and spent more than an hour with him; the next morning, Judge Beniamin accompanied his son to a small private clinic near Zurich, where Roberto spent the next six months, emerging to begin an apprentice-ship in a pottery workshop near Milan.

The favour, spontaneously offered on Brunetti's part, had rested between him and the Judge for those years, much in the way a pair of shoes that cost too much will lie in the bottom of a closet and be forgotten about until they are kicked aside or stepped on accidentally, only then to be remembered with a wince that the buyer could so foolishly have fallen into such a false bargain.

The phone at the Judge's chambers was answered on the third ring by a woman's voice. Brunetti give his name and asked to speak to Judge Beniamin.

After a minute, the Judge came on to the line. '*Buon giorno*, commissario. I've been expecting your call.'

'Yes,' Brunetti said simply. 'I'd like to speak to you, your honour.'

'Today?'

'If it's convenient for you.'

'I can give you a half-hour, this afternoon at five. Will that be sufficient?'

'I think so, your honour.'

'I'll expect you, then. Here,' the Judge said and hung up.

The main criminal court house of the city lies at the foot of the Rialto Bridge, not the San Marco side but the side that holds the fruit and vegetable market.

In fact, those who go early to the market can sometimes see men and women in handcuffs and shackles being led into and out of the various entrances to the court, and not infrequently machine-gun-carrying carabinieri stand amidst the crates of cabbages and grapes, guarding the people who are taken inside. Brunetti showed his warrant card to the armed guards at the door and climbed the two flights of broad marble stairs to Judge Beniamin's chambers. Each landing had a large window that looked across to the Fondazione dei Tedeschi, under the Republic the commercial centre for all German traders in the city, now the Central Post Office. At the top of the stairs, two carabinieri wearing flak jackets and carrying assault rifles stopped him and asked to see his identification.

'Are you wearing a weapon, commissario?' one of them asked after a close examination of his warrant card.

Brunetti regretted having forgotten to leave the gun in his office: it had been open season on judges in Italy for so long that everyone was nervous and, too late, very cautious. He slowly pulled his jacket open and held the sides far from his body to allow the guard to take the pistol from him.

The third door on the right was Beniamin's. Brunetti knocked twice and was told to enter.

In the years that had passed since his visit to Judge Beniamin's home, the two men had passed one another occasionally on the street, nodding to one another, but it had been at least a year since Brunetti had seen the Judge, and he was shocked at the change in him.

Though the Judge was no more than a decade older than Brunetti, he now looked old enough to be his father. Deep lines ran from the sides of his nose down past his mouth before disappearing beneath his chin. His eyes, once a deep brown, seemed cloudy, as though someone had forgotten to dust them. And, wrapped in the flowing black robes of his calling, he seemed more trapped than dressed, so much weight had he lost.

'Have a seat, commissario,' Benjamin said. The voice was the same, deep and resonant, a singer's voice.

'Thank you, your honour,' Brunetti said and took his place in one of the four chairs in front of the Judge's desk.

'I'm sorry to tell you that I have less time than I thought I would have.' After he spoke, the Judge paused for a moment, as if just hearing what he had said. He gave a small, sad smile and added, 'This afternoon, that is. So if we can be quick, I'd be very grateful to you. If not, we can talk again in two days if it's necessary.'

'Of course, your honour. It goes without saying that I appreciate your agreeing to see me.' He paused and the men's eyes met, each fully aware of how formulaic this sentence was.

'Yes,' was all the Judge answered.

'Carlo Trevisan,' Brunetti said.

'Specifically?' asked the Judge.

'Who profits from his death? What was his relationship with his brother-in-law? With his wife? Why did his daughter tell a story, about five years ago, that her parents were afraid she would be kidnapped? And what, if any, association did he have with the Mafia?'

Judge Beniamin had taken no notes, had simply listened to the questions. He propped his elbows on his desk and showed the back of his hand to Brunetti, his five fingers splayed out.

'Two years ago, another lawyer, Salvatore Martucci, joined his firm, bringing with him his own clients. Their agreement stipulated that, next year, Martucci would be made an equal partner in the practice. There is talk that Trevisan was no longer willing to honour this contract. With Trevisan dead, Martucci is in sole charge of the practice.' Judge Beniamin's thumb disappeared.

'The brother-in-law is slick, very slick. It is an unproven rumour which would make me criminally liable for a charge of slander were I to repeat, but anyone wanting to avoid paying taxes on international business or to know whom to bribe so that shipments arrive here without customs inspection knows he's the best man to see.' The top half of his forefinger disappeared.

'The wife is having an affair with Martucci.' His middle finger joined the others.

'About five years ago, Trevisan – and this, too, is merely rumour – was involved in some sort of financial dealings with two men from the Palermo Mafia, very violent men. I do not know the nature of his involvement, whether it was criminal or not, even whether it was voluntary or not, but I do know that these men were interested in him, or he was interested in them, because of the possibility that Eastern Europe would soon open up, and there would consequently be more

161

business between Italy and those countries. The Mafia has been known to kidnap or kill the children of people who oppose their business offers. It is said that for a time Trevisan was a very frightened man, but it is also said that the fear went away.' Pulling the tops of his two remaining fingers into his fist, the judge said, 'I think that answers all of your questions.'

Brunetti got to his feet. 'Thank you, your Honour.'

'You're welcome, commissario.'

No mention was made of Roberto, dead of an overdose a year ago, nor was any made of the cancer that was destroying the Judge's liver. Outside the office, Brunetti retrieved his pistol from the guard and left the court building.

Chapter Eighteen

The first thing Brunetti did when he arrived at his office the next morning was to dial Barbara Zorzi's home number. After the beep, he said, 'Dottoressa, this is Guido Brunetti. If you're there, please pick up. I need to talk to you about the Trevisans again. I've learned that . . .'

'Yes?' she said, cutting in but not surprising him by failing to exchange pleasantries or greetings.

'I'd like to know if Signora Trevisan's visit to your office had anything to do with a pregnancy.' Before she could answer, he added, 'Not her daughter's, her own.'

'Why do you want to know this?' she asked.

'The autopsy report said her husband had had a vasectomy.'

'How long ago?'

'I don't know. Does that make a difference?'

There was a long pause before she spoke again. 'No, I suppose it doesn't. Yes, when she came to me two years ago, she thought she was pregnant. She was forty-one at the time, so it was possible.'

'Was she?'

'No.'

'Was she particularly disturbed about it?'

'At the time, I thought not, well, not more than a woman her age would be, who thought all of that was behind her. But now I suppose I have to say that, yes, she was.'

'Thank you,' Brunetti said simply.

'Is that all?' Her surprise was audible.

'Yes.'

'You aren't going to ask if I knew who the father was?'

'No. I think if you had thought it was anyone other than Trevisan, you would have told me the other day.'

She didn't answer for a moment, but when she did, she drew the first word out. 'Yes, I probably would have.'

'Good.'

'Perhaps.'

'Thank you,' Brunetti said and hung up.

Next he called Trevisan's office and attempted to arrange an appointment with Avvocato Salvatore Martucci, but he was told that Signor Martucci had gone to Milan on business and would return Commissario Brunetti's call as soon as he returned to Venice. No new papers lay on his desk, and so he contented himself with the list he had made the day before and with reflecting upon his conversation with the Judge.

Not for a moment did it occur to Brunetti to question the truth of anything Judge Beniamin had told him nor to spend any time attempting to confirm it. Given, then, Trevisan's probable involvement with the Mafia, his death began to look even more like an execution: as sudden and anonymous as a bolt of lightning. From his name, Martucci would probably turn out to be a Southerner: Brunetti warned himself against the prejudice that would carry that fact towards certain assumptions, especially should Martucci turn out to be Sicilian.

That left the daughter, Francesca, and her story of her parents' fear of kidnapping. Before he left the house that morning, Brunetti had told Chiara that the police had straightened out the kidnapping story and didn't need any more help from her. Even the most remote possibility that someone might learn of Chiara's interest in a matter that had to do with the Mafia caused Brunetti profound uneasiness, and he knew that a display of casual uninterest was the best way to dissuade her from asking more questions.

He was brought back from these thoughts by a knock at his door. '*Avanti*,' he called and raised his eyes to see Signora Elettra pushing open the door to allow a man to enter. 'Commissario,' she said as she came in, 'I'd like you to meet Signor Giorgio Rondini. He'd like to have a few words with you.'

The man she ushered in towered at least a head above her, though it was unlikely that he weighed much more than she. As gaunt as the subject of an El Greco portrait, Signor Rondini added to that resemblance with a pointed dark beard and black eyes that looked out at the world from beneath thick brows.

'Please have a seat, Signor Rondini,' Brunetti said, getting to his feet. 'How may I be of service to you?'

While Rondini was lowering himself into a chair, Signorina Elettra went back to the door she had left open and paused there for a moment. She stood immobile until Brunetti glanced across at her, when she pointed a finger at the now-seated man and mouthed, as if dealing with the newly deaf, 'Gi-or-gio.' Brunetti gave her the slightest of nods and said, '*Grazie*, signorina,' as she left, closing the door behind her.

For a time, neither man spoke. Rondini looked around the office, and Brunetti looked down at the list on his desk. Finally Rondini spoke: 'Commissario, I've come to ask your advice.'

'Yes, Signor Rondini?' Brunetti asked, looking up.

'It's about the conviction,' he said and stopped.

'The conviction, Signor Rondini?' Brunetti asked.

'Yes, because of that day on the beach.' He gave Brunetti a small smile of encouragement, prodding Brunetti to remember something he must have known about.

'I'm sorry, Signor Rondini, but I'm not familiar with the conviction. Could you tell me something more about it?'

Rondini's smile disappeared, replaced by a pained, embarrassed look.

'Elettra didn't tell you?'

'No, I'm afraid she hasn't spoken to me about it.' When Rondini's expression became even more grim at hearing this, Brunetti added, smiling, 'Other than to explain to me what a great help you've been to us, of course. It's because of your help that we've made the progress we have.' The fact that there was no real progress in the case didn't make the remark necessarily a lie, not that this would have stopped Brunetti from saying it.

When Rondini didn't say anything, Brunetti prodded him: 'Perhaps you could tell me a little bit about it, and then I can see how I can help you.'

Rondini's hands came together in his lap, the fingers of the right gently massaging those of the left. 'As I said, it's about the conviction.' He looked up and Brunetti smiled, nodding his head encouragingly. 'For indecent exposure.' Brunetti's smile didn't change; Rondini seemed encouraged by that.

'You see, commissario, I was on the beach two summers ago, at the Alberoni.' Brunetti's smile didn't change, even at the name of the beach out at the end of the Lido so popular with gays that it had come to be known as 'Sin Beach'. The smile didn't change, but his eyes studied Rondini, and his hands, with sharpened attention.

'No, no, commissario,' Rondini said with a shake of his head. 'It's not me. It's my brother.' He stopped and shook his head again in mingled embarrassment and confusion. 'I'm just making it worse.' Again, he smiled, even more nervously, and sighed once. 'Let me start again.' Brunetti greeted this idea with a nod. 'My brother's a journalist. That summer he was doing an article about the beach, and he asked me to go out there with him. He thought that way we'd look like a couple and people would leave us alone. That is, leave us alone but talk to him.' Again, Rondini stopped and glanced down at his hands, now floundering about in his lap.

When he said nothing and gave no indication that he would speak again, Brunetti asked, 'Is that where it happened?' When Rondini neither looked up nor answered, Brunetti prodded. 'The incident?'

Rondini took a deep breath and started talking again. 'I went for a swim, but then it began to get cold, so I decided to change back into my clothes. My brother was way down the beach, talking to someone, and I thought I was alone. Well, there was no one within about twenty metres of the blanket. So I sat down and took off my swimming trunks, and just as I was pulling my trousers on, two policemen came up to me and told me to stand up. I tried to pull my trousers on, but one of the policemen stepped on them, so I couldn't.' As he spoke, Rondini's voice grew tighter, Brunetti couldn't tell whether with embarrassment or anger.

One of Rondini's hands moved up to his chin and began to rub absently at his beard. 'So I tried to put my swimming trunks back on, but one of them picked them up and held them.' Rondini stopped.

'Then what happened, Signor Rondini?'

'I stood up.'

'And?'

'And they wrote up a summons against me, accusing me of public indecency.'

'Did you explain to them?'

'Yes.'

'And?'

'They didn't believe me.'

'What about your brother? Did he come back?'

'No, it all happened in about five minutes. By the

time he got back, they'd written out the summons and they were gone.'

'What did you do about it?'

'Nothing,' Rondini said and looked Brunetti in the eye. 'My brother told me not to worry, that they had to inform me if they were going to do anything about it.'

'And did they?'

'No. Or at least I never heard anything. Then, two months later, a friend called and told me he'd seen my name in that day's *Gazzettino*. There'd been some sort of legal process, but I was never notified. No fine, nothing. I never heard anything, not until they sent me a letter saying that I'd been convicted.'

Brunetti considered this for a moment, not finding it at all strange. A misdemeanour like this could very easily slip through the cracks of the justice system, and a man could find himself convicted without ever having been formally accused. What he did not understand was why Rondini was coming to him about it.

'Have you tried to get the decision changed?'

'Yes. But they told me that it was too late, that I had to do something about it before the proceedings. It wasn't a trial or anything like that.' Brunetti nodded, familiar with this system of ruling on misdemeanours. 'But it means I've been convicted of a crime.'

'A misdemeanour,' Brunetti corrected him.

'But still convicted,' Rondini insisted.

Brunetti tilted his head to one side and raised his eyebrows in a gesture he hoped was both sceptical and dismissive. 'I don't think you have anything to worry about, Signor Rondini.'

'I'm getting married,' Rondini said, an answer that baffled Brunetti completely.

'I'm afraid I don't follow you.'

Rondini's voice grew tight as he said, 'My fiancée. I don't want her family to learn that I was convicted of indecent exposure on a homosexual beach.'

'Does she know about it?' Brunetti asked.

He saw Rondini begin to give one answer, then change it. 'No. I didn't know her when it happened, and since then there's never been a time when it seemed right to tell her. Or a way. With my brother and my friends, it's just a funny story now, but I don't think she'd like it.' Rondini shrugged away any uneasiness he might have with this fact and added, 'And her family would like it even less.'

'And you've come to me to see if I can do anything about it?'

'Yes. Elettra has talked about you a lot, said you were very powerful here at the Questura.' Rondini's voice was rich with deference when he said this; worse, it was equally filled with hope.

Brunetti shrugged this compliment away. 'What sort of thing did you have in mind?'

'I need two things,' Rondini began. 'I'd like you to change my record,' he began, but as soon as he saw Brunetti begin to object, he added, 'I'm sure you can do something as simple as that.'

'It means altering an official government document,' Brunetti said in a voice he hoped he managed to make sound severe.

'But Elettra says that's . . .' Rondini began but stopped immediately.

Brunetti was afraid of how that sentence might have ended, so he said, 'This might be something that sounds a great deal easier than it is.'

Rondini looked up at him then, his gaze bold, his objection evident but unspoken. 'May I tell you the second thing?'

'Of course.'

'I need a letter explaining that the original complaint was mistaken and that I was absolved in court. In fact, it would help if the letter apologized for my trouble.'

He was tempted to dismiss the idea as impossible, but instead Brunetti asked, 'Why do you need this?'

'For my fiancée. And for her family. If they should ever learn about it.'

'But if the record is changed, why would you need the letter?' Brunetti asked but immediately corrected himself, adding, 'If the record can be changed, that is.'

'Don't worry about the record, dottore.' Rondini spoke with such absolute authority that Brunetti was forced to recall that he worked in the computer office of SIP, and then he remembered the small rectangular box on Signorina Elettra's desk.

'And from whom should this letter come?'

'I'd like it to come from the Questore,' Rondini began but quickly added, 'but I know that's impossible.' Brunetti noticed that, at the first sign they had apparently struck a bargain and had only to haggle about the details, Rondini's hands had ceased to move and lay quiet in his lap; he seemed even to relax in his chair.

'Would a letter from a commissario suffice?'

'Yes, I think so,' Rondini said.

'And what about cancelling the report in our files?' Rondini waved a hand. 'A day. Two.'

Brunetti didn't want to know which of them, Rondini or Elettra, would do it, so he didn't ask. 'Later in the week, I'll run a check on your name and see if there's a file on you.'

'There won't be,' Rondini assured him, but there was no arrogance in the claim, nothing more than simple certainty.

'When I know that, I'll write the letter.'

Rondini got to his feet. He extended his hand across Brunetti's desk. As the two men shook hands, Rondini said, 'If I can ever do you a favour, commissario, anything at all, just remember where I work.' Brunetti saw him to the door and, when he was gone, went down to speak to Signorina Elettra.

'You spoke to him?' she asked when Brunetti went in.

Brunetti wasn't sure whether to be offended by her assumption that he would so casually discuss the altering of official state documents and the writing of entirely fraudulent letters.

He opted for irony. 'I'm surprised you bothered to have him speak to me at all. That you didn't just take care of it all yourself.'

Her smile blossomed. 'Well, of course, I thought of doing that, but I thought it would be helpful if you spoke to him.'

'Because of changing the records?' he asked.

'Oh, no, either Giorgio or I could do that in a minute,' she said in an entirely dismissive tone.

'But isn't there some sort of secret password that prevents people from getting into our computer?'

She hesitated a moment before she answered. 'There's a password, yes, but it's not very secret.'

'Who knows it?'

'I've no idea, but it would be very easy to find.'

'And use?'

'Probably.'

Brunetti chose not to follow that thought. 'Then because of the letter?' he asked, assuming that she would know about Rondini's request for one.

'Oh, no, dottore. I could just as easily have written that for him. But I thought it would be good for him to meet you, to show him that you're willing to help him with this.'

'In case we need more information from SIP?' he asked, irony abandoned.

'Exactly,' she said and smiled in real delight, for the commissario had begun to understand how things worked.

Chapter Nineteen

All thoughts of Signor Rondini, however, were wiped from Brunetti's mind by the news that pulled him, half-shaved, from the bathroom the next morning. Ubaldo Lotto, the brother of Carlo Trevisan's widow, had been found shot dead in his car, parked on a side road that led off the state highway between Mestre and Mogliano Veneto. He appeared to have been shot three times, at close range, apparently by someone who was sitting beside him in the front seat of his car.

The body had been discovered at about five that morning by a local resident who, his car slowed by the heavy mud formed by the night's rain and by the large car parked at the side of the narrow road, had not liked what he saw when he passed: the driver slumped over the steering wheel, the motor of the car still running. He had stopped, walked back to peer inside, and then, seeing the blood pooled on the front seat, had called the police. When they arrived, the police cordoned off the area and began to search for traces of the killer or killers. There were signs that another car had been parked behind Lotto's, but the heavy autumn rain had washed away all hope of taking an impression of the tyre tracks. The first policeman to open the door gagged at the smell of blood, faecal matter, and some heavy scent he took to be the victim's aftershave, all blended together and exaggerated by the heater of the car, which had run at its highest setting during the hours Lotto lay in his death's embrace across the steering wheel. Carefully, the crime-scene crew examined the area around the car and then, when it had been towed to the police garage in Mestre, pored over the vehicle to extract and label fibres, hairs, and any other particles of matter that might provide information about the person who had sat beside Lotto on the front seat when he died.

The car had already been towed when Brunetti and Vianello, driven in a car from the Mestre police, arrived at the scene of the killing. From the back seat, all they saw was a narrow country lane and trees that still dripped with water, even though the rain had stopped at dawn. At the police garage, they saw a maroon Lancia sedan, its front seat covered with stains which were slowly turning the same colour as the car. And at the morgue they met the man who had been called to identify the body and who turned out to be Salvatore Martucci, the surviving partner of Trevisan's law firm. A flash from Vianello's eyes and a slight nod in Martucci's direction told Brunetti that this was the same lawyer Vianello had spoken to, the one who had displayed so little grief in the aftermath of Trevisan's murder.

Though thin and wiry, Martucci was taller than most Southerners, and his hair, which he wore shorter than was the current style, was reddish blond: this combination of qualities made him appear a throwback to the hordes of invading Normans who had swept across the island for generations and whose heritage could still be found, centuries later, in the piercing green eyes of many Sicilians as well as in the occasional French phrases that lingered in their dialect.

When Vianello and Brunetti got there, Martucci was just being led out of the room in which the bodies were kept. It struck them both that it would take very little for Martucci to look like a corpse himself: his eyes were ringed with flesh so dark it looked bruised and emphasized the terrible pallor of his complexion.

'Avvocato Martucci?' Brunetti began, stopping in front of him.

The lawyer looked at Brunetti, apparently without seeing him, then at Vianello, whom he seemed to notice, though he might have recognized no more than the familiar blue uniform.

'Yes?' he said.

'I'm Commissario Guido Brunetti. I'd like to ask you a few questions about Signor Lotto.'

'I don't know anything,' Martucci answered. Though he spoke in a monotone, his Sicilian accent was still marked.

'I realize this must be a very difficult time for you, Signor Martucci, but there are certain questions we must ask you.'

'I don't know anything,' Martucci repeated.

'Signor Martucci,' Brunetti said, standing steady beside Vianello so as to block Martucci's passage down the hallway, 'I'm afraid that if you don't speak to us, we'll have no choice but to ask the same questions of Signora Trevisan.'

'What's she got to do with this?' Martucci asked, head shooting up, eyes flashing back and forth between Brunetti and Vianello.

'The murdered man is her brother. Her husband died, in the same way, less than a week ago.'

Martucci looked away from them while he considered this. Brunetti was curious to see whether Martucci would question that similarity, insist that it meant nothing. But he simply said, 'All right, what do you want to know?'

'Perhaps we could go into one of the offices,' Brunetti said, having already asked the coroner if he could use his deputy's room.

Brunetti turned away and walked down the corridor, and Martucci fell into step behind him, followed by Vianello, who still had neither spoken nor acknowledged having already spoken to Martucci. Brunetti opened the door to the office and held it for Martucci. When the three men were seated, Brunetti said, 'Perhaps you could tell us where you were last night, Signor Martucci.'

'I don't see why that's necessary,' Martucci answered in a voice more confused than resistant.

'We will want to find out where everyone who knew Signor Lotto was last night, Signor Martucci. Such information is, as you must know, necessary in any murder investigation.'

'I was at home,' Martucci answered.

'Was anyone with you?'

177

'No.'

'Are you married, Signor Martucci?'

'Yes. But I'm separated from my wife.'

'Do you live alone?'

'Yes.'

'Do you have children?'

'Yes. Two.'

'Do they live with you or with your wife?'

'I don't see what any of this has to do with Lotto.'

'We are interested in you at the moment, Signor Martucci, not in Signor Lotto,' Brunetti answered. 'Do your children live with your wife?'

'Yes, they do.'

'Is yours a legal separation, leading towards a divorce?'

'We've never discussed it.'

'Could you explain that a bit further for me, Signor Martucci?' Brunetti asked, though it was a common enough situation.

When he spoke, Martucci's voice had the dead calm of truth. 'Even though I'm a lawyer, the thought of going through a divorce terrifies me. My wife would oppose any attempt I might make to get one.'

'Yet you've never discussed it?'

'Never. I know my wife well enough to know what her answer would be. She would not consent, and there are no grounds on which I could divorce her. If I tried to do so against her will, she would take everything I own.'

'Are there grounds on which she might divorce you, Signor Martucci?' Brunetti asked. When Martucci gave no answer, Brunetti rephrased the question, turning to euphemism, 'Are you seeing anyone, Signor Martucci?'

Martucci's answer was immediate. 'No.'

'I find that hard to believe,' Brunetti said with a smile of camaraderie.

'What does that mean?' Martucci said.

'You're a handsome man, in the prime of life, a professional, clearly a successful man. Certainly there are many women who would find you attractive and would welcome your attentions.'

Martucci said nothing.

'No one?' Brunetti repeated.

'No.'

'And so you were home alone last night?'

'I've already told you that, commissario.'

'Ah, yes, so you have.'

Martucci stood abruptly. 'If you have no further questions, I'd like to leave.'

With a soft wave of his hand, Brunetti said, 'Just a few more questions, Signor Martucci.'

Seeing the look in Brunetti's eyes, Martucci sat back down.

'What was the nature of your relationship with Signor Trevisan?'

'I worked for him.'

'For him or with him, Avvocato Martucci?'

'Both, I suppose you could say.' Brunetti prodded him with an inquisitive look and Martucci continued, 'First one and then the other.' He looked at Brunetti, but seeing that this was not enough, continued, 'I began working for him, but last year we agreed that, at the end of the year, I would become a partner in the firm.'

'An equal partner?'

Martucci kept both his voice and his eyes level. 'We hadn't discussed that.'

Brunetti found this an unusual lapse, especially on the part of lawyers. A lapse or, given that the only other witness to the agreement was dead, something else.

'And in the event of his death?' Brunetti asked.

'We didn't discuss that.'

'Why?'

Martucci's voice hardened. 'I think that's self-evident. People don't plan to die.'

'But they do die,' Brunetti remarked.

Martucci ignored him.

'And now that Signor Trevisan has died, will you assume the responsibility for the practice?'

'If Signora Trevisan asks me to, I will.'

'I see,' Brunetti remarked in a voice he strove to make entirely level. 'So you've, in a sense, inherited Signor Trevisan's clients?'

Martucci's attempt to keep his temper was visible. 'If those clients wish to retain me as their lawyer, yes.'

'And do they?'

'It is still too soon after Signor Trevisan's death to be able to know that.'

'And Signor Lotto,' Brunetti said, changing course. 'What was his relationship to or involvement in the practice?'

180

the streams of hot air that flowed up
he Nike of Samothrace had stepped
l, regained her head, and begun to
of the Louvre, she would have looked

said as she reached him.
estore, sir. He said he'd like very much

h to,' Brunetti found himself repeat-
the phrasing of the message. Paola
t a Dickens character who predicted
things by announcing that the wind
n a certain quarter; Brunetti could
which character, or which quarter,
that, when Patta 'would like' to talk
could be said to be coming from that

office?' Brunetti asked, turning and
the stairs beside the young woman.
d he's spent much of the morning on
too, was often a sign of a looming

Questore Patta called in response to
'Good morning, Brunetti,' he said
nate entered the office. 'Have a seat,
a few things I'd like to discuss with
remarks from Patta even before he sat
ti immediately on his guard.
e room and took his usual seat. 'Yes,
ked, taking his notebook from his
thus to display the seriousness with

'He was our accountant and business manager,' Martucci answered.

'Of both you and Signor Trevisan, when you worked
together?'

'Yes.'

'And after Signor Trevisan's death, did Signor Lotto
remain as your accountant?'

'Certainly. He was intimately familiar with the business. He'd worked for Carlo for more than fifteen years.'

'And were you planning to retain him as your
accountant and business manager?'

'Of course.'

'Did Signor Lotto have any legal claim to the practice
or to part of it?'

'I'm afraid I don't understand.'

This seemed strange to Brunetti, not only because
the question was straightforward enough but because
Martucci was a lawyer and certainly should have understood it. 'Was there any way in which the legal practice
was incorporated, and did Signor Lotto own any part
of it?' Brunetti asked.

Martucci thought about this for a while before he
answered. 'To the best of my knowledge, no, but they
might have had some sort of separate agreement
between themselves.'

'What sort of agreement might that have been?'

'I have no idea. Whatever they decided on.'

'I see,' Brunetti said and then asked, voice entirely
conversational, 'And Signora Trevisan?'

Martucci's silence showed that he had been expecting the question. 'What about her?'

'Did she retain any interest in the business?'

'That would depend upon the stipulations of Carlo's will.'

'You didn't draw it up?'

'No, he did that himself.'

'And you have no idea of its contents?'

'No, of course not. Why should I?'

'I thought that, as his partner . . .' Brunetti began and allowed a vague, encompassing flourish of his hands to complete the sentence for him.

'I was not his partner and would not have been so until the beginning of next year.'

'Yes, of course,' Brunetti agreed. 'I thought that, given your association, you might have had some idea of the contents.'

'None at all.'

'I see.' Brunetti got to his feet. 'I think that will be all for now, Signor Martucci. I'm very grateful for your co-operation.'

'That's all?' Martucci asked as he stood. 'I can go?'

'Of course,' Brunetti said and then, as if in proof of his good faith, went to the door and held it open for the lawyer. After mutual goodbyes, the lawyer left the office. Brunetti and Vianello waited a few minutes and then left the building, heading back towards Venice.

By the time the police launch delivered them to the landing in front of the Questura, Brunetti and Vianello had agreed that, though Martucci had seemed prepared for questions about Signora Trevisan and had responded to them coolly, the questions about her late husband and their partnership had obviously made him nervous.

Vianello had v
didn't have to
bours, friends,
was any confir
the previous n
yet, and becau
effects upon th
be difficult to

As they wer
Questura, Brun
Vianello. 'The

'What, sir?'

'The gas tan
left in it, and
got it filled. T
the motor ran.
shot.'

Vianello no
much, but if th
of the time of
point, there w
time of death.

Vianello we
up the steps to
top of the st
emerging from
down the steps
missario. The
Brunetti stopp
the steps towa
gossamer, trail

her shoulders by
the staircase. If
from her pedest
descend the step
much like this.

'Um?' Brunet

'The Vice-Qu
to speak to you.

'Like very m
ing, impressed b
often joked abo
the arrival of ba
was coming fro
never remembe
but he did kno
to him, the win
same quarter.

'Is he in his
going back dow

'Yes, he is, a
the phone.' Thi
storm.

'Avanti,' Vice
Brunetti's knock
when his subor
please. There ar
you.' Three civi
down put Brun

He crossed th
sir?' Brunetti a
pocket, hoping

which he wanted Patta to believe he treated this meeting.

'I'd like you to tell me what you know about the death of Rino Favero.'

'Favero, sir?'

'Yes, an accountant in Padua who was found dead in his garage last week.' Patta waited a length of time he would consider a pregnant pause and added, 'A suicide.'

'Ah, yes, Favero. I was told that he had Carlo Trevisan's phone number written in his address book.'

'I'm sure he had many phone numbers written in his address book,' Patta said.

'Trevisan's was listed without a name.'

'I see. Anything else?'

'There were some other numbers. We're trying to check them.'

'We, commissario? We?' Patta's voice was filled with nothing more than polite curiosity. A person less familiar with the Vice-Questore would hear only that, not the implied menace.

'The police in Padua, that is.'

'And have you found out what these numbers are?'

'No, sir.'

'Are you investigating Favero's death?'

'No, sir,' Brunetti replied honestly.

'Good.' Patta looked down at his desk and placed a telephone memo to one side, then looked at the paper below it. 'And Trevisan? What have you to report there?'

'There's been another killing,' Brunetti said.

'Lotto? Yes, I know. You think they're related?'

Brunetti took a long breath before answering. The two men were business partners and were killed in the same way, perhaps with the same weapon, and Patta asked if the crimes were related. 'Yes, sir. I do.'

'I think, then, that you had best devote your time and energies to investigating their deaths and leave this business of Favero to the people in Padua, where it belongs.' Patta moved a second piece of paper to the side of his desk and glanced down at a third.

'Is there anything else, sir?' Brunetti asked.

'No, I think that will be all,' Patta said, not bothering to look up.

Brunetti put the notebook in his pocket, got up, and left the office, unsettled by Patta's civility. Outside, he stopped at Signorina Elettra's desk. 'You have any idea who he's been talking to?'

'No, I don't, but he's having lunch at Do Forni,' she said, naming a restaurant once famous for its food, now for its prices.

'Did you make the reservation for him?'

'No, I didn't. In fact, one of those phone calls must have contained a better invitation because he asked me to cancel his own reservation at Corte Sconto,' she said, naming a restaurant of similar cost. Before Brunetti could muster the bravado to ask an employee of the police to compromise her principles, Signorina Elettra suggested, 'Perhaps I could call this afternoon and ask if they've found the Vice-Questore's notebook. Since he never carries one, that's unlikely. But I'm sure they'll

186

tell me who he was sitting with if I explain I'd like to call whoever he was with and ask if they found it.'

'I'd be very grateful,' Brunetti said. He had no idea if this information would be important in any way, but he had, over the years, found it useful to have an idea of what Patta was doing and whom he was seeing, especially during those rare periods when Patta chose to treat him politely.

Chapter Twenty

An hour after Brunetti returned to his office, he received a phone call from della Corte, at a phone booth in Padua. At least that's what it sounded like to Brunetti, who at times had difficulty hearing what the other man said, so loud was the noise of horns and traffic that followed his voice down the line.

'We've found the restaurant where he had dinner the night he died,' della Corte said, and Brunetti needed no explanation to know that the pronoun referred to Favero.

Brunetti jumped over questions of where and how the police had found out and asked the only question that had bearing on the case: 'Was he alone?'

'No,' della Corte said eagerly. 'He was with a woman, about ten years younger than himself. Very well dressed and, from what the waiter said, very attractive.'

'And?' Brunetti insisted, realizing how little help that description would be in recognizing her.

'One second,' della Corte said. 'Here, I've got it. She was about thirty-five, blonde hair, cut neither short nor long. Just about Favero's height.' Remembering the description of Favero on the autopsy report, Brunetti

'He was our accountant and business manager,' Martucci answered.

'Of both you and Signor Trevisan, when you worked together?'

'Yes.'

'And after Signor Trevisan's death, did Signor Lotto remain as your accountant?'

'Certainly. He was intimately familiar with the business. He'd worked for Carlo for more than fifteen years.'

'And were you planning to retain him as your accountant and business manager?'

'Of course.'

'Did Signor Lotto have any legal claim to the practice or to part of it?'

'I'm afraid I don't understand.'

This seemed strange to Brunetti, not only because the question was straightforward enough but because Martucci was a lawyer and certainly should have understood it. 'Was there any way in which the legal practice was incorporated, and did Signor Lotto own any part of it?' Brunetti asked.

Martucci thought about this for a while before he answered. 'To the best of my knowledge, no, but they might have had some sort of separate agreement between themselves.'

'What sort of agreement might that have been?'

'I have no idea. Whatever they decided on.'

'I see,' Brunetti said and then asked, voice entirely conversational, 'And Signora Trevisan?'

Martucci's silence showed that he had been expecting the question. 'What about her?'

'Did she retain any interest in the business?'

'That would depend upon the stipulations of Carlo's will.'

'You didn't draw it up?'

'No, he did that himself.'

'And you have no idea of its contents?'

'No, of course not. Why should I?'

'I thought that, as his partner . . .' Brunetti began and allowed a vague, encompassing flourish of his hands to complete the sentence for him.

'I was not his partner and would not have been so until the beginning of next year.'

'Yes, of course,' Brunetti agreed. 'I thought that, given your association, you might have had some idea of the contents.'

'None at all.'

'I see.' Brunetti got to his feet. 'I think that will be all for now, Signor Martucci. I'm very grateful for your co-operation.'

'That's all?' Martucci asked as he stood. 'I can go?'

'Of course,' Brunetti said and then, as if in proof of his good faith, went to the door and held it open for the lawyer. After mutual goodbyes, the lawyer left the office. Brunetti and Vianello waited a few minutes and then left the building, heading back towards Venice.

By the time the police launch delivered them to the landing in front of the Questura, Brunetti and Vianello had agreed that, though Martucci had seemed prepared for questions about Signora Trevisan and had responded to them coolly, the questions about her late husband and their partnership had obviously made him nervous.

Vianello had worked with Brunetti for so long that he didn't have to be told to run the usual checks – neighbours, friends, wife – on Martucci's story to see if there was any confirmation of his presence in his own home the previous night. The autopsy hadn't been performed yet, and because of the intense heat in the car and its effects upon the body, the exact time of death would be difficult to determine.

As they were crossing the broad entrance hall of the Questura, Brunetti stopped in his tracks and turned to Vianello. 'The gas tank,' he said suddenly.

'What, sir?' he asked.

'The gas tank. Have them measure how much gas is left in it, and then find out, if you can, when he last got it filled. That might give some idea of how long the motor ran. Might help them calculate when he was shot.'

Vianello nodded. It might not narrow things down much, but if the autopsy failed to give a clear indication of the time of death, it might help. Not that, at this point, there was any compelling need to ascertain the time of death.

Vianello went off on his errand, and Brunetti went up the steps towards his office. Before he got to the top of the steps, however, he met Signora Elettra, emerging from the end of the corridor and turning down the steps towards him. 'Oh, there you are, commissario. The Vice-Questore has been asking for you.' Brunetti stopped and gazed up at her as she descended the steps towards him. A long saffron scarf, as light as gossamer, trailed behind her, borne aloft at the level of her shoulders by the streams of hot air that flowed up the staircase. If the Nike of Samothrace had stepped from her pedestal, regained her head, and begun to descend the steps of the Louvre, she would have looked much like this.

'Um?' Brunetti said as she reached him.

'The Vice-Questore, sir. He said he'd like very much to speak to you.'

'Like very much to,' Brunetti found himself repeating, impressed by the phrasing of the message. Paola often joked about a Dickens character who predicted the arrival of bad things by announcing that the wind was coming from a certain quarter; Brunetti could never remember which character, or which quarter, but he did know that, when Patta 'would like' to talk to him, the wind could be said to be coming from that same quarter.

'Is he in his office?' Brunetti asked, turning and going back down the stairs beside the young woman.

'Yes, he is, and he's spent much of the morning on the phone.' This, too, was often a sign of a looming storm.

'*Avanti*,' Vice-Questore Patta called in response to Brunetti's knock. 'Good morning, Brunetti,' he said when his subordinate entered the office. 'Have a seat, please. There are a few things I'd like to discuss with you.' Three civil remarks from Patta even before he sat down put Brunetti immediately on his guard.

He crossed the room and took his usual seat. 'Yes, sir?' Brunetti asked, taking his notebook from his pocket, hoping thus to display the seriousness with

'Lotto? Yes, I know. You think they're related?'

Brunetti took a long breath before answering. The two men were business partners and were killed in the same way, perhaps with the same weapon, and Patta asked if the crimes were related. 'Yes, sir. I do.'

'I think, then, that you had best devote your time and energies to investigating their deaths and leave this business of Favero to the people in Padua, where it belongs.' Patta moved a second piece of paper to the side of his desk and glanced down at a third.

'Is there anything else, sir?' Brunetti asked.

'No, I think that will be all,' Patta said, not bothering to look up.

Brunetti put the notebook in his pocket, got up, and left the office, unsettled by Patta's civility. Outside, he stopped at Signorina Elettra's desk. 'You have any idea who he's been talking to?'

'No, I don't, but he's having lunch at Do Forni,' she said, naming a restaurant once famous for its food, now for its prices.

'Did you make the reservation for him?'

'No, I didn't. In fact, one of those phone calls must have contained a better invitation because he asked me to cancel his own reservation at Corte Sconto,' she said, naming a restaurant of similar cost. Before Brunetti could muster the bravado to ask an employee of the police to compromise her principles, Signorina Elettra suggested, 'Perhaps I could call this afternoon and ask if they've found the Vice-Questore's notebook. Since he never carries one, that's unlikely. But I'm sure they'll

186

which he wanted Patta to believe he treated this meeting.

'I'd like you to tell me what you know about the death of Rino Favero.'

'Favero, sir?'

'Yes, an accountant in Padua who was found dead in his garage last week.' Patta waited a length of time he would consider a pregnant pause and added, 'A suicide.'

'Ah, yes, Favero. I was told that he had Carlo Trevisan's phone number written in his address book.'

'I'm sure he had many phone numbers written in his address book,' Patta said.

'Trevisan's was listed without a name.'

'I see. Anything else?'

'There were some other numbers. We're trying to check them.'

'We, commissario? We?' Patta's voice was filled with nothing more than polite curiosity. A person less familiar with the Vice-Questore would hear only that, not the implied menace.

'The police in Padua, that is.'

'And have you found out what these numbers are?'

'No, sir.'

'Are you investigating Favero's death?'

'No, sir,' Brunetti replied honestly.

'Good.' Patta looked down at his desk and placed a telephone memo to one side, then looked at the paper below it. 'And Trevisan? What have you to report there?'

'There's been another killing,' Brunetti said.

realized that this would make her tall for a woman. 'The waiter said she was very well dressed, very expensively. He didn't hear her say much, but she sounded as expensive as the clothing – at least that's how he described her.'

'Where were they?'

'In a restaurant over near the university.'

'How'd you find out?'

'None of the people who work there reads the *Gazzettino*, so they didn't see Favero's picture when the story appeared. The waiter didn't see it until this morning, when he went to get his hair cut and found it on a pile of old newspapers. He recognized Favero from the photo and called us. I just spoke to them but haven't gone over to speak to him yet. I thought you might like to come with me when I do.'

'When?'

'It's a restaurant. Lunch?'

Brunetti glanced down at his watch. It was twenty to eleven. 'It'll take me half an hour to get to the railway station,' he said. 'I'll get the first train leaving after that. Can you meet me?'

'I'll be there,' della Corte said and hung up.

And so he was, waiting on the platform when the train pulled in. Brunetti pushed his way through the crowd of university students who milled around on the platform, trying to push their way up on to the train the instant its doors opened.

The two men shook hands and left the platform, heading down the stairs that would carry them under the tracks and up out of the station to the police car that stood, motor running and driver in place, at the curb.

As the car crawled through the gagging traffic of Padua, Brunetti asked, 'Has anyone from your place been in touch with my boss?'

'Patta?' della Corte asked, pronouncing the name with a soft explosion of breath that could mean anything. Or nothing.

'Yes.'

'Not that I know of. Why?'

'He's suggested that I leave the investigation of Favero's death to you. Of his suicide. I wondered if the suggestion came from the people here.'

'Could have,' della Corte said.

'Have you had any more trouble?'

'No, not really. Everyone's treating it like it was a suicide. Anything I do is on my own time.'

'Like this?' Brunetti asked, waving a hand to encompass the car.

'Yes. I'm still free to eat lunch wherever I please.'

'And invite a friend from Venice?' asked Brunetti.

'Exactly,' della Corte agreed just as the car pulled up to the curb in front of the restaurant. The uniformed driver sprang out and opened the door, held it while the two men got out. 'Go and have some lunch, Rinaldi,' della Corte said. 'Be back at three.'

The young man saluted and climbed back into the car.

Two miniature Norfolk pines in large terracotta pots flanked the door to the restaurant, which opened as they drew near. 'Good afternoon, gentlemen,' a dark-

190

suited man with a long face and basset eyes said as they came inside.

'Good afternoon,' the captain said. 'Della Corte. I called to reserve a table for two.'

'Your table is ready, if you'd like to come this way.'

The man paused to pick up two long menus from a desk near the door before leading them into a room so small it held no more than six or seven tables, all but one of which were taken. Through a high arch, Brunetti saw a second room, it too filled with what looked like businessmen. Because the high windows allowed so little light, both rooms were softly lit from lighting hidden in the oak beams that ran across the ceiling. They walked past a round table covered with antipasti of all types: salami, shellfish, prosciutto, octopus. The man led them to a table in a corner, held Brunetti's chair for him, and then placed the menus in front of them. 'May I offer you a Prosecco, gentlemen?' he asked.

Both nodded, and he left them.

'He the owner?' Brunetti asked.

'Yes.'

'What's he so worried about?'

'Everyone's worried when the police come to ask questions,' della Corte said, picking up the menu and turning his attention to it. He held it at arm's length and read through it, then put it down, saying, 'I'm told the duck is very good here.'

Brunetti studied the menu long enough to see that nothing sounded better. He closed it and set it down beside his plate just as the owner returned with a bottle of Prosecco. He filled the two narrow glasses that stood to the right of their plates and then passed the bottle to a waiter who came up behind him.

'Have you decided, capitano?' he asked.

'I'd like the fettuccine with truffles,' della Corte said. Brunetti nodded to the owner. 'And then the duck.' Brunetti nodded again.

'I suggest the Merlot del Piave,' the owner said. When della Corte nodded, the owner gave the most minimal of bows and backed away from their table.

Della Corte picked up his glass and sipped at the sparkling wine. Brunetti did the same. Until their first course came, the men talked of much and nothing, della Corte explaining that the recent elections would probably result in a complete upheaval of the police in Padua, at least at the highest levels.

Brunetti remembered his own poor behaviour in the last mayoral election in Venice and said nothing. He had found both candidates unappealing – the philosopher with no government experience proposed by the ex-Communists and the businessman put up by the Lega – and so he had emerged from the voting booth without having been able to vote, something he had never confessed to Paola, who was so happy at the victory of the philosopher that she never bothered to ask him whom he had voted for. Maybe all of these new elections would force things to begin to change. Brunetti doubted it, had been around government and the people who ran it too long to think that any changes would ever be more than cosmetic.

He brought his attention back to the table, and their

plates of fettuccine, glistening with the sheen of butter. The owner came back, carrying a small truffle on a white plate in one hand, a metal grater in the other. He bent over della Corte's plate and shaved at the truffle, rose, and bent over Brunetti's plate and did the same. The woody, musty odour wafted up from the still-steaming fettuccine, enveloping not only the three men, but the entire area around them. Brunetti twirled the first forkful and began to eat, giving in whole-heartedly to the sensual delight of the butter, the perfectly cooked noodles, and the savoury, heady taste of the truffles.

Della Corte was obviously a man who refused to spoil food with talk, and so they said little until the meal was finished, the duck almost as good as the truffles – for Brunetti, nothing was as good as truffles – and they sat with small glasses of calvados in front of them.

It was at that point that a short, happily stout man approached their table. He wore the white jacket and black cummerbund that their own waiter had worn. 'Signor Germani said you'd like to speak to me, capitano.'

'Was it you I spoke to this morning?' della Corte asked, pushing out a chair and waving the man into it.

The waiter pulled the chair out a bit more in order to accommodate his substantial paunch and sat. 'Yes, sir, it was.'

'I'd like you to repeat what you told me for my colleague here,' he said, nodding in Brunetti's direction.

Looking at della Corte, he began. 'As I told you on the phone, sir, I didn't recognize him when I first saw his picture in the paper. But then, when the barber was cutting my hair, it just came to me who he was, right out of the blue. So I called the police.'

Della Corte smiled and nodded as if to compliment the waiter on his sense of civic responsibility. 'Go on,' he said.

'I don't think I can tell you much more than I told you this morning, sir. He was with a woman. I described her to you on the phone.'

Della Corte asked him, 'Could you repeat what you told me?'

'She was tall, as tall as he was. Light eyes and skin, and light hair, not blonde, but almost. She was the same one he was here with before.'

'When were they here before?' della Corte asked.

'Once about a month ago, and once back in the summer, I forget when. I just remember that it was hot, and she wore a yellow dress.'

'How did they behave?' della Corte asked.

'Behave? You mean their manners?'

'No, I mean how they behaved towards one another.'

'Oh, do you mean was there anything between them?'

'Yes,' della Corte said and nodded.

'I don't think so,' the waiter said and paused to consider the question. After a moment's pause, he continued, 'It was obvious that they weren't married.' Even before della Corte could ask, the waiter explained, 'I don't know what it is that makes me say that, but I've watched a million couples here over the years, and there's just a way people who are married behave with one another. I mean, whether it's a good marriage or a bad one, even if they hate one another, they're always comfortable with one another.' He waved the subject away as too complex to explain. Brunetti knew exactly what he meant but, like him, could never hope to explain it.

'And these people didn't give you that idea?' Brunetti asked, speaking for the first time.

The waiter shook his head.

'Do you know what they talked about?'

'No,' the waiter said, 'but whatever it was, they both seemed very happy about it. At one point during the meal, he showed her some papers. She looked at them for a while. That's when she put on her glasses.'

'Do you have any idea what the papers were?' della Corte asked.

'No. When I brought their pasta, she gave them back to him.'

'And what did he do with them?'

'He must have put them in his pocket. I didn't notice.' Brunetti glanced across at della Corte, who shook his head, signalling that no papers had been found on Favero.

'Could you tell us a bit more about what she looked like?' della Corte asked.

'Well, as I told you, she was somewhere in her thirties. Tall, light hair, but not natural. She had the colouring for it, light eyes, so maybe she was just helping it a little.'

'Anything else?' Brunetti asked, smiling and then

sipping at his calvados to suggest that the question had no special importance.

'Well, now that I know he's dead, and by his own hand, I don't know whether I noticed it at the time or I started to think it after I found out what happened to him.' Neither Brunetti nor della Corte asked anything. 'Well, something wasn't right between them.' He reached forward and brushed some crumbs from the table, caught them in his hand, and then, seeing no place to put them, slipped them into the pocket of his jacket.

In the face of the silence of the two policemen, he continued, speaking slowly, thinking this out for the first time. 'It was about halfway through the meal, when she was looking at the papers. She glanced up from them and gave him a look.'

'What kind of look?' della Corte finally asked after a long silence.

'I don't know. It wasn't angry or anything like that. She just looked at him like he was in a zoo or something, like she'd never seen anything like him. You know, like he was of a different species or had stepped out of a spaceship. I don't know if I'm making the idea clear,' he said, letting his voice trail off inconclusively.

'Did it seem like the look was threatening in any way?'

'Oh, no, not at all,' he shook his head in an effort to convince them. 'That's what was so strange about it, that there was no anger in it. There was just nothing in it.' He stuffed his hands in his pockets and gave an awkward grin. 'I'm sorry. I'm not explaining this well.'

'Did he notice it?' Brunetti asked.

'No, he was pouring some more wine. But I saw it.'

'What about the other times?' Brunetti asked. 'Did they get on well?'

'Oh, yes. They always got on well. I don't mean to suggest that they didn't get on well that night, either. They were always very friendly but in a sort of semi-formal way.'

'Were there any papers the other times?'

'No, nothing like that. They seemed like friends, no, like business associates having a meal together. That's what it was like, the way two men who have to meet for business meet. Maybe that's why I always found it so strange, such an attractive woman, and he was a handsome man, but there was none of that tension that you like to see between a man and a woman, none of that at all. Yes, now that I think about it, that's what was so strange.' He smiled now, having finally figured it out.

'Do you remember what wine they drank?' Brunetti asked. Both the waiter and della Corte gave him puzzled glances.

The waiter thought about it for a while. 'Barolo,' he finally answered. 'A good, hearty red. Went well with the bistecche. And then Vin Santo with the dessert.'

'Did he leave the table at any time?' Brunetti asked, thinking about just how hearty those wines were and about how easy it is to drop something in a glass.

'I don't remember. He might have.'

'Do you remember if he paid with a credit card?' Brunetti asked.

'No, he paid with cash this time, and I have it in my mind that he paid with cash those other times, too.'

'Do you know if he's come other times? Other than when you saw them?'

'I asked the other waiters, but no one remembers them. But it's not likely. We're closed Tuesday and Wednesday, and I'm here all of the other days. Haven't missed a day of work in thirteen years. So if they came, I was here, and I don't remember seeing them except for last week and those two other times. She's a woman I'd remember.'

Della Corte glanced across the table at Brunetti, but he shook his head. He had no more questions, not for now. Della Corte reached into his pocket and took out a small visiting card. 'If you think of anything else, you can reach me at the Questura,' della Corte said, handing him the card. Then, in a voice he made casually neutral, he added, 'Be sure to ask for me specifically.'

The waiter pocketed it, stood, and started to walk away from their table. Suddenly he stopped and came back towards them. 'Do you want her glasses?' he asked without preamble.

'Excuse me?' della Corte said.

'Her glasses. She left them here, on the chair beside her. She must have taken them off after she looked at the papers and then forgot to take them with her. We found them after they left. Do you want them?'

Della Corte recovered himself immediately. 'Yes, of course.'

The waiter disappeared and was back in a few moments, carrying a pair of wire-framed glasses in one hand. He held them up and, with almost childlike delight, said, 'Look.' With that, he held them by the ends of the earpieces and twisted them round, as though the frame were made of rubber and this a very clever trick. Pretzel-like, they bent, and then, when he released the pressure, immediately sprang back to their original shape. 'Isn't that remarkable?' he asked.

The waiter handed the glasses to della Corte and went back across the restaurant, towards the door that led to the kitchen.

'Why don't they break?' della Corte asked, holding the glasses in one hand and twisting at them with the other, bending them just as the waiter had.

'Titanium,' Brunetti answered, though the question had been entirely rhetorical.

'What?' della Corte asked.

'Titanium,' Brunetti repeated. 'My wife bought a new pair of reading glasses last month, and she told me about these. May I?' he asked, reaching for them. Della Corte handed them over, and Brunetti brought them close to his eyes, searching for a manufacturer's sign. He found it, inside the right earpiece, up close to the hinge. 'See,' he said, extending them to della Corte.

'What is it?' della Corte asked. 'I don't have my own glasses with me.'

'It's Japanese,' Brunetti said. 'At least I think it is. It's only the Japanese who make these.'

'The Japanese?' della Corte asked. 'They make glasses?'

'They make the frames,' Brunetti explained. 'And these frames, I'd say, cost almost a million lire. At least that's what my wife told me. If they're titanium, and I think these are,' he said, twisting them once more into a painful shape and then releasing them suddenly and watching them snap back into shape, 'then that's what they cost.'

Brunetti's smile blossomed and he looked down at the glasses as though they had been transformed back into a million lire, and he'd been told to keep them.

'What are you smiling at?' della Corte asked.

'Frames that cost a million lire,' Brunetti explained, 'especially frames that are imported from Japan, ought to be very easy to trace.'

The same million lire appeared, but this time they were in della Corte's smile.

Chapter Twenty-One

It was Brunetti's suggestion that they take the glasses to an optician and have the prescription of the lenses examined to make it even easier to identify them. Because the frames were not only expensive but imported, they should have been easy to trace, but this was to ignore the fact that della Corte, having been ordered to treat Favero's death as a suicide, had to use his own time to search for the optician who sold them, just as it was to ignore the possibility that they had been purchased in some city other than Padua.

Brunetti did what he could, assigning one of his junior officers the task of phoning all of the opticians in the Mestre-Venice area to ask if they carried those particular frames and, if so, whether they had ever filled them with that prescription. He then returned his attention to the Trevisan-Lotto-Martucci triangle, his interest centred on the survivors, both of whom would profit in some way from Trevisan's death. The widow would probably inherit, and Martucci might well inherit the widow. Lotto's murder, however, was difficult to fit into any pattern Brunetti envisioned that involved Martucci and Signora Trevisan. He did not for a moment question the fact that husbands and wives would want to, and often did, kill one another, but he found it difficult to believe that a sister would kill a brother. Husbands, even children, can be replaced, but one's aged parents can never produce another son. Antigone had sacrificed her life to this truth. Brunetti realized he needed to speak to both Signora Trevisan and Avvocato Martucci again, and he thought it would be interesting to speak to them together and see how things fell out.

Before he did anything about that, however, he turned his attention to the papers that had accumulated on his desk. There was, as promised, the list of Trevisan's clients, seven close-typed pages that held names and addresses in perfect and perfectly neutral alphabetical order. He glanced through it quickly, running his eyes down the column of names. At a few, he whistled under his breath: it appeared that Trevisan had planted his standard firmly among the ranks of the wealthiest citizens of the city as well as among those who passed for its nobility. Brunetti flipped back to the first page and began to read the names carefully. He realized that the attention he was giving them would, to a non-Venetian, pass for sober reflection; anyone bred on the incestuous rumours and cabals of the city would realize that he was doing no more than dredging up gossip, slur, and slander as he considered each name. There was Baggio, the Director of the port, a man accustomed to power and its ruthless employment. There was Seno, owner of the largest glass-making workshop on Murano, employer of more than three hundred people, a man whose competitors seemed to share the common misfortune of being hit by strikes and unexplained fires. And there was Brandoni, Conte Brandoni, the exact source of whose immense wealth was as obscure as the origin of his title.

Some of the people on the list did have the most blameless, even the highest, of reputations; what Brunetti found peculiar was the promiscuity of names, the revered rubbing elbows with the suspect, the most highly honoured mingling with the equivocal. He turned back to the Fs and searched for his father-in-law's name, but Conte Orazio Falier was not listed. Brunetti laid the list aside, knowing that they would have no choice but to question all of them, one by one, and reproving himself for his reluctance to call his father-in-law to ask what he knew about Trevisan. Or about his clients.

Below the list, there was a painfully typed and inordinately long message from Officer Gravini, explaining that the Brazilian whore and her pimp had appeared at Pinetta's bar the previous night and that he had 'initiated' an arrest. 'Initiated?' Brunetti heard himself asking aloud. That's the sort of thing that came of allowing university graduates into the ranks. When Brunetti called downstairs and asked where they were, he learned that both had been brought over from the gaol that morning and were being kept in separate rooms on Officer Gravini's recommendation in case Brunetti wanted to question them.

Next was a fax from the police in Padua, reporting that the bullets recovered from Lotto's body came from a .22 calibre pistol, though no tests had yet been performed to determine whether it was the same pistol used on Trevisan. Brunetti knew that any tests would do no more than confirm what he already knew in his blood.

Below that were more sheets of fax papers, these bearing the SIP letterhead and containing the phone records he had asked Signorina Elettra to obtain from Giorgio. At the thought of Rondini and the many lists he had provided, Brunetti remembered the letter he had to write and the fact that he had not yet bothered to do so. The fact that Rondini felt he needed such a letter to give to his fiancée left Brunetti bemused that he would want to marry her, but he had long ago abandoned the idea that he understood marriage.

Brunetti admitted to himself that he also had no idea of what he hoped to learn from either Mara or her pimp, but he decided to go and speak to them anyway. He walked down to the first floor, which contained three separate cell-like rooms in which the police routinely interviewed suspects and others brought in for questioning.

Outside one of the rooms stood Gravini, a handsome young man who had joined the force a year ago, having spent the previous two trying to find someone who would give a job to a twenty-seven-year-old university graduate with a degree in philosophy and no previous work experience. Brunetti often wondered what had impelled Gravini to that decision, which philosopher's precepts had moved him to take on the jacket, pistol, and cap of the forces of order. Or, the thought sneaked out from nowhere and leaped into Brunetti's mind, perhaps Gravini had found in Vice-Questore Patta the living manifestation of Plato's philosopher king.

'Good morning, sir,' Gravini said, snapping out a quick salute and demonstrating no surprise at the fact that his superior arrived laughing to himself. Philosophers, it is rumoured, bear with these things.

'Which of them's in here?' Brunetti asked, nodding his head at the door behind Gravini.

'The woman, sir.' Saying this, Gravini handed Brunetti a dark-blue file. 'The man's record's in here, sir. Nothing on her.'

Brunetti took the file and glanced at the two pages stapled to the inside cover. There was the usual: assault, selling drugs, living off the earnings of a prostitute. Franco Silvestri was one of thousands. After reading through it carefully, he handed the file back to Gravini.

'Did you have any trouble bringing them in?'

'Not her, sir. It was almost as if she was expecting it. But the man tried to make a run for it. Ruffo and Vallot were with me, outside, and they grabbed him.'

'Well done, Gravini. Whose idea was it to take them along?'

'Well, sir,' Gravini said, with a low cough. 'I told them what I was going to do, and they offered to come along. On their own time, you understand.'

'You get along well with them, don't you, Gravini?'

'Yes, sir, I do.'

'Good, good. Well, let's have a look at her.'

Brunetti let himself into the grim little room. The only light came from a small, dirty window high on one wall, far higher than a person could hope to jump, and from a single 60-watt bulb in a wire-covered fixture in the centre of the ceiling.

Mara sat on the edge of one of the three chairs. There was no other furniture, no table, no sink, nothing but three straight-backed chairs and, on the floor, a scattering of cigarette butts. She looked up when Brunetti came in, recognized him, and said, 'Good morning' in a relaxed voice. She looked tired, as if she'd not slept well the night before, but she didn't look particularly disturbed to find herself here. On the back of a chair hung the same leopard-skin jacket she had worn the other night, but her blouse and skirt were new, though they both looked as though she had slept in them. Her make-up had worn off or she had washed it off; either way, its absence made her look younger, little more than an adolescent.

'You've done this before, I imagine?' Brunetti asked, sitting in the third chair.

'More times than I can count,' she said, and then asked, 'Do you have any cigarettes? I've finished mine, and the cop out there won't open the door.'

Brunetti stepped over to the door and tapped on it three times. When Gravini opened it, Brunetti asked him if he had some cigarettes, then took the pack the officer handed him and brought it back to Mara.

'Thank you,' she said, pulled a plastic lighter from the pocket of her skirt and lit one. 'My mother died of these,' she said, holding it up and waving it back and forth in front of her, studying the trail of smoke it left. 'I wanted to put that on her death certificate, but the doctors wouldn't do it. They put "cancer", but it should have been "Marlboro".' She begged me never to start smoking, and I promised her I never would.'

'Did she find out that you smoked?'

Mara shook her head. 'No, she never found out, not about the cigarettes and not about a lot of things.'

'Like what?' Brunetti asked.

'Like I was pregnant when she died. Only four months, but it was the first time and I was young, so it didn't show.'

'She might have been happy to know,' suggested Brunetti. 'Especially if she knew she was dying.'

'I was fifteen,' Mara said.

'Oh,' Brunetti said and looked away. 'Did you have others?'

'Other what?' she asked, confused.

'Other children. You said it was the first.'

'No, I meant it was the first time I was pregnant. I had the baby, but then I had a miscarriage with the second and since then I've been careful.'

'Where is your child?'

'In Brazil, with my mother's sister.'

'Is it a boy or a girl?'

'A girl.'

'How old is she now?'

'Six.' She smiled at the thought of the child. She looked down at her feet and then up at Brunetti, began to speak, stopped, and said, 'I have a picture of her if you'd like to see it.'

'Yes, I would,' he said, pulling his chair closer.

She tossed the cigarette on to the floor and reached into her blouse to pull out a gold-plated locket the size of a 100-lire coin. Pressing a tab on the top, she sprang it open and held it out to Brunetti, who bent forward to examine it. On one side, he saw a round-faced baby swaddled to within an inch of its life and on the other a little girl with long dark braids, standing stiff and formal, wearing what looked like a school uniform. 'She goes to school with the sisters,' Mara explained, bending her head down awkwardly to look at the photo. 'I think it's better for them.'

'Yes, I think so, too,' Brunetti agreed. 'We sent our daughter to the sisters until she finished middle school.'

'How old is she?' Mara asked, closing the locket and putting it back inside her blouse.

'Fourteen.' Brunetti sighed. 'It's a difficult age,' he said before he remembered what Mara had told him only moments before.

She, luckily, seemed to have forgotten it, too, and said only, 'Yes, it's hard. I hope she's a good girl.'

Brunetti smiled, proud to say it. 'Yes, she is. Very good.'

'Do you have other children?'

'A son, he's seventeen.'

She nodded, as if she knew more than she wanted to know about seventeen-year-old boys.

A long moment passed. Brunetti waved a hand around the room. 'Why this?' he asked.

Mara shrugged. 'Why not?'

'If you've got a child in Brazil, this is a long way to come to work.' He smiled when he said it, and she took no offence.

'I make enough money to send to my aunt, enough

to pay for the school, and good food, and new uniforms whenever she needs them.' Her voice was tight with pride or anger, Brunetti couldn't tell which.

'And in São Paulo, couldn't you make money there? So that you wouldn't have to be away from her?'

'I left school when I was nine because someone had to take care of the other children. My mother was sick for a long time, and I was the only girl. Then, after my daughter was born, I got a job in a bar.' She saw his look and answered, 'No, it wasn't that kind of place. All I did was serve drinks.'

When it seemed she was going to say nothing else, Brunetti asked, 'How long did you keep that job?'

'Three years. It paid our rent and for our food, for me and Ana and for my aunt, who took care of her. But it didn't pay for much else.' She stopped again, but, to Brunetti, her voice had taken on the rhythms of story-telling.

'And then what?'

'And then Eduardo, my Latin Lover,' she said bitterly and crushed at one of the butts on the floor with her toe, reducing it to fragments of paper and tobacco.

'Eduardo?'

'Eduardo Alfieri. At least that's what he told me his name was. He saw me in the bar one night, and he stayed after closing and asked me if I wanted to go for a coffee. Not a drink, mind you, for coffee, like I was a respectable girl he was asking for a date.'

'And what happened?'

'What do you think happened?' she asked, voice bitter for the first time. 'We had that coffee, and then

209

he came back to the bar every night, always asking me out for coffee when it closed, always respectful, always polite. My grandmother would have approved of him, he was so respectful. It was the first time a man had ever treated me as something other than something to fuck, so I did what any girl would do, I fell in love with him.'

'Yes,' Brunetti said. 'Yes.'

'And he said he wanted to marry me, but I would have to come to Italy for that and meet his family. He told me he would arrange everything, a visa and a job when I got here. He told me it would be no trouble to learn Italian.' She gave a rueful grin then. 'That's probably the only true thing he told me, the bastard.'

'What happened?'

'I came to Italy. I signed all the papers and I got on Alitalia and, the first thing you know, I was in Milan, and Eduardo was there to meet me at the airport.' The look she gave Brunetti was level and open. 'You've heard this a thousand times, I suppose?'

'Something like it, yes. Trouble with the papers?'

She smiled, almost with humour, at the memory of her former self, her former innocence. 'Exactly. Trouble with the papers. Bureaucracy. But he was going to take me to his apartment, and everything would be all right. I was in love, so I believed him. That night, he asked me to give him my passport so he could take it the next day, when he went to get the papers for the marriage.' She reached for a cigarette but then put it back in the pack. 'Do you think I could have a coffee?' she asked.

Again Brunetti went to the door and tapped on it, this time asking Gravini to bring some coffee and sandwiches.

When he went back to his seat, she was smoking again. 'I saw him once more, only once. He came back that night and told me that there was serious trouble with my visa, and he couldn't marry me until it was settled. I don't know when I stopped believing him and realized what was going on.'

'Why didn't you go to the police?' Brunetti asked.

Her astonishment was unfeigned. 'The police? He had my passport, and then he showed me that one of the papers I'd signed – he'd even gone to the trouble to have my signature notarized, said we'd have less trouble in Italy if I did – it said that he'd lent me 50 million lire.'

'And then?' Brunetti asked.

'He told me that he'd found me a job in a bar, and all I had to do was work there until the money was paid back.'

'And?'

'Eduardo took me to see the man who owned the bar, and the man said I could have a job. It paid, I think, a million lire a month, but then the man explained that he would have to take money out for the room where I could live over the bar. I couldn't live anywhere else because I didn't have a passport or a visa. And he said he'd have to take out for the food and for the clothing he'd give me. Eduardo never brought my suitcases, so all I had was the clothes I was wearing. It worked out that I would be making about 50,000 lire a month.

I couldn't speak the language, but I could count; I knew that when that got sent back to my aunt, it would be less than thirty dollars. That's not a lot for an old woman and a baby to live on, not even in Brazil.'

There was a knock and then the door opened. Brunetti went over and took a tin tray from Gravini. As he went back to Mara, she pulled the third chair between them and motioned to Brunetti to set the tray down there. They both stirred sugar into their coffee. He nodded down at the sandwiches that lay on the plate, but she shook her head.

'Not until I finish,' she said, and sipped at her coffee. 'I wasn't stupid; I knew the choices I had. So I went to work at the bar. It was hard the first couple of times, but then I got used to it. That was two years ago.'

'What happened between then and now? To bring you to Mestre?' Brunetti asked.

'I got sick. Pneumonia, I think. I hate this cold weather,' she said, shivering unconsciously at the mere thought of it. 'While I was in the hospital, the bar burned down. Someone said it was arson. I don't know. I hope it was. But when it was time for me to get out, Franco', she said, nodding off to her left, as if she knew Franco was in the next cell, 'came and paid the bill and brought me back here. I've been working for him ever since.' She finished her coffee and set the cup back on the tray.

It was a story Brunetti had heard more times than he cared to remember, but this was the first time he'd heard it told with not even a trace of self-pity, with no attempt to turn the teller into an unwilling victim of overwhelming forces.

'Did he', Brunetti asked, nodding his head towards the same wall, though Franco, as it happened, was lodged behind the opposite one, 'have anything to do with the bar in Milan or the one where you work now? Or with Eduardo?'

She stared down at the floor. 'I don't know.' Brunetti said nothing and she finally added, 'I think he bought me. Or bought my contract.' She looked up then and asked, 'Why do you want to know?'

Brunetti saw no reason to lie to her. 'We found the phone number of the bar where you're working now in the course of another investigation. We're trying to find out how they're related.'

'What's the other investigation?' she asked.

'I can't tell you that,' Brunetti said. 'But, so far, it has nothing to do with you or Eduardo or anything about that.'

'Can I ask you a question?' she said.

Whenever Chiara asked him that, Brunetti was in the habit of telling her that she couldn't very well ask him an answer but, instead, he said, 'Of course.'

'Does it have anything to do with . . .' she began and then paused, looking for the right word. 'Well, with some of us who have died?'

'I don't know who you mean by "us",' Brunetti said.

'Whores,' she explained.

'No.' His answer was instant and she believed him. 'Why do you ask?'

'No special reason. We hear things.' She reached out

and picked up a sandwich, bit delicately at one end, and then brushed absently at the crumbs that cascaded down the front of her blouse.

'What sort of things do you hear?'

'Just things,' she said, taking another bite.

'Mara,' he began, not certain what tone to use. 'If there's something you'd like to tell me, or ask me, it will rest between us.' Then, before she could speak, he added, 'Not if it's about a crime. But if you just want to tell me something or find out about something, it's between us.'

'Not official?'

'No, not official.'

'What's your name?' she asked.

'Guido,' he answered.

She smiled at the thought that he had used his own name. 'Guido the Plumber?'

He nodded.

She took another bite and, still chewing, said, 'We hear things,' then looked down and brushed at the new crumbs. 'You know, the word travels, when things happen. So we hear things, but it's hard, ever, to be sure where we heard it or who said it.'

'What is it you heard, Mara?'

'That someone had been killing us.' As soon as she said it, she shook her head. 'No, that's wrong. Not killing us. But we've been dying.'

'I don't understand the difference,' Brunetti said.

'There was that young one. I can't remember her name, the little Yugoslavian. She killed herself in the summer and then Anja, the one from Bulgaria, she got it out in the field. I didn't know the little one, but I did know Anja. She'd go with anyone.'

Brunetti remembered these crimes and remembered that the police had never even discovered the victims' names.

'And then that truck.' She paused and looked at him. The conjunction of words struck a chord, but Brunetti could produce no clear memory.

When he said nothing, she continued, 'One of the girls said she'd heard – she couldn't remember where – that the girls were coming down here. I forget from where.'

'To work as prostitutes?' he asked and immediately regretted the question.

She pulled back from him and stopped speaking. The expression in her eyes changed as veils were lowered. 'I don't remember.'

Her voice told Brunetti that he had lost her, that his question had severed the fine thread that held them together momentarily.

'Did you ever say anything about this?' he asked.

'To the police?' she finished the question for him with a snort of disbelief. She tossed the remnant of sandwich she still held down on to the tray. 'Are you going to charge me with anything?' she asked.

'No,' Brunetti said.

'Then can I go?' The woman he'd spoken to was gone, replaced by the whore who had taken him back to her room.

'Yes, you're free to go whenever you want.' Before she could get to her feet, Brunetti asked, 'Is it safe for you to leave before he does?' – again nodding towards the wall behind which Franco was not.

'Him,' she said, puffing out her cheeks with contempt.

Brunetti went over to the door, and tapped on it. 'The signorina is leaving now,' he said, when Gravini opened the door.

She picked up her jacket, passed in front of Brunetti, and left without saying a word. When she was gone, Brunetti looked at Gravini. 'Thanks for the coffee,' he said, taking back the file which Gravini was still holding.

'It's nothing, dottore.'

'If you'll get the tray, I'll talk to the man now.'

'Should I get some more cigarettes, sir? Or coffee?' Gravini asked.

'No, I don't think so. Not until I get my 50,000 lire from Franco,' Brunetti said and let himself into the room.

One glance was enough to tell Brunetti all he needed to know about Franco: Franco was a tough guy, Franco ate nails, Franco wasn't afraid of cops. But from the papers in his hand and from what della Corte had said, Brunetti knew that Franco was a heroin addict who had been in police custody for more than ten hours.

'Good morning, Signor Silvestri,' Brunetti said pleasantly, quite as though he'd come to talk of the weekend soccer results.

Silvestri unfolded his arms and looked at Brunetti, recognizing him immediately. 'Plumber,' he said and spat on the floor.

'Please, Signor Silvestri,' Brunetti said patiently as he pulled out one of the two empty chairs and sat. He opened the file again and looked down at the papers, flipped the top sheet over and looked at the one beneath it. 'Assault, and living off the earnings of a whore, and I notice here that you were arrested for selling drugs in, let me see', he said, flipping back to the first page and reading the date, 'January of last year. Now, two charges of accepting money offered to a prostitute will cause you a certain amount of trouble, but I suspect that . . .'

Silvestri cut him off. 'Look, let's get on with it, all right, Mr Plumber? Charge me, and I'll call my lawyer, and then he'll come down here and get me out.' Brunetti glanced idly in his direction and noticed the way Silvestri held his hands clenched together at his sides, saw the thin film of perspiration on his brow.

'I'd certainly be more than happy to do that, Signor Silvestri, but I'm afraid what we have here is a far more serious matter than any of the charges in your file.' Brunetti closed the file and tapped it against his knee. 'In fact, it's something far beyond the competence of the city police force.'

'What's that supposed to mean?' As Brunetti watched, the other man forced himself to relax his hands, open them, and place them casually, palms down, on his lap.

'It means that, for some time, the bar you frequent with your, ah, with your colleagues has been under surveillance, and they've had a tap on the phone.'

'They?' Silvestri asked.

'SISMI,' Brunetti explained. 'Specifically the anti-terrorism squad.'

'Anti-terrorism?' Silvestri repeated stupidly.

'Yes, it seems that the bar was used by some of the people involved in the bombing of the museum in Florence,' Brunetti said, inventing as he went along. 'I suppose I shouldn't tell you this, but as you seem to be caught up in it, I don't see why we shouldn't speak of it.'

'Florence?' Silvestri could do no more than repeat what he heard.

'Yes, from what little I've been told, the phone in the bar has been used to pass on messages. Those boys have had a tap on it for a month or so. Everything according to the rules – orders from a judge.' Brunetti waved the folder in the air. 'When my men arrested you last night, I tried to tell those others that you were just a little fish, one of ours, but they won't listen to me.'

'What does that mean?' Silvestri asked in a voice from which all anger had disappeared.

'It means they're going to hold you under the anti-terrorism law.' Brunetti closed the file and got to his feet. 'It's just a misunderstanding between services, you understand, Signor Silvestri. They'll hold you for forty-eight hours.'

'But my lawyer?'

'You can call him then, Signor Silvestri. It'll only be forty-eight hours and you've already passed', Brunetti began, pushing back his cuff to look at his watch, 'ten of them. So you just have to wait a day and a half, and you'll be free to call your lawyer, and I'm sure he'll have you out of here in no time at all.' Brunetti smiled.

'Why are you here?' Silvestri asked, suspicious.

'Since it was one of my men who arrested you, I felt that, well, I felt that I was the one, you might say, to get you into this, so I thought the least I could do was come by and explain it to you. I've dealt with the fellows from SISMI before,' Brunetti said wearily, 'and there's no talking sense to them. The law says they can keep you for forty-eight hours without notifying anyone, and I guess we'll just have to live with it.' He looked down at his watch again. 'It'll pass like nothing, Signor Silvestri, I'm sure. If you'd like any magazines, just let my man outside know, all right?' Saying that, Brunetti got to his feet and started towards the door.

'Please,' Silvestri said, certainly the first time in his life he'd addressed that word to a policeman. 'Please don't go.'

Brunetti turned round and tilted his head to one side in open curiosity. 'Have you thought of some magazines you'd like? *Panorama*? *Architectural Digest*? *Famiglia Christiana*?'

'What do you want?' Silvestri said, voice harsh but not with anger. The film of sweat on his brow stood out in thick beads.

Brunetti saw that there was no further necessity to play with him. So much for tough Franco, hard as nails.

Voice severe and level, Brunetti demanded, 'Who calls you on the phone in that bar and who do you call?'

Silvestri ran both hands up across his face and

through his thick hair, plastering his forelock to his skull. He rubbed his mouth with one hand, pulling repeatedly at the edge, as if attempting to remove a stain. 'There's a man who calls and tells me when new girls will arrive.'

Brunetti said nothing.

'I don't know who he is or where he calls from. But he calls me every month or so and tells me where to pick them up. They're already broken in. I just have to get them and set them to work.'

'And the money?'

Silvestri said nothing. Brunetti turned and headed towards the door.

'I give it to a woman. Every month. When he calls me, he tells me where to meet the woman, and when, and I give her the money.'

'How much?'

'All of it.'

'All of what?'

'Everything that's left after I pay for the rooms and pay the girls.'

'How much is that?'

'It depends,' he said evasively.

'You're wasting my time, Silvestri,' Brunetti said, unleashing his anger.

'Some months it's 40 or 50 million. Some months it's less.' Which, to Brunetti, meant that some months it was more.

'Who's the woman?'

'I don't know. I've never seen her.'

'What do you mean?'

'He tells me where her car will be parked. It's a white Mercedes. I have to come at it from behind, open the back door, and put the money on the back seat. Then she drives away.'

'And you've never seen her?'

'She wears a scarf. And sunglasses.'

'Is she tall? Thin? White? Black? Blonde? Old? Come on, Silvestri, you don't have to see a woman's face to know this.'

'She's not short, but I don't know what colour hair she has. I've never seen her face, but I don't think she's old.'

'What licence plates does the car have?'

'I don't know.'

'Didn't you see it?'

'No. I always do it at night, and the lights in the car are off.' He was sure Silvestri was lying, but Brunetti could also sense that he was near the end of what he would tell.

'Where do you meet her?'

'On the street. Mestre. Once in Treviso. Different places. He tells me where to go when he calls.'

'And the girls. How do you pick them up?'

'Same way. He tells me a street corner and how many there'll be, and I meet them with my car.'

'Who brings them?'

'No one. I get there, and they're waiting.'

'Just like that? Like sheep?'

'They know better than to try anything,' Silvestri said, voice suddenly savage.

'Where do they come from?'

'All over.'

'What does that mean?'

'Lots of cities. Different countries.'

'How do they get here?'

'What do you mean?'

'How do they come to be part of your . . . part of your delivery?'

'They're just whores. How do you expect me to know? For Christ's sake, I don't talk to them.' Suddenly Silvestri jammed his hands into his pockets and demanded, 'When are you going to get me out of here?'

'How many have there been?'

'No more,' Silvestri shouted, getting up from the chair and moving towards Brunetti. 'No more. Get me out of here.'

Brunetti didn't move and Silvestri backed off a few steps. Brunetti tapped on the door, which was quickly opened by Gravini. Stepping out in the hall, Brunetti waited while the officer closed the door, then said, 'Wait an hour and a half, then let him go.'

'Yes, sir,' Gravini said and saluted the back of his superior as Brunetti walked away.

Chapter Twenty-Two

His session with Mara and her pimp hadn't put Brunetti in the most favourable of moods for dealing with Signora Trevisan and her late husband's business partner, to call Martucci by but one of the offices he filled, but he made the necessary phone call to the widow, insisting that it was imperative to the progress of his investigation that he have a few words with her and, if possible, with Signor Martucci. Their separate accounts of where they had been the night Trevisan was murdered had been checked: Signora Trevisan's maid confirmed that her mistress had not gone out that evening, and a friend of Martucci's had phoned him at 9.30 and found him at home.

Long experience had told Brunetti that it was always best to allow people to select the place in which they were to be interviewed: they invariably selected the place in which they felt most comfortable, and thus they enjoyed the erroneous belief that control of location equalled control of content. Predictably, Signora Trevisan selected her home, where Brunetti arrived at the precise hour, 5.30. His spirit still roughened from his encounter with Franco Silvestri, Brunetti was predisposed to disapprove of whatever hospitality might be offered him: a cocktail would be too cosmopolitan, tea too pretentious.

But after Signora Trevisan, today dressed in sober navy blue, led him into a sitting room that contained too few chairs and too much taste, Brunetti realized he had presumed too much upon his sense of his own importance and that he was to be treated as an intruder, not a representative of the state. The widow offered him her hand, and Martucci stood when she led Brunetti into the room, but neither bothered to rise above the bare requirement of civility. Their solemn manner and long faces, Brunetti suspected, were meant to demonstrate the grief he was intruding upon, shared grief at the departure of a beloved husband and friend. But Brunetti had been rendered sceptical of both by his conversation with Judge Beniamin, and perhaps he had been rendered sceptical of humanity in general by his brief conversation with Franco Silvestri.

Quickly, Brunetti reeled off his formulaic thanks for their having agreed to talk to him. Martucci nodded; Signora Trevisan gave no sign of having heard him.

'Signora Trevisan,' Brunetti began, 'I would like to obtain some information about your husband's finances.' She said nothing, asked for no explanation. 'Could you tell me what becomes of your husband's law practice?'

'You can ask me about that,' Martucci interrupted.

'I did, two days ago,' Brunetti said. 'You told me very little.'

'We've had more information since then,' Martucci said.

'Does that mean you've read the will?' Brunetti asked, quietly pleased to see how much his tastelessness surprised them both.

Martucci's voice remained calm and polite. 'Signora Trevisan has asked me to serve as her lawyer in the settling of her husband's estate, if that's what you mean.'

'That answer will do as well as another, I suppose,' Brunetti said, interested that Martucci could not easily be baited. Must come of practising corporate law, Brunetti reflected, where everyone's forced to be polite. Brunetti continued, 'What happens to the law firm?'

'Signora Trevisan retains 60 per cent.'

Brunetti said nothing for so long that Martucci was forced to add, 'And I retain 40.'

'May I ask when this will was drawn up?'

'Two years ago,' Martucci answered with no hesitation.

'And when did you join Signor Trevisan's firm, Avvocato Martucci?'

Signora Trevisan turned her very pale eyes on Brunetti and spoke for the first time since they came into the room. 'Commissario, before you become too exercised in pursuit of your own vulgar curiosity, might I inquire as to the final goal of these questions?'

'If they have a goal, signora, it is in gaining information to help in finding the person who murdered your husband.'

'It would seem to me', she began, propping her elbows on the arms of her chair and pressing her hands into a steeple in front of her, 'that this would be true only if some connection existed between the conditions

225

of his will and his murder. Or am I being too simple-minded for you?' When Brunetti failed to answer immediately, she graced him with a sliver of a smile. 'It *is* possible for things to be too simple-minded for you, isn't it, commissario?'

'I'm certain it is, signora,' Brunetti said, glad he had managed to provoke at least one of them. 'Hence I like to ask questions with simple answers. This one has a number, how long Signor Martucci worked for your husband.'

'Two years,' Martucci answered.

Brunetti turned his attention back to the lawyer, intent on him now, and asked, 'And if I might ask about the other dispositions of the will?'

Martucci started to answer, but Signora Trevisan held up a hand to silence him. 'I'll answer this, avvocato.' Then, turning to Brunetti, she said, 'The bulk of Carlo's property, as is entirely common under the law, is left to me, as his widow, and to his children in equal shares. There are some other bequests to relatives and friends, but the bulk comes to us. Does that satisfy your curiosity?'

'Yes, signora, it does.'

Martucci shifted in his seat, preparing to rise, and said, 'If that's all you came for . . .'

'I have some other questions,' Brunetti said, turning to Signora Trevisan, 'for you, signora.'

She nodded without bothering to answer him and gave a calming glance in Martucci's direction.

'Do you have a car?'

'I'm afraid I don't understand your question,' she said after a short pause.

Brunetti repeated, 'Do you have a car?'

'Yes.'

'What kind?'

'I don't see what sense this makes,' Martucci interrupted.

Ignoring him, Signora Trevisan said, 'It's a BMW. Three years old. Green.'

'Thank you,' Brunetti said, face impassive, and then asked, 'Your brother, signora, does he leave a family?'

'No. He and his wife never had children.'

Martucci interrupted again. 'I'm sure your records must tell you that.'

Ignoring him, Brunetti asked, choosing his words carefully, 'Did your brother have anything to do with prostitutes?'

Martucci jumped to his feet, but Brunetti ignored him; his attention was riveted on Signora Trevisan. Her head shot up when she heard the question, and then, almost as though listening to an echo of it, she looked away from him for a moment, then brought her eyes back to his. Two very slow beats passed before her face displayed any anger, and then she said in a loud, declamatory voice, 'My brother had no need for whores.'

Martucci caught the tail of her anger and used it to swing his own towards Brunetti. 'I will not permit you to insult the memory of Signora Trevisan's brother. Your accusation is disgusting and offensive. We don't have to listen to your insinuations.' He paused to gather breath, and Brunetti could almost hear his lawyer's mind spring into action. 'Furthermore, your remark is slanderous, and I have Signora Trevisan as a witness to what you've said.' He looked from one to the other for a response, but neither had paid the least attention to his explosion.

Brunetti never glanced away from Signora Trevisan, nor did she make any attempt to avoid his eyes. Martucci started to speak again, but then stopped, confused at the attention they seemed to be paying to one another, missing the fact that what engaged them was not the slanderous potential of Brunetti's last remark but, rather, its exact phrasing.

Brunetti waited until the others realized that he wanted an answer, not righteous indignation. He saw her consider the question and how to answer it. He thought he saw some revelation move from her eyes to her lips, but just as she was about to speak, Martucci started up again. 'I demand an apology.' When Brunetti didn't bother to answer him, Martucci took two steps towards Brunetti until he stood between him and Signora Trevisan, blocking their view of one another. 'I demand an apology,' he repeated, looking down at Brunetti.

'Of course, of course,' Brunetti said with singular lack of interest. 'You can have as many apologies as you like.' Brunetti got to his feet and stepped to Martucci's side, but Signora Trevisan had looked away and didn't bother to look up at him. One glance told him that Martucci's interruption had served to drive all urge towards confidence from her; Brunetti saw there was no sense in repeating himself.

'Signora,' he said, 'if you decide to answer my question, you'll find me at the Questura.' Saying nothing else, he stepped around Martucci and left the room, then let himself out of the house without bothering to call the maid, who was nowhere to be seen.

As he walked home, Brunetti thought about how close he had just come to that moment of contact that he sometimes managed to create between himself and a witness or a suspect, that delicate point of balance when some chance phrase or word would suddenly spur a person to reveal something they had tried to keep hidden. What had she been about to say, and what had Lotto had to do with prostitutes? And the woman in the Mercedes? Was she the woman who had dinner with Favero the night he was killed? Brunetti asked himself what could happen during dinner to make a woman so nervous or forgetful that she would leave behind a pair of glasses worth more than a million lire. And had it been something that happened during dinner or what she knew was going to happen after dinner that made her nervous? The questions swirled around Brunetti, Furies calling to him and mocking him because he didn't know the answers and, worse, because he didn't even know which questions were important.

When he left the Trevisan apartment, Brunetti turned automatically toward the Accademia Bridge and home. He was so preoccupied with his thoughts that it took him some time to notice that the street seemed crowded. He glanced down at his watch, puzzled that there should be so many people in this part of the city more than a half-hour before the shops closed. He looked at them more carefully and saw that they were Italians: both men and women were too well dressed and groomed to be anything else.

He abandoned any thought of hurrying and allowed the flow to carry him towards Campo San Stefano. From the bottom of the closest bridge, he heard amplified sound but could not distinguish it clearly.

Down the narrow slot of the last *calle* they pulled him and then, suddenly, freed him into the darkening *campo*. Directly in front of him was the statue Brunetti had always thought of as the Meringue Man, so starkly white and porous was the marble from which he was carved. Other people, seeing the pile of books that seemed to issue from beneath his coat, called him something more indelicate.

To Brunetti's right, a wooden platform had been erected along the side of the church of San Stefano. A few wooden chairs stood on it; the front corners held enormous speakers. From three wooden poles at the back of the platform hung the limp flags bearing the Italian tricolor, the lion of San Marco, and the newly minted symbol of what had once been the Christian Democratic party.

Brunetti moved over closer to the statue and stepped behind the low metal fence that encircled its base. About a hundred people stood in front of the platform; from that group three men and a woman broke away and walked up the steps of the platform. Loud music suddenly blared forth. Brunetti thought it was the national anthem, but the volume and the static made it difficult to tell.

A man in jeans and a bomber jacket handed a microphone with a long hanging wire up to one of the men on the platform. He held it at his side for a while, smiled at the crowd, shifted the microphone to his left hand, and shook hands with the people on the platform. From below, the man in the jacket lifted a hand and made a cutting gesture, but the music didn't stop.

The man on the platform held the microphone up to his mouth and said something, but the music rode above it and made it incomprehensible. He held the microphone out at arm's length and tapped at it with one hand, but this came through as six muffled pistol shots.

A pod of people broke away from the crowd and went into a bar. Six more walked around towards the front of the church and disappeared up Calle della Mandorla. The man in the bomber jacket clambered up on to the platform and did something to the wires at the back of one of the speakers. That speaker went suddenly dead, but music and static continued to blare forth from the other. He walked hurriedly across the platform and knelt behind the other speaker.

Some more people drifted away. The woman on the platform walked down the steps and disappeared into the crowd, quickly followed by two of the men. When the noise didn't stop, the man in the jacket got to his feet and had a huddled conference with the man with the microphone. By the time Brunetti turned his attention away from them, only a handful of people remained in front of the platform.

He climbed back over the low fence and headed towards the Accademia Bridge. Just as he was passing in front of the small florist's kiosk at the end of the *campo*, the music and static came to a sudden halt, and a man's voice, amplified by nothing more than anger, called out, '*Cittadini, Italiani*', but Brunetti didn't stop, nor did he bother to turn around.

He realized that he wanted to talk to Paola. He had, as always and as was against the regulations, kept her informed about the progress of the investigation, had given her his impressions of the people he questioned and the answers they gave him. This time, because there had been no one standing naked in guilt's spotlight at the very beginning, Paola had refrained from naming the person she believed to be the murderer, a habit Brunetti had never been able to break her of. Devoid of that *a priori* certainty, she served as the perfect listener: prodding him with questions, forcing him to explain things so clearly that she would understand. Often, forced to explain some lingering uneasiness, he better understood it himself. This time, she had suggested nothing, hinted nothing, displayed no suspicion of any of the people he mentioned. She listened, interested, and that was all she did.

When he got home, he found that Paola wasn't there yet, but Chiara was waiting for him. 'Papà,' she called from her room when she heard him open the door. A second later, she appeared at the door of her room, a magazine hanging open in her hand. He recognized the yellow-bordered cover of *Airone*, just as he recognized in its lavish photos, glossy paper, and simple prose style more signs of the American magazine it so closely imitated.

'What is it, sweetheart?' he asked, bending down to kiss the top of her head and then turning to hang his coat in the closet near the door.

'There's a competition, Papà, and if you win it, you get a free subscription.'

'But don't you already have a subscription?' he asked, having given it to her for Christmas.

'That's not the point, Papà.'

'What is the point, then?' he asked, making his way down the hallway towards the kitchen. He flipped on the light and went over to the refrigerator.

'The point is winning,' she said, following him down the hall and making Brunetti wonder if the magazine might be a bit too American for his daughter.

He found a bottle of Orvieto, checked the label, put it back, and pulled out the bottle of Soave they had begun with dinner the night before. He took down a glass, filled it, and took a sip. 'All right, Chiara, what's the contest?'

'You have to name a penguin.'

'Name a penguin?' Brunetti repeated stupidly.

'Yes, look here,' she said, holding the magazine out towards him with one hand and pointing down towards a photo with the other. As she did, he saw a picture of what looked to be the fuzzy mass that Paola sometimes emptied from the vacuum cleaner. 'What's that?' he asked, taking the magazine and turning it towards the light.

'It's the baby penguin, Papà. It was born last month at the Rome Zoo, and it doesn't have a name yet. So they're offering a prize to whoever comes up with the best name for it.'

Brunetti pulled open the magazine and looked more closely at the photo. Sure enough, he saw a beak and two round black eyes. Two yellow flippers. On the opposite page was a full-grown penguin, but Brunetti looked in vain for some familial resemblance between the two.

'What name?' he asked, flipping through the magazine and watching hyenas, ibis, and elephants stream past him.

'Spot,' she said.

'What?'

'Spot,' she repeated.

'For a penguin?' he asked, flipping back to the original article and staring at the photos of the adult birds. Spot?

'Sure. Everyone else is going to call him "Flipper" or "Waiter".' No one else will think of calling him Spot.'

That, Brunetti allowed, was probably true. 'You could always save the name,' he suggested, putting the bottle back in the refrigerator.

'What for?' she asked and took the magazine back.

'In case there's a contest for a zebra,' he said.

'Oh, Papà, you're so silly sometimes,' she said and

went back towards her room, little aware of how much her judgement pleased him.

In the living room, he picked up his book, left face down when he went to bed the night before. While waiting for Paola, he might as well fight the Peloponnesian War again.

She came home an hour later, let herself into the apartment, and came into the living room. She tossed her coat over the back of the sofa and flopped down next to him, her scarf still around her neck. 'Guido, you ever consider the possibility that I'm insane?'

'Often,' he said and turned a page.

'No, really. I've got to be, working for those cretins.'

'Which cretins?' he asked, still not bothering to look up from the book.

'The ones who run the university.'

'What now?'

'They asked me, three months ago, to give a lecture in Padua, to the English Faculty. They said it would be on the British novel. Why do you think I was reading all those books for the last two months?'

'Because you like them. That's why you've read them for the last twenty years.'

'Oh, stop it, Guido,' she said, digging a gentle elbow into his ribs.

'So what happened?'

'I went into the office today to pick up my mail, and they told me that they'd got it all wrong, that I was supposed to be lecturing on American poetry, but no one thought to tell me about the change.'

'And so, which is it?'

'I won't know until tomorrow. They'll go ahead and tell Padua about the new topic if Il Magnifico approves it.' Both of them had always taken delight in this most wonderful of holdovers from the academic Stone Age, the fact that the Rector of the university was addressed as 'Il Magnifico Rettore', the only thing Brunetti had learned in twenty years on the fringes of the university that had managed to make academic life sound interesting to him.

'What's he likely to do?' Brunetti asked.

'Toss a coin, probably.'

'Good luck,' Brunetti said, putting down his book. 'You don't like the American stuff, do you?'

'Holy heavens, no,' she explained, burying her face in her hands. 'Puritans, cowboys, and strident women. I'd rather teach the Silver Fork Novel,' she said, using the English words.

'The what?' Brunetti asked.

'Silver Fork Novel,' she repeated. 'Books with simple plots written to explain to people who made a lot of money how to behave in polite company.'

'For yuppies?' Brunetti asked, honestly interested.

Paola erupted in laughter. 'No, Guido, not for yuppies. They were written in the eighteenth century, when all the money poured into England from the colonies, and the fat wives of Yorkshire weavers had to be taught which fork to use.' She was quiet for a few minutes, considering what he said. 'But if I think about it for a minute, with a little updating, there's no reason the same couldn't be said of Bret Easton Ellis.' She put her face in his shoulder and gave herself up to giggles,

236

laughing herself weak at a joke Brunetti didn't understand.

When she stopped laughing, she took the scarf from her neck and tossed it on the table. 'And you?' she asked.

He put his book face down on his knees and faced her. 'I talked to the whore and her pimp and then to Signora Trevisan and her lawyer.' Slowly, attentive to his story and careful to get the details right, he told her everything that had happened that day, finishing with Signora Trevisan's reaction to his question about the prostitutes.

'Did her brother have anything to do with prostitutes?' Paola repeated, careful to duplicate Brunetti's exact phrasing. 'And you think she understood what you meant?'

Brunetti nodded.

'But the lawyer misunderstood?'

'Yes, but I don't think it was deliberate. He just didn't get it, that the question was ambiguous and didn't mean that he had sex with them.'

'She did, though?'

Brunetti nodded again. 'She's much brighter than he is.'

'Women usually are,' Paola said and then asked, 'What do you think he might have had to do with them?'

'I don't know, Paola, but her reaction tells me that, whatever it was, she knew about it.'

Paola said nothing, waiting for him to think it through. He took one of her hands in his, kissed the palm, and let it fall to his lap, where she left it, waiting still.

'It's the only common thread,' he began, talking more to himself than to her. 'Both of them, Trevisan and Favero, had the number of the bar in Mestre, and that's the place where a pimp is running a string of girls, and there's always a supply of new ones. I don't know about Lotto, except that he ran Trevisan's business for him.'

He turned Paola's hand over and ran his forefinger across the faint blue veins visible on the back.

'Not a lot, is it?' Paola finally asked.

He shook his head.

'The one you talked to, Mara, what did she ask you about the others?'

'She wanted to know if I knew anything about a girl who died in Treviso, and she said something about girls in a truck. I don't know what she meant.'

Like an aged carp slowly swimming towards the light of day, a memory stirred in the recesses of Paola's mind, a memory that had to do with a truck and with women. She rested her head against the back of the sofa and closed her eyes. And saw snow. And that small detail was enough to bring the memory to the surface.

'Guido, early this autumn – I think it was when you were in Rome for the conference – a truck ran off the highway, up near Udine, I think. I forget the details – I think it skidded on the ice and went off a cliff or something. Anyway, there were women in the back of the truck, and they were all killed, eight or ten of them. It was strange. The story was in the papers one day,

238

but then it disappeared, and I never saw anything else about it.' Paola felt his hand grip hers a bit more firmly. 'Was she talking about that, do you think?'

'I remember something about it, a reference to it in a report from Interpol about women who are being brought here as prostitutes,' Brunetti said. 'The driver was killed, wasn't he?'

Paola nodded. 'I think so.'

The Udine police would have a report; he could call them tomorrow. He tried to remember more about the report from Interpol, or perhaps it had been from some other agency – God alone knew where it was filed. Time enough for all of this tomorrow.

Paola pulled gently on his hand. 'Why do you use them?'

'Hum?' Brunetti asked, not really paying attention.

'Why do you use whores?' Then, before he could misunderstand, she clarified the question, 'Men, that is. Not you. Men.'

He picked up their joined hands and waved them in the air, a vague, aimless gesture. 'Guiltless sex, I guess. No strings, no obligations. No need to be polite.'

'Doesn't sound very appealing,' Paola said, and then added, 'But I suppose women always want to sentimentalize sex.'

'Yes, you do,' Brunetti said.

Paola freed her hand from his and got to her feet. She glanced down at her husband for a moment, then went into the kitchen to begin dinner.

Chapter Twenty-Three

Brunetti spent the first part of his work day hunting through his files for the Interpol report on prostitution and waiting for the operator to put his call through to the police in Udine. The operator was quicker than Brunetti, and he spent fifteen minutes listening to a captain of the carabinieri describe the accident, then ended the conversation with a request that they fax him all of the documents relevant to the case.

It took him twenty minutes to locate the report about the international traffic in prostitutes and a half-hour to read it. He found it a sobering experience, and he found the last line, 'It is estimated by various police and international organizations that there could be as many as half a million women involved in this traffic', almost impossible to believe. The report catalogued something that he, like most police officials in Europe, knew was going on; the shocking part was the enormity and complexity of it.

The pattern wasn't far from what Mara said she had experienced: a young woman from a developing country was offered the promise of a new life in Europe – sometimes the reason was love, sweet love, but most often the promise was work as a domestic servant, sometimes as an entertainer. There, in Europe, she was told, she would have a chance at a decent life, could earn enough money to send back to her family, perhaps even some day bring her family to live with her in that earthly paradise.

Upon arrival, their various discoveries were much like Mara's, and they learned that the work contract they had signed before leaving was often an agreement to repay as much as $50,000 to the person responsible for bringing them to Europe. And so they found themselves in a foreign country, having given their passport to the person who brought them in, persuaded that they were breaking the law by their mere presence and thus subject to arrest and long sentences because of the debt they had incurred by signing the contract. Even at this, many objected and showed no fear of arrest. Gang rape usually subdued them. If not, greater violence often proved persuasive. Some died. Word travelled. There was little resistance.

And so the brothels of the developed world filled up with dark-haired, dark-skinned exotics: Thai women, whose gentle modesty was so flattering to a man's sense of superiority; those mixed-race Dominicans, and we all know how much those blacks love it; and not least the Brazilians, those hot-blooded Cariocas, born to be whores.

The report went on to state that, transportation costs being what they are, a new market opportunity was seen opening up in the East as thousands of blonde, blue-eyed women lost their jobs or saw their savings gobbled up by inflation. Seventy years of the physical privations of Communism had prepared them to fall easy prey to the blandishments of the West, and so they migrated in cars and trucks, on foot, and sometimes even on sleds, all seeking the great El Dorado that was their Western neighbour, but finding, instead, when they arrived, that they were without papers, without rights, and without hope.

Brunetti believed it all and was staggered by the final number: half a million. He flipped to the back pages and read through the names of the people and organizations that had compiled the report; they were enough to persuade him to believe the number, though it still remained intolerable. There were entire provinces of Italy that didn't have half a million women living in them. Their numbers could populate whole cities.

When he finished it, he set the report in the centre of his desk, then pushed it farther away from him, as if fearing its power of contamination. He opened his drawer and pulled out a pencil, took a piece of paper, and quickly made a list of three names: one was a Brazilian police major whom he had met while on a police seminar in Paris some years ago; one was the owner of an import-export firm with offices in Bangkok; and the third was Pia, a prostitute. All of them, for one reason or another, were in Brunetti's debt, and he could think of no better way of calling in those debts than by asking them for information.

He spent the next two hours on the phone, running up a bill that was later made to evaporate by a few key strokes on the central computer at the SIP offices. At the end of that time, he knew little more than he had already read in the report, but he knew it more fully, more personally.

Major de Vedia in Rio was unable to share Brunetti's concern and incapable of understanding his indignation. After all, seven of his officers had that week been arrested for working as an execution squad for Rio merchants, who paid them to kill the street children who blocked access to their shops. 'The lucky ones are the ones who go to Europe, Guido,' he said before he hung up. His contact in Bangkok was just as uncomprehending. 'Commissario, more than half of the whores here have Aids. The girls who get out of Thailand are the lucky ones.'

The most valuable source was Pia, whom he found at home, kept there by her golden retriever, Luna, who was about to give birth to her first litter. She knew all about the business, was surprised that the police were bothering with it. When she learned that Brunetti's interest had been provoked by the death of three businessmen, she laughed long and loud. The girls, she explained after she caught her breath, came in from all over; some worked the streets, but many were kept in houses, where better control could be kept over them. Yes, they got banged around a fair bit, if not by the men who ran them, then by some of the men who used them. Complain? To whom? They had no papers, they were persuaded that their mere presence in Italy was a crime; some never even learned to speak Italian. After all, it's not as if they were engaged in a profession where sparkling conversation counted for very much.

Pia felt no particular animus towards them, though

she didn't hide the fact that she minded the competition. She and her friends, none of whom had a pimp, at least had some sort of economic stability – an apartment, a car, some even had their own homes – but these foreign women had none, and so they could not afford to reject a client, no matter what he demanded. They and the women who were addicts were the worst off, would accept anything, could be forced to do anything. Powerless, they became the targets of brutality and, worse, the vectors of disease.

He asked her how many there were in the Veneto area and, with a laugh, she told him he didn't know how to count that high. But then Luna gave a bark so loud that even Brunetti could hear it, and Pia said she had to go.

'Who's in charge, Pia?' he asked, hoping to get one more answer from her before she hung up.

'It's big business, dottore,' she said, using the English words. 'You might as well ask who runs the banks or the stock market. It's the same men with the good haircuts and the custom-made suits. Church on Sunday, go to the office every day, and when no one's looking, count up how much they've made from the women who work on their backs. We're just another commodity, dottore. Wait long enough, we'll be listed on the futures market.' Pia laughed, made a rude suggestion about what the futures could be named, Luna howled, and Pia hung up.

On the same piece of paper, Brunetti began to do some simple sums. He decided to estimate the average price of a trick at 50,000 lire, then had to admit that he had no idea how many a day there might be. He decided that selecting ten would simplify his multiplication, so he made it ten. Even with the weekend off, which he doubted was a luxury these women were permitted, it came to $2\frac{1}{2}$ million lire a week, 10 million lire a month. He decided to simplify things and settled on 100 million lire a year, then cut it in half to make up, however roughly, for any errors he might have made in his previous calculations. After that, when he tried to multiply by half a million, he ceased having a name for the sum and had to settle for counting the zeros: there were, he thought, fifteen of them. Pia was right: this was indeed big business.

Instinct and experience told him that there was no more information to be had from either Mara or her pimp. He called down to Vianello and asked whether they'd located the optician who had sold the glasses found in the Padua restaurant. Vianello covered the phone with his hand, sound disappeared, and then the sergeant's voice came back, tight with what sounded like anger or even something stronger. 'I'll be up in a minute, dottore,' he said and put the phone down.

When the sergeant came in, his face was still red with what Brunetti knew from long experience was the aftermath of rage. Vianello closed the door softly behind him, and came over to Brunetti's desk. 'Riverre,' he said by way of explanation, naming the black nemesis of his life, indeed, of the entire staff of the Questura.

'What's he done?'

'He found the optician yesterday, made a note of it, but left it on his own desk until just now when I asked about it.' Had he been in a better mood, Brunetti would have quipped that at least Riverre had bothered to make a note this time, but he found himself without either patience or good humour. And long experience had taught them both that, in the issue of Riverre's incompetence, comment was unnecessary.

'Which one?'

'Carraro, in Calle della Mandora.'

'Did he get a name?'

Vianello bit at his lower lip, his hands tightened into involuntary fists. 'No, he was content merely to discover that the glasses had been sold, with that prescription. That's all he was told to do, he said, so that's what he did.'

Brunetti pulled out the phone book and quickly found the number. The optician, when he answered, said that he had been expecting another call from the police and immediately gave Brunetti the name and address of the woman who had bought those glasses. From the way he spoke, it seemed that he believed the police were interested in no more than seeing that her glasses were returned to her. Brunetti did nothing to disabuse him of this idea.

'But I don't think you'll find her at home,' Dr Carraro volunteered. 'I think she'll be at work.'

'And where is that, dottore?' Brunetti asked, voice warm with concern.

'She has a travel agency over near the university, halfway between it and the shop that sells carpets.'

'Ah, yes, I know it,' Brunetti said, recalling a poster-filled window he had passed countless times. 'Thank you, dottore, I'll see that the glasses are returned to her.'

Brunetti put down the phone, looked up at Vianello, and said, 'Regina Ceroni. Name mean anything to you?'

Vianello shook his head.

'She runs that travel agency over by the university.'

'Do you want me to come with you, sir?' Vianello asked.

'No, I think I'll go over before lunch and return Signora Ceroni's glasses to her.'

Brunetti stood in the late-afternoon drizzle of mid-November and looked at the sun-swept beach. A hammock stretched between two enormous palm trees, and in it lay a young woman wearing, so far as he could make out, only the bottom of her bikini. Beyond her, soft waves broke on the sandy beach, while a lapis sea stretched out to the horizon. All this could be his for a week for a mere 1,800,000 lire, double occupancy, air fare included.

He pushed open the door to the agency and went in. An attractive young woman with dark hair sat at a computer. She glanced up at him and smiled pleasantly.

'*Buon giorno,*' he said, returning her smile. 'Is Signora Ceroni here?'

'And who may I say is calling?'

'Signor Brunetti.'

She held up a hand in a waiting gesture, pushed a few more keys, and then stood up. To her left, the printer chattered into life, and what appeared to be an airline ticket began to emerge.

'I'll tell her you're here, Signor Brunetti,' she said, turning towards the back of the office, where there was a single door, closed now. She knocked and entered without waiting. A few moments later, she came out and held the door for Brunetti, signalling him to enter.

The inner office was far smaller than the outer, but what it lacked in space it more than made up for in style. The desk was, he thought, teak, polished to a glassy sheen, its absence of drawers proclaiming that it needed no excuse of utility to explain its presence. The carpet was a pale gold Isfahan silk, similar to one lying on the floor of Brunetti's father-in-law's study.

The woman who sat behind both of these had light hair pulled back on both sides and held in place by a carved ivory comb. The simplicity of the style contrasted with both the fabric and the cut of her suit, dark-grey raw silk with heavily padded shoulders and very narrow sleeves. She appeared to be in her thirties, but because of her skill with make-up and the general elegance of her bearing, it was difficult to tell which end she was closer to. She wore a pair of thick-rimmed glasses. The left lens had a small semi-circular chip in the lower corner, little wider than a pea.

She looked up as he came in, smiled without opening her mouth, removed her glasses and placed them on the papers in front of her, but said nothing. The colour of her eyes, he noticed, was so exactly that of her suit that it could not have been coincidental. Looking at her, Brunetti found himself thinking of the description

Figaro gives of the woman with whom Count Almaviva is in love: light hair, rosy cheeks, eyes that speak.

'*Si?*' she asked.

'Signora Ceroni?'

'Yes.'

'I've brought you your glasses,' Brunetti said, taking them from his pocket but not looking away from her.

Her face filled with instant pleasure that made her even lovelier. 'Oh, wonderful,' she said and got to her feet. 'Wherever did you find them?' Brunetti heard a slight accent, perhaps Slavic, certainly Eastern European.

Without saying anything, he passed them across the desk to her. She accepted the leather case and set it on top of the desk without looking inside.

'Aren't you going to check that they're yours?' he asked.

'No, I recognize the case,' she said. Then, smiling again, 'But how did you know they were mine?'

'We called the opticians in the city.'

'We?' she asked. But then she remembered her manners and said, 'But please, sit down. I'm afraid I'm being very impolite.'

'Thank you,' Brunetti said and sat in one of the three chairs that stood in front of her desk.

'I'm sorry,' she said, 'but Roberta didn't tell me your name.'

'Brunetti, Guido Brunetti.'

'Thank you, Signor Brunetti, for going to all of this trouble. You certainly could have called me, and I would have been very glad to go and pick them up.

249

There's no need for you to have come all the way across the city to give them to me.'

'Across the city?' Brunetti repeated.

His question surprised her, but for only a moment. She dismissed it, and her own surprise at it, with a wave of her hand. 'Just an expression. The agency is sort of out of the way over here.'

'Yes, of course,' he said.

'I don't know how to thank you.'

'You could tell me where you lost them.'

She smiled again. 'Why, if I knew where I lost them, then they wouldn't have been lost, would they?'

Brunetti said nothing.

She gazed across the desk at him, but he said nothing. She looked down at the glasses case and pulled it towards her. She took the glasses out and, just as had Brunetti in the restaurant, wiggled one earpiece, then pulled them both sharply to the sides; again, the glasses bent but did not break.

'Remarkable, isn't it?' she asked without looking at him.

Brunetti remained silent.

In the same entirely casual voice, she said, 'I didn't want to get involved.'

'With us?' Brunetti asked, assuming that, if she knew that he had to cross the city to get to her, then she knew where he had come from.

'Yes.'

'Why?'

'He was a married man.'

'In a few years, we'll be in the twenty-first century, signora.'

'What do you mean?' she asked, looking up at him in real confusion.

'That married or not married hardly means much any more.'

'It did to his wife,' she said fiercely. She folded the glasses and slipped them back into the leather case.

'Not even when he was found dead?'

'Especially not then. I didn't want there to be any suspicion that I had anything to do with it.'

'Did you?'

'Commissario Brunetti,' she said, managing to surprise him by the use of his title, 'it took me five years to become a citizen of this country and, even now, I have no doubt that my citizenship could very easily be taken away from me at the first moment I came to the attention of the authorities. Because of that, I want to do nothing that will bring me to their attention.'

'You're receiving our attention now.'

She pursed her lips in involuntary vexation. 'I had hoped to avoid it.'

'Yet you knew you had left the glasses there?'

'I knew I lost them that day, but I hoped it was somewhere else.'

'Were you having an affair with him?'

He watched her weigh this, and then she nodded.

'How long had it gone on?'

'Three years.'

'Did you have any intention of changing things?'

'I'm afraid I don't understand your question.'

251

'Did you have hopes of marrying him?'

'No. The situation suited me as it was.'

'And what was that situation?'

'We saw one another every few weeks.'

'And did what?'

She looked up at him sharply. 'Again, I don't understand your question.'

'What did you do when you saw him?'

'What is it lovers usually do, Dottor Brunetti?'

'They make love.'

'Very good, dottore. Yes, they make love, which is what we did.' Brunetti sensed that she was angry, but it didn't seem to him that her anger was directed at, or caused by, his questions. 'Where?' he asked.

'I beg your pardon.'

'Where did you make love?'

Her lips tightened and her answer squeezed from between them. 'In bed.'

'Where?'

Silence.

'Where was the bed? Here in Venice or in Padua?'

'In both places.'

'In an apartment or a hotel?'

Before she could answer, the phone on her desk gave a discreet buzz, and she answered it. She listened for a moment, said, 'I'll give you a call this afternoon,' and hung up. The break in the rhythm of the questions had been minimal, but it had been enough to allow her to regain her composure.

'I'm sorry, commissario, would you repeat your last question?' she asked.

He repeated it, knowing that the interruption provided by the phone call had given her enough time to think about the answer she'd given. But he wanted to hear her change it. 'I asked you where you made love.'

'Here in my apartment.'

'And in Padua?'

She feigned confusion. 'What?'

'In Padua, where did you meet?'

She gave him a small smile. 'I'm afraid I misunderstood your question. We usually met here.'

'And how frequently were you able to see one another?'

Her manner warmed, as it always did just before people began to lie. 'Actually, there really wasn't very much of an affair left, but we liked one another and were still good friends. So we saw one another for dinner every so often, either here or in Padua.'

'Do you remember the last time you were together here in Venice?'

She turned aside and considered how to answer his question. 'Why, no, I don't. I think it must have been some time during the summer.'

'Are you married, signora?' he asked.

'I'm divorced,' she answered.

'Do you live alone?'

She nodded.

'How did you learn of Signor Favero's death?'

'I read it in the paper, the morning after it happened.'

'And didn't call us?'

'No.'

'Even though you'd seen him the night before?'

'Especially because of that. As I explained a moment ago, I have no reason to put my trust in the authorities.'

In his worst moments, Brunetti suspected that no one did, but that was perhaps an opinion best not revealed to Signora Ceroni.

'Where do you come from originally, signora?'

'Yugoslavia. From Mostar.'

'And how long ago did you come to Italy?'

'Nine years.'

'Why did you come?'

'I came originally as a tourist, but then I found work and decided to stay.'

'In Venice?'

'Yes.'

'What sort of work did you do?' he asked, though he knew that this information would be available somewhere in the records of the Ufficio Stranieri.

'At first, I worked in a bar, but then I got a job in a travel agency. I knew several languages, and so it was easy for me to find work.'

'And now this?' he asked, waving his hand to encompass the small office in which they sat. 'Is it yours?'

'Yes.'

'How long have you owned it?'

'Three years. It took me more than four years to save enough money to give a deposit to the old owners. But now it's mine. That's another reason I didn't want any trouble.'

'Even if you have nothing to hide?'

'If I might be frank, commissario, it has never been my experience that agencies of the state pay much attention to whether people have things to hide or not. Quite the contrary, in fact. And because I know nothing about the details of Signor Favero's death, I made the judgement that there was no information I could provide to the police, and so I did not call you.'

'What did you talk about at dinner that night?'

She paused and looked aside, thinking back to the evening. 'What friends talk about. His business. Mine. His children.'

'His wife?'

Again, she brought her lips together in evident disapproval. 'No, we did not discuss his wife. Neither of us thought that in good taste.'

'What else did you talk about?'

'Nothing that I can remember. He talked about buying a new car and didn't know what kind to get, but I couldn't help him there.'

'Because you don't drive?'

'No, there's no need for it here, is there?' she asked with a smile. 'And I know nothing about cars. Like most women.'

Brunetti wondered why she made this obvious appeal to his male sense of superiority; it seemed out of character in a woman who so easily established her own equality with a man.

'The waiter in the restaurant where you had dinner said that he showed you some papers during dinner.'

'Ah, yes. That's when I took out the glasses. I need them for reading.'

'What were the papers?'

She paused, either in memory or invention. 'It was the prospectus for a company he wanted me to invest in. Because the agency is making a profit, he wanted me to start to use the money I made – "put it to work" – those were his words. But I wasn't interested.'

'Do you remember what sort of company it was?'

'No, I'm afraid I don't. I don't pay much attention to that sort of thing.' Brunetti doubted this. 'Is it important?' she asked.

'We found quite a number of files in the trunk of his car,' Brunetti lied, 'and we'd like to get some idea of whether any of them have special importance.'

He watched as she started to ask about the papers and then changed her mind.

'Can you remember anything particular about that evening? Did he seem troubled or upset about anything?' It occurred to Brunetti that almost anyone would find it strange that it had taken him so long to get around to this question.

'He was more quiet than usual, but that could have been because he was working so much. He said a number of times that he was very busy.'

'Did he mention anything in particular?'

'No.'

'And after dinner, where did you go?'

'He drove me to the railway station, and I came back to Venice.'

'Which train?'

She thought for a moment before answering. 'It got in about eleven, I think.'

'The one Trevisan took,' Brunetti said and saw the name register.

'The man who was killed last week?' she asked after a short pause.

'Yes. Did you know him?' Brunetti asked.

'He was a client here. We handled his travel arrangements, for himself and for the people who worked for him.'

'Strange, isn't it?' Brunetti asked.

'Isn't what strange?'

'That two men you know should die in the same week.'

Her voice was cool, uninterested. 'No, I don't find it particularly strange, commissario. Certainly, you don't mean to suggest there's some sort of connection between the two.'

Instead of answering her question, he got to his feet. 'Thank you for your time, Signora Ceroni,' he said, reaching across the desk to shake her hand.

She stood and came around the desk, moving gracefully. 'It is I who should thank you for having taken the trouble to return my glasses to me.'

'It was our duty,' he said.

'None the less, I thank you for taking the trouble.' She went with him to the door, opened it, and allowed him to pass in front of her to the outer office. The young woman still sat at the desk, and a long sheet of tickets hung suspended from the printer. Signora Ceroni walked with him to the front door of the agency. He opened it, turned and shook hands again, and then headed back up towards home. Signora Ceroni stood in front of the beach until he turned the corner and disappeared.

Chapter Twenty-Four

When he arrived at the Questura, Brunetti stopped first in Signorina Elettra's office and dictated the letter to Giorgio – he couldn't help thinking of him that way now – in which he apologized for what he called 'clerical inaccuracies' on the part of the Questura. The letter would suffice, he hoped, for Giorgio's fiancée and her family while at the same time remaining sufficiently vague so as not to commit him to having actually done anything.

'He'll be very glad to get this,' Signorina Elettra said, looking down at the page of shorthand notes on her desk.

'And the record of his arrest?' Brunetti asked.

She glanced up at him, eyes two limpid pools. 'Arrest?' She took a sheaf of computer print-out from beside her pad and passed it across to Brunetti. 'Your letter ought to pay him back for this.'

'The numbers in Favero's book?' he asked.

'The very same,' she said, unable to disguise her pride.

He smiled, her pleasure immediately contagious. 'Have you looked at it?' he asked.

'Just briefly. He's got names, addresses, and I think

he's managed to get the dates and times of all calls going through to all of those numbers from any phones in Venice or Padua.'

'How does he do it?' Brunetti asked, voice reverent with the awe he felt at Giorgio's ability to pry information from SIP; the files of the secret services were easier to penetrate.

'He went to school in the United States for a year, to study computers, and while he was there, he joined a group of something called "ackers". He keeps in touch with them, and they trade information about how to do things like this.'

'Does he do this at work, using the SIP lines?' Brunetti asked, his awe and gratitude so strong as to erase the fact that what Giorgio did was probably illegal.

'Of course.'

'Bless him,' Brunetti said with all the fervour of a person whose phone bill for any given period never corresponded to the use given the phone.

'They're all over the world, these "ackers",' Signorina Elettra added, 'and I don't think there's much that can be hidden from them. He told me he contacted people in Hungary and Cuba to do this. And someplace else. Do they have phones in Laos?'

He was no longer listening but was reading down through the long columns of times and dates, of places and names. Patta's name, however, broke through: '. . . wants to see you'.

'Later,' he said and left her office, going back to his own, reading all the way. Inside, he closed the door and went over to stand in the light coming through the window. He stood there, poised like a Roman senator of the time of the Caesars, hands spread wide, slowly studying a long report from the far-flung cities of the Empire. This one did not deal with troop disposition or the shipment of spices and oil. Instead, it told only when two relatively inconspicuous Italians might have called and spoken to people in Bangkok, the Dominican Republic, Belgrade, Manila, and a handful of other cities, but it was no less interesting for that. Pencilled in the margin of the sheets were the locations of the public call boxes from which some of the calls were made. Though some of the calls were made from the offices of both Trevisan and Favero, many more were made from a public phone on the same street as Favero's office in Padua and still more from another one located in a small *calle* that ran behind Trevisan's office.

At the bottom, Brunetti read the names under which the phones were listed. Three, including the one in Belgrade, belonged to travel agencies, and the Manila number belonged to a company named Euro-Employ. At the name, all of the events since Trevisan's death turned into shards of coloured glass in an immense kaleidoscope seen only by Brunetti. And this single name was the final turn of the cylinder that jogged the separate pieces and forced them into a pattern. It was not yet complete, not yet fully in focus, but it was there, and Brunetti understood.

He pulled his address book from his desk drawer, rifling through the pages for the phone number of Roberto Linchianko, a lieutenant-colonel in the Philippine military police, a man who had attended a two-week police seminar in Lyons three years ago and with whom Brunetti had formed a friendship that had lasted since then, though their only communication had been by phone and fax.

His buzzer rang. He ignored it and picked up the phone, got an outside line, and dialled Linchianko's home phone number, though he had no idea at all what time it was in Manila. Six hours ahead, as it turned out, which meant he caught Linchianko just as he was about to go to bed. Yes, he knew Euro-Employ. His disgust came down the wire, leaping across the oceans. Euro-Employ was only one of the agencies engaged in the trade of young women, and it was hardly the worst. All of the papers the women signed before they went off to 'work' in Europe were entirely legal. The fact that the papers were signed by the 'X' of an illiterate or by a woman that didn't speak the language of the contract in no way compromised their legality, though none of the women who managed to return to the Philippines thought or sought to bring a legal claim against the agency. In any case, so far as Linchianko knew, very few returned. As to how many were sent, he estimated that there were between fifty and a hundred a week, just from Euro-Employ, and named the agency that booked their tickets, a name already familiar to Brunetti from its presence on the list. Before he hung up, Linchianko promised to fax Brunetti the official police file on both Euro-Employ and the travel agency as well as the personnel files he had kept for years on all of the employment agencies working in Manila.

Brunetti had no personal contacts in any of the other cities on the list from SIP, but what he learned from Linchianko was more than enough to tell him what he would find there.

In all of his reading of Roman and Greek history, one of the things that had always puzzled Brunetti was the ease with which the ancients had accepted slavery. The rules of war were different then, he knew, as had been the economic basis of the society, and so slaves were both available and necessary. Perhaps it was a possibility that it might happen to you, should your country lose a war, that made the idea acceptable – no more than a spin of the wheel of fate could make you a slave or master. But no one had spoken against it, not Plato and not Socrates, or, if anyone had, what they said and wrote had not survived.

And today, to the best of his knowledge, no one spoke against it, either, but today the silence was based on the belief that slavery had ceased to exist. He had listened to Paola voice her radical politics for decades, had grown almost deaf to her hurling about terms like 'wage slave' and 'economic chains', but now those clichés rose up to haunt him, for what Linchianko had described to him could be given no other name but slavery.

The full flood of his interior rhetoric was cut off by the repeated buzz of the intercom on his desk.

'Yes, sir,' he said as he picked it up.

'I'd like to talk to you,' said a disgruntled Patta.

'I'll be right down.'

Signorina Elettra was no longer at her desk when Brunetti went downstairs, so he went into Patta's office with no idea of what to expect, not that the possibilities were ever more than a few: after all, how many manifestations could displeasure take?

Today, he was to learn that he was not the target of Patta's dissatisfaction, only the means by which it was to be conveyed to the lower orders. 'It's that sergeant of yours,' Patta began after telling Brunetti to take a seat.

'Vianello?'

'Yes.'

'What do you think he's done?' Brunetti asked, not conscious until after he had spoken of the scepticism implicit in his question.

Patta did not overlook it. 'I think he's been abusive to one of the patrolmen.'

'Riverre?' Brunetti asked.

'Then you've heard about it and done nothing?' Patta asked.

'No, I've heard nothing. But if there's anyone who deserves abuse, it's Riverre.'

Patta threw up his hands in a visible manifestation of his irritation. 'I've had a complaint from one of the officers.'

'Lieutenant Scarpa?' Brunetti asked, unable to disguise his dislike for the Sicilian who had come up to Venice with his patron, the Vice-Questore, and who served as much as spy as assistant.

'It's not important who made the complaint. What is important is that it was made.'

'Was it an official complaint?' Brunetti asked.

'That's irrelevant,' Patta said with swift anger. With Patta, anything he didn't want to hear was irrelevant, regardless of its truth. 'I don't want any trouble with the unions. They won't put up with this sort of thing.'

Brunetti, disgusted with this latest example of Patta's cowardice, came close to asking him if there were any threat before which he would not bow down, but he cautioned himself, yet once again, against the rage of fools and, instead, said, 'I'll speak to them.'

'Them?'

'Lieutenant Scarpa, Sergeant Vianello, and Officer Riverre.'

Patta came close, he could tell, to objecting to this, but then, no doubt realizing that the problem, even if not solved, was at least out of his hands, said instead, 'And this Trevisan thing?'

'We're working on it, sir.'

'Any progress?'

'Very little.' At least none he wanted to discuss with Patta.

'Well, take care of this problem with Vianello. Let me know what happens.' Patta turned his attention back to the papers in front of him, his equivalent of a polite dismissal.

Signorina Elettra was no longer at her desk, so Brunetti went down to Vianello's office, where he found the sergeant reading that day's *Gazzettino*.

'Scarpa?' Brunetti asked when he came in.

Vianello crumpled the pages of the newspaper together and pressed it down on the desk with an unverifiable remark about Lieutenant Scarpa's mother.

'What happened?'

With one hand, Vianello began to smooth out the pages of his newspaper. 'I was talking to Riverre, and Lieutenant Scarpa came in.'

'Talking to?'

Vianello shrugged. 'Riverre knew what I meant, and he knew he should have given you that woman's name sooner. I was telling him that when the lieutenant came in. He didn't like the way I was talking to Riverre.'

'What were you saying?'

Vianello folded the paper closed and then in half, then pushed it to the side of his desk. 'I called him an idiot.'

Brunetti, who knew Riverre was one, found nothing strange in this.

'What did he say?'

'Who, Riverre?'

'No, the lieutenant.'

'He said I could not speak to my subordinates that way.'

'Did he say anything else?'

Vianello didn't answer.

'Did he say anything else, sergeant?'

Still no answer.

'Did you say anything to him?'

Vianello's voice was defensive. 'I told him that the matter was between me and one of my officers, that it didn't concern him.'

Brunetti knew he didn't have to waste time telling Vianello how foolish this was.

'And Riverre?' Brunetti asked.

'Oh, he's come to me already and told me that, as far as he remembers our conversation, I was telling him a joke. About a Sicilian.' Vianello permitted himself a small smile here. 'The lieutenant, as Riverre now remembers the incident, came in just as I was giving the punch line, about how stupid the Sicilian was, and the lieutenant didn't understand – we were speaking dialect – and thought I was talking to Riverre.'

'Well, that seems to take care of that,' Brunetti said, though he didn't like the fact that Scarpa had taken his complaint to Patta. Vianello already had enough against him in that quarter, just by virtue of his so often working with Brunetti, and didn't need the opposition of the lieutenant as well.

Abandoning the issue, Brunetti asked, 'Do you remember something about a truck that went off the road, up in Tarvisio, this autumn?'

'Yes. Why?'

'Do you remember when it was?'

Vianello paused for a moment before he answered. 'September 26th. Two days before my birthday. First time it's ever snowed that early up there.'

Because it was Vianello, Brunetti didn't have to ask him if he was sure of the date. He left the sergeant to return to his newspaper and went back to his office and to the computer sheets. A call had been made from Trevisan's office to the number in Belgrade at nine in the morning of 26 September, a call that lasted three minutes. The following day, another call had been made to the same number, but this one came from the call box in the *calle* behind Trevisan's office. This one had lasted twelve minutes.

The truck went off the road; its shipment was destroyed. Surely, the purchaser would want to know if it had been his cargo scattered out there in the snow, and there would be no better way to find out than to call the shipper. Brunetti shivered involuntarily at the possibility that people might think of those girls as a shipment, their sudden deaths as a loss of cargo.

He paged ahead to the date of Trevisan's death. Two calls had been made from the office on the day after Trevisan's death, both to the Belgrade number. If the first calls had been made to report a loss of cargo, could these later calls mean that, with Trevisan's death, the business passed to new hands?

Chapter Twenty-Five

Brunetti tried to quiet his uneasiness by hunting through the papers that had accumulated on his desk during the last two days. He found that Lotto's widow had, indeed, been interviewed and had said she spent the night of Lotto's death in the civil hospital, at the bedside of her mother, who was dying of cancer. Both of the ward sisters verified that she had been there all through the night. Vianello had interviewed her, and he had gone on, with his usual precision, to ask about the nights of both Trevisan's and Favero's deaths. She was in the hospital the first night, at home the second. Both nights, however, her sister from Torino was with her, and so Signora Lotto ceased to have a place in Brunetti's imagination.

Suddenly he found himself wondering if Chiara was still engaged in her hare-brained attempt to get information from Francesca, and as he thought about it, he was overcome with something akin to disgust. He could allow himself the luxury of righteous indignation about men who used teenagers as whores, yet he had felt no equal repugnance to turn his own child into a spy. Until now.

His phone rang and he answered it with his name.

It was Paola, voice wildly out of pitch, calling his name. In the background, he heard even wilder noises, high voiced.

'What is it, Paola?'

'Guido, come home. Now. It's Chiara,' Paola cried, voice raised to be heard over the wailing that came from somewhere else in the house.

'What's happened? Is she all right?'

'I don't know, Guido. She was in the living room, and then she began to scream. She's in her room, and the door's locked.' He could hear the panic in Paola's voice, like an undercurrent that pulled at her, and then at him.

'Is she all right? Did she hurt herself?' he asked.

'I don't know. But you can hear her. She's hysterical, Guido. Please come home. Please. Now.'

'I'll be there as soon as I can,' he said and put the phone down. He grabbed his coat and ran from his office, already calculating the fastest way to get home. Outside, there was no police launch tied up to the *embarcadero* in front of the Questura, so he turned to the left and started to run, coat flapping wide behind him. He turned the corner and started up the narrow *calle*, trying to decide whether to go across the Rialto Bridge or to take the public gondola. In front of him, three young boys walked arm in arm. As he approached them, he shouted out, '*Attenti*', voice so loud as to remove all politeness from the call. The boys scattered to the sides and Brunetti hurled past them. By the time he got to Campo Santa Maria Formosa, he was winded and had to slow to a shambling trot. Near the Rialto, he got caught in foot traffic and found himself, at one point, shoving past a tourist by pushing her knapsack roughly out of the way. Behind him, he heard the girl call out in angry German, but Brunetti ran on.

Out from under the underpass and into Campo San Bartolomeo, he cut off to the left, deciding to take the gondola and avoid the bridge, heavy now with late-afternoon traffic. Luckily, a gondola was pulled up at the stop, two old ladies standing at the back. He ran across the wooden landing and stepped down into the gondola. 'Let's go,' he called to the gondoliere who stood in the back, leaning against his oar. 'Police, take me across.'

Casually, as if he did this every day of the week, the gondoliere in the front pushed against the railing of the steps leading down to the boat, and the gondola slipped backwards into the Grand Canal. The one in the back shifted his weight and leaned into his oar; the gondola turned and started across the canal. The old women, strangers, grabbed at one another in fear and sat down on the low seat that ran across the back of the boat.

'Can you take me to the end of Calle Tiepolo?' Brunetti asked the man in front.

'You really police?' the gondoliere asked.

'Yes,' he said, digging into his pocket and showing them his warrant card.

'All right.' Saying this, he turned to the women in the back and said, in Veneziano, 'We've got a detour, Signore.'

The old women were too frightened by what was happening to say anything.

Brunetti stood, blind to the boats, blind to the light, blind to anything but their slow passage across the canal. Finally, after what seemed hours, they pulled up at the end of Calle Tiepolo, and the two gondoliere held the boat steady while Brunetti climbed up to the embankment. He shoved 10,000 lire into the hand of the man in front and turned up the *calle*, running.

Brunetti had got his wind back in the gondola and raced up the *calle* towards home, then up the first three flights of stairs. He took the fourth and fifth quickly, gasping, legs throbbing. He heard the door above him open, and he looked up to see Paola at the door, holding it open for him.

'Paola,' he began.

Before he could say anything more, she shouted down at him, 'I hope you'll be happy to see what your little detective found out for you. I hope you'll be happy to see the world you're taking her into with your questions and your investigations.' Her face was flushed and she was explosive with rage.

He let himself into the apartment and shut the door behind him. Paola turned away from him and walked down the hall. He called her name, but she ignored him and went into the kitchen, slamming the door. He went down to Chiara's door and stood outside it. Silence. He listened for sobs, for some sound that she was in there. Nothing. He went back up the hall and knocked on the kitchen door. Paola opened it and glared at him, stony-eyed.

'Tell me about this,' he said. 'Tell me what's going on.'

He had often seen Paola angry, but he had never seen her like this, shaking with rage or with some deeper emotion.

Instinctively Brunetti kept his distance from her, and keeping his voice calm, repeated, 'Tell me what's going on.'

Paola gritted her teeth and sucked air through them. The tendons in her neck were strained and stood out in her flesh. He waited.

Her voice, when it came, was so tight as to be almost inaudible. 'She came home this afternoon and said she had something she wanted to watch on the VCR. I was busy in my study, so I told her to go and watch it herself but keep the volume down.' Paola stopped speaking for a moment and looked at him steadily. Brunetti said nothing.

She pulled more air in through her teeth and continued. 'After about a quarter of an hour, she started to scream. When I came out of the study, she was in the hall, hysterical. You heard her. I tried to hold her, to talk to her, but she couldn't stop screaming. She's in her room now.'

'What happened?'

'She brought home a tape, and she watched it.'

'Where did she get the tape?'

'Guido,' she began, still breathing heavily but more slowly now, 'I'm sorry for what I said.'

'It doesn't matter. Where did she get the tape?'

'From Francesca.'

'Trevisan?'

'Yes.'

'Did you see it?'

She nodded.

'What is it?'

This time she shook her head from side to side. Awkwardly, she raised an arm and pointed back towards the living room.

'Is she all right?'

'Yes. She let me into her room a couple of minutes ago. I gave her some aspirin and told her to lie down. She wants to talk to you. But you have to look at the tape first.'

Brunetti nodded and turned towards the living room, where the television and VCR were. 'Should you be with her, Paola?'

'Yes,' Paola said and turned back down the corridor towards Chiara's room.

In the living room, Brunetti found the television and VCR both turned on, a tape in place, played out to the end. He pushed the rewind button and straightened up, waiting and listening to the snake-like hiss of tape from the machine. He thought of nothing, concentrated on emptying his mind of all possibility.

The faint click brought him back. He pushed the play button and moved away from the screen, seating himself on a straight-backed chair. There were no credits, no introductory graphic, no sound. The luminous grey disappeared, and the screen showed a room with two windows high up on one wall, three chairs, and a table. The lighting came from the windows and, he thought, from some source of light that stood behind whoever held the camera, for it was evident from the faint unsteadiness of the picture that the camera was hand-held.

A noise came from the television, and the camera panned over to reveal a door, which opened, allowing three young men to push into the room, laughing and joking and shoving at one another. When they were just inside the room, the last one turned and reached back through the door. He pulled a woman into the room, and three other men crowded in behind her.

The first three appeared to be in their early teens, two others were perhaps Brunetti's age, and the last, the one who followed the woman into the room, was perhaps in his thirties. All wore shirts and pants that had a faintly military look, and all wore thick-soled boots that laced up above the ankle.

The woman appeared to be in her late thirties or early forties and was wearing a dark skirt and sweater. She wore no make-up, and her hair hung loose and tangled, as though it had been pulled free from a bun or a kerchief. Though the film was in colour, it was impossible to tell the colour of her eyes save that they were dark, and terrified.

Brunetti could hear the men talking, but he couldn't understand what they said. The three youngest ones laughed at something one of the older ones said, but the woman turned to him and stared at him after he spoke, as if unable, or unwilling, to believe what she had heard. With unconscious modesty, she folded her hands across her chest and lowered her head.

For a long moment, no one spoke and no one moved, and then a voice called out, very close to the camera, but none of the people in the screen had spoken. It took Brunetti a moment to realize that it must have been the cameraman who spoke. From the tone, it must have been a command or some sort of encouragement. When he spoke, the woman's head shot up and she looked towards the camera, but not into the lens, a bit to the left, at the person who held it. The voice near the camera spoke again, this time louder, and this time the men moved in response to it.

Two of the young ones came up on either side of the woman and grabbed her by the arms. The one in his thirties came up to her and said something. She shook her head from side to side, and he punched her. He didn't slap her; he punched her just in front of the ear. And then, quite calmly, he took a knife from his belt and slit her sweater open, all down the front. She started to scream, and he hit her again, then pulled the sweater free from her body, leaving her naked from the waist up. He ripped a sleeve from the sweater and, when she opened her mouth to speak to him or to scream, he shoved it into her mouth.

He spoke to the two men who held her, and they lifted her up on to the table. He gestured to the two older ones. They moved quickly around the table and grabbed her feet, pinning her legs to the table. The one with the knife used it again, this time to slash her skirt from the hem to the waistband. He peeled it away from her, as if breaking open a new book to the centre pages.

The cameraman spoke again, and the man with the knife moved around to the other side of the table; his body had been blocking the lens. He set the knife down on the edge of the table and unzipped his pants. He wore no belt. He clambered up on to the table and lay on top of the woman. The two men who held her legs had to back off a way so as not to be kicked by him as he thrust into her. He lay on top of her for a few minutes, then climbed down the other side of the table. One of the young ones went next, and then the other two.

The sound grew confused, for the men were calling to one another and laughing, and the cameraman seemed to be egging them on. Like a low continuo, the woman moaned and whimpered through all of this, but it was almost impossible to pick up the sound she made.

The last to use her were the two middle-aged men. One of them baulked at the table and shook his head, but this was met with hoots of derision, and so he too climbed on the table and took his turn. The last one, the oldest, was so eager that he pushed the other one from her body and mounted her.

When all six were done, the camera moved for the first time and came in very close. It moved lovingly up and down her body, pausing here and there, wherever there was blood. It paused on her face. Her eyes were closed, but the voice that Brunetti was now thinking of as the cameraman's called softly to her, and she opened her eyes, just inches from the camera. He heard her gasp and heard her head crack against the table as she pulled it roughly to the side in a vain attempt to hide from the camera.

The lens pulled back and more of her body came into the screen. When he was back in his original position, the cameraman called out again, and the first one who had used her picked up the knife. The cameraman spoke again, more urgently, and the one with the knife, as casually as if he had been asked to prepare the chicken for that night's dinner, drew the blade across the woman's throat. Blood splattered across his arm and hand, and the other men laughed at the foolish look that filled his face as he leaped back from her body. They were still laughing as the camera slid in for one last look at her body. It didn't have to be particular any more: there was plenty of blood now. The screen darkened.

The tape continued to play, but the only sound was its quiet whirr and a faint humming sound that Brunetti, after a moment's confusion, realized was coming from himself. He stopped and tried to get up, but he was prevented by his hands, which he couldn't release from the edge of the chair. He looked down at them, fascinated, and willed his fingers to relax. After a moment, they did, and he got to his feet.

He had recognized enough of the language to know it was Serbo-Croat. Months ago, he had read a brief article in *Corriere della Sera* about these tapes, made in the death traps that the cities of Bosnia had become, made and then brought out to be reproduced and sold. He had, at the time, chosen not to believe what he read, unable, even with what he had seen for these last decades, or perhaps unwilling, to believe his fellow man capable of this last obscenity. And now, like St Thomas the Doubter, he had plunged his hand into the open wound, and so he had no choice but to believe.

He turned off the television and the VCR. He went down the corridor to Chiara's room. The door was open and he went in without knocking. Chiara lay propped up on her pillows. She had one arm wrapped about Paola, who sat on the side of the bed, and in the other she held to herself a much chewed and battered toy beagle which she had had since her sixth birthday.

'*Ciao, Papà,*' she said as he came in. She looked up at him but she didn't smile.

'*Ciao, angelo,*' he said and came to stand closer to the bed. 'I'm sorry you saw that, Chiara.' He felt as stupid as the words.

Chiara looked at him sharply, seeking a reproach in his words, but found none, only a searing remorse she was too young to recognize. 'Did they really kill her, Papà?' she asked, destroying at once his hope that she had fled from the video before the end.

He nodded. 'I'm afraid so, Chiara.'

'Why?' Chiara asked, voice as filled with confusion as horror.

His mind flew up and away from the room. He tried to think noble thoughts, tried to think of something to say that would assure his child, convince her that, however wicked what she had seen, the world was a place where things like that were random, and humanity remained good by instinct and impulse.

'Why, Papà? Why would they do that?'

'I don't know, Chiara.'

'But they really killed her?' she asked.

'Don't talk about it,' Paola interrupted her and bent to kiss the side of her head, pulling her closer.

Undeterred, Chiara repeated, 'Did they, Papà?'

'Yes, Chiara.'

'She really died?'

Paola looked up at him, trying to silence him with her eyes, but he answered, 'Yes, Chiara, she really died.'

Chiara pulled the battered dog on to her lap and stared down at it.

'Who gave you the tape, Chiara?' he asked.

She pulled at one of the dog's long ears, but not roughly, remembering that this was the one that was ripped. 'Francesca,' she finally answered. 'She gave it to me before class this morning.'

'Did she say anything about it?'

She picked up the dog and held it, standing upright, on her lap. Finally she answered, 'She said she'd heard I was asking questions about her because of what happened to her father. She thought I was doing it for you because you're a cop. And then she told me to look at the tape if I wanted to see why someone might want to kill her father.' She tilted the dog from side to side and made it walk towards her.

'Did she say anything else, Chiara?'

'No, Papà, just that.'

'Do you know where she got the tape?'

'No. That's all she said, that it would show why someone would want to kill her father. But what does Francesca's father have to do with that?'

'I don't know.'

Paola stood, so abruptly that Chiara let go of the beagle and it fell to the floor. Paola bent and snatched it up with one hand and stood holding it for a moment, clutching the tattered thing in a death grip. Then, very slowly, she bent down and returned it to Chiara's lap, ran her hand across the top of her daughter's head, and left the room.

'Who were they, Papà?'

'I think they were Serbs, but I'm not sure. Someone who knows the language will have to listen to them, and then we'll know.'

'What will you do about it, Papà? Will you arrest them and send them to prison?'

'I don't know, darling. It won't be easy to find them.'

'But they should go to prison, shouldn't they?'

'Yes.'

'What do you think Francesca meant about her father?' A possibility occurred to Chiara and she asked, 'That wasn't him holding the camera, was it?'

'No, I'm sure it wasn't.'

'Then what did she mean?'

'I don't know. That's what I have to find out.' He watched her try to tie the dog's ears together. 'Chiara?'

'Yes, Papà?' She looked up at him, certain that he would say something that would make it all right, that would fix it and make it be as though it hadn't happened.

'I think you better not talk to Francesca any more.'

'And not ask any more questions?'

'No, not that, either.'

She absorbed this, then asked hesitantly, 'You're not mad at me, are you?'

Brunetti stooped down beside the bed. 'No, I'm not mad at you at all.' He wasn't sure if he could control his voice and so paused a moment, then said, pointing to the dog, 'Be careful you don't pull Bark's ear off.'

'He's a silly dog, isn't he?' Chiara asked. 'Whoever heard of a dog with bald spots?'

Brunetti rubbed a finger across the dog's nose. 'Most dogs don't get chewed, Chiara.'

She smiled at that and swung her legs out from under the covers. 'I think I better do my homework now,' she said, standing up.

'All right. I'll go talk to your mother.'

'Papà?' she said as he went towards the door.

'Hum?' he asked.

'Mamma's not mad at me, either, is she?'

'Chiara,' he answered, voice not entirely steady, 'you are our greatest joy.' Before she could say anything, he deepened his voice and added, 'Now do your homework.' Brunetti waited to see her smile before he left the room.

In the kitchen, Paola stood at the sink, whirling something around in the vegetable centrifuge. When he came in, she looked up and said, 'The whole world could fall down, and still we'd have to have dinner, I suppose.' He was relieved to see her smile when she said it. 'Chiara all right?'

Brunetti shrugged. 'She's doing her homework. I don't know how she is. What do you think? You know her better than I do.'

She took her hand off the knob that spun the centrifuge and looked at him. The whirring sound filled the room, and when it slowed to a stop, she asked, 'Do you really believe that?'

'Believe what?'

'That I know her better than you do?'

'You're her mother,' Brunetti said, as if that would explain it.

'Oh, Guido, you're such a goose at times. If you were a coin, Chiara would be the other side.'

Hearing Paola say that made him feel, strangely enough, very tired. He pulled one of the chairs out and sat down at the table. 'Who knows? She's young. Maybe she'll forget.'

'Will you?' Paola asked, coming to sit opposite him.

Brunetti shook his head. 'I'll forget the details of the film, but I'll never forget that I saw it, never forget what it means.'

'That's what I don't understand,' Paola said. 'Why would anyone want to see such a thing? It's obscene.' She paused a moment and then added, voice filled with surprise at finding herself using such a term, 'It's evil. That's what's so horrible about it: I feel as though I'd looked through a window and seen human evil looking back at me.' After a moment, she asked, 'Guido, how could those men do that? How could they do that and continue to think of themselves as human?'

Brunetti never had answers to what he thought of as Big Questions. Instead of trying, he posed his own, 'What about the cameraman, and what about the people who will pay to watch it?'

'Pay?' Paola asked. 'Pay?'

Brunetti nodded. 'I think that's what this is, a video made to be sold. The Americans call them "snuff films". People really get killed. I've read about them. Interpol had a report a few months ago. They found some in America, in Los Angeles, I think. In a film studio, they were being reproduced and then sold.'

'Where do they come from?' Paola asked, her astonishment now replaced by horror.

'You saw the men, in uniforms. I think it was Serbo-Croat they spoke.'

'Jesus help us all,' Paola whispered. 'And that poor woman.' She covered her mouth with one hand. 'Guido, Guido.'

He got to his feet. 'I have to go talk to her mother again,' he said.

'Did she know?'

Brunetti had no idea; he knew only that he was tired, tired to the point of pain, with Signora Trevisan and her barely concealed contempt and her protestations of ignorance. He suspected that, if Francesca had given the tape to Chiara, then the girl was far clearer than her mother on separating fact from fiction. When he thought that the girl must have known what was on the tape, he was filled with a horror of the unclean at the thought of having to question her, but all he had to do was summon up the memory of the look in the woman's eyes when she opened them and saw the camera lens staring down at her, and he knew that he would hound the girl and her mother to the fiery pit itself to find out what they knew.

Chapter Twenty-Six

Signora Trevisan backed away from Brunetti the instant she opened the door, as if responding to some refulgent ferocity that expanded out and filled the air around him. He stepped into the apartment and slammed the door closed behind him, almost glad to see her flinch away from the sharp sound it made.

'No more, Signora,' Brunetti said. 'No more evasions and no more lies about what you knew and didn't know.'

'I don't know what you're talking about,' she said, pumping up her voice with an anger so patently false that it could not cover the fear that lurked there. 'I've spoken to you once already, and . . .'

'And lied and lied and done nothing but lie to me,' Brunetti said, letting his anger rise. 'No more lies, or I'll have you and your lover down at the Questura and the Guardia di Finanza going over every bank transaction you've made for the last ten years.' He took a step towards her, and she backed away from him, putting one hand out in front of her to push back his rage.

'I still don't know . . .' she began, but Brunetti cut

her off with a hand thrust up so savagely that it succeeded in scaring even himself.

'Don't even think about lying to me, signora. My daughter's seen the tape, the one from Bosnia.' He raised his voice above whatever protest it was she started to make. 'My daughter's fourteen, and she's seen that tape.' Relentlessly, as she backed away from him, he followed her down the hall. 'You will tell me everything you know about this, no lies, none, or you will regret it every one of your living days.'

She looked at him, eyes as terrified, he realized, as the woman in the tape's had been, but even that resemblance left him cold.

Not the jaws, nothing more sinister than a door, opened behind her, and her daughter's head popped out. 'What is it, Mamma?' Francesca asked and then looked at Brunetti. She recognized him instantly but said nothing.

'Go back in your room, Francesca,' her mother said, amazing Brunetti by the coolness of her voice. 'Commissario Brunetti has to ask a few more questions.'

'About Papà and Zio Ubaldo?' she asked, making no attempt to disguise her interest.

'I said I'd talk to him, Francesca.'

'I'm sure you will,' the girl said and went back into her room, closing her door quietly.

In the same calm voice, Signora Trevisan said, 'All right,' and turned towards the room in which their previous interviews had taken place.

Inside, she sat, but Brunetti remained standing, moving uneasily from foot to foot while she spoke or taking short steps back and forth, too torn by emotion to remain still.

'What do you want to know?' she asked as soon as she was seated.

'The films.'

'They're made in Bosnia. Sarajevo, I think.'

'I know that.'

'Then what do you want to know?' she asked, feigning ignorance, but doing it badly.

'Signora,' he said, standing still for a moment, 'I am warning you that I will destroy you if you don't tell me what I want to know.' He watched the tone register. 'The tapes. Tell me.'

She adjusted her voice and managed to sound, now, like a hostess who has been much put upon by a particularly fractious guest. 'They're made there, and then some are sent to France, where they're reproduced. Others go to the United States, and the same thing happens there. Then they're sold.'

'Where?'

'In shops. Or through the mails. There are lists.'

'Who has these lists?'

'The distributors.'

'And who are they?'

'I don't know their names. The master films get sent to postboxes in Marseilles and Los Angeles.'

'Who makes the originals?'

'Someone in Sarajevo. I think he works for the Serbian army, but I'm not sure.'

'Did your husband know who he is?' He saw her begin to answer and added, 'I want the truth, signora.'

'Yes, he knew.'

'Whose idea was it to make these films?'

'I don't know. I think Carlo might have seen one. He liked things like that. And then I think the idea came to him to distribute them. He was already distributing other things through the mail and in shops in Germany.'

'What things?'

'Magazines.'

'What sort of magazines?'

'Pornographic.'

'Signora, pornographic magazines are available on every news-stand in this city. What sort of pornography?'

Her voice was so low that he had to lean forward to hear it. 'Children.' She said nothing else, only the one word.

Brunetti said nothing, waiting for her to continue. 'Carlo said that there was nothing illegal about it.' It took Brunetti a moment to realize that she was serious.

'How did your daughter come by this film?'

'Carlo kept the master tapes in his study. He liked to watch the new ones before he had them sent off.' Her voice grew sharp with disapproval as she said, 'I suppose she got in there and took one. It never would have happened if Carlo were still here.'

Brunetti did not presume to interfere with a widow's grief and so asked, instead, 'How many tapes have there been?'

'Oh, I don't know. A dozen or so, perhaps twenty.'

'All the same?'

'I don't know. I have no idea what you mean by "the same".'

'Tapes in which women are raped and murdered.'

She gave him a look rich with disgust at his daring to speak of such ugly things. 'I think so.'

'You think so or you know so?'

'I suppose I know so.'

'Who else was involved in this?'

Her answer was immediate. 'I wasn't involved.'

'Aside from your husband and your brother, who else was involved?'

'I think that man in Padua.'

'Favero?'

'Yes.'

'Who else?'

'With the tapes, no one else that I know of.'

'And with the other thing, with the prostitutes, who else?'

'I think there was a woman. I don't know who she was, but I know Carlo used her to help transfer new girls.' Brunetti heard how naturally she answered his questions about 'the girls', so casually admitting to full knowledge of her husband's traffic in prostitutes.

'From where?'

'All over. I don't know.'

'Who was she?'

'I don't know. They said very little about her.'

'What did they say?'

'Nothing, nothing.'

'What did they say about her?'

'I don't remember. Ubaldo said something once, I think, but I really don't remember.'

'What did he say?'

'He called her "The Slav", but I don't know what he meant.'

To Brunetti, it seemed clear what he had meant. 'Was she a Slav?'

She lowered her voice and looked away from him before she answered, 'I think so.'

'Who is she? Where does she live?'

He watched her weigh this question before she answered, watched her try to predict how much trouble an honest answer would cost her. He wheeled away from her and took two steps, then as suddenly wheeled again and came to stand in front of her. 'Where is she?'

'I think she lives here.'

'In Venice?'

'Yes.'

'What else do you know?'

'She has a job.'

'Signora, most people have jobs. What is hers?'

'She arranges, that is, she arranged Ubaldo's and Carlo's flights.'

'Signora Ceroni?' Brunetti asked, surprising Signora Trevisan by his question.

'I think so.'

'What else did she do for them?'

'I don't know,' she said, but before he could move any closer to her, she said, 'I really don't know. I heard them talk to her on the phone a few times.'

'About plane tickets?' he asked, making no attempt to disguise his sarcasm.

'No, about other things. Girls. Money.'

'Do you know her?'

'No, I've never met her.'

'Did you ever hear her name used when they talked about the tapes?'

'They never talked about the tapes. Not really. They just said things, and I understood what they meant.'

He didn't bother to contradict her, certain as he was that this was going to become the truth around which her future would be constructed – to suspect is not to know, and if you don't know, then you aren't responsible, not in any real way, for what happens. His certainty grew so strong that Brunetti's soul sickened with it, and he knew he could no longer stay in the same room with this woman. With no explanation, he turned and left her, closing the door behind him. He could not bear the thought of speaking to the girl, and so he left the apartment, left them both there to begin constructing a convenient future.

The darkness and cold into which Brunetti emerged served to quiet him. He looked down at his watch and saw that it was after nine. He should be both hungry and thirsty, he knew, but his rage had driven both from him.

He couldn't remember the home address that they had got for Signora Ceroni beyond that it was in San Vio and that, when he had seen it, he had wondered how close it would be to the Church of La Salute. He checked it in a phone book in a bar and took the No.

1 boat across the Grand Canal to the Salute stop. He found the house not only near the church, but looking out at it from the other side of the small canal that ran along the side of the church. Her name was on the bell. He rang it and, after a minute or so, heard a woman's voice asking who it was. He gave his name and, with no further questions, she buzzed him in.

He paid no attention to the hallway, to the stairs, or to what sort of greeting she gave him at the door. She led him into a large living room, one wall of which was covered with books. Soft lighting glowed down from lights that must have been concealed behind the beams that ran across the ceiling. None of this interested him. Nor her loveliness nor the soft elegance of her clothing.

'You didn't tell me you knew Carlo Trevisan,' he said when they were seated facing one another.

'I told you he was a client of mine.' As he forced himself to calm down, he began to take notice of her, of the beige dress, the carefully combed hair, the silver buckles on her shoes.

'Signora,' Brunetti said with a weary shake of his head, 'I'm not talking about his being a client of yours. I'm talking about your being in business with him or working for him.'

She tilted her chin up and, mouth slightly ajar, stared off to one side of the room, as if he'd asked her to make a difficult decision. After what seemed a long time, she spoke. 'I told you, the last time we spoke, that I do not want to become involved with the authorities.'

'And I told you that you already are.'

'So it seems,' she said without humour.

'What did you do for Signor Trevisan?'

'If you know that I worked for him, then you probably have no need to ask me that.'

'Answer the question, Signora Ceroni.'

'I collected money for him.'

'What money?'

'The money that was given to him by various men.'

'Money from prostitutes?'

'Yes.'

'You know this is illegal, living off the earnings of a prostitute?'

'Of course I know it,' she said angrily.

'Yet you did it?'

'I just told you that I did.'

'What else did you do for him?'

'I see no reason I should make your job any easier for you, commissario.'

'Did you have anything to do with the tapes?' he asked.

If he had struck her, her response could have been no stronger. She got halfway up from her seat and then, remembering where she was and who he was, sat down again. Brunetti sat and looked at her, making a list of the things that had to be done: find her doctor and see if she had ever been prescribed Roipnol; show her photo to the people who had been on the train with Trevisan and see if they recognized her; check the phone records from her office and home; send her name, photo, and fingerprints to Interpol; check credit-card receipts to see if she had ever rented a car and thence knew how to drive. In short, do all the things he should have done the instant he found out whose glasses they were.

'Did you have anything to do with the tapes?' he asked again.

'You know about them?' she asked, and then, aware of how redundant the question was, asked, 'How did you find out?'

'My daughter saw one. Trevisan's daughter gave it to her and said it might explain why someone would want to have killed her father.'

'How old is your daughter?' she asked.

'Fourteen.'

'I'm sorry,' Signora Ceroni said and looked down at her hands. 'I'm really sorry.'

'You know what's on the tapes?' he asked.

She nodded. 'Yes, I know.'

He made no attempt to keep his disgust from his voice, 'And you helped Trevisan sell them?'

'Commissario,' she said, getting to her feet, 'I don't want to discuss this any further. If you have formal questions to ask me, you can do it at the Questura, in the presence of my lawyer.'

'You killed them, didn't you?' he asked before he thought about it.

'I'm afraid I have no idea what you're talking about,' she said. 'And now, if you have no further questions, I'll wish you good evening.'

'Was it you on the train, the woman with the fur hat?'

She had started towards the door, but when he asked

her that, she faltered and came down heavily on her left foot. She quickly regained her balance and her composure and continued towards the door. She opened it and held it open for him. 'Good evening, commissario.'

He paused in front of her at the door, but her gaze was level and cool. He left without saying anything.

When he left the building, he walked away from it without turning to look up towards what he thought must be her windows. Instead, he crossed the bridge in front and turned right into the first *calle*. There he stopped, wishing, not for the first time, that he had a portable phone. He summoned up memory and waited until the street map of the area that every Venetian carried around in his mind appeared in his. As he thought about it, he realized that he would have to go down to the second *calle* and then swing around to the left, to a narrow *calle* that ran in at the back of her house if he was to get to where he wanted to be: at the end of the *calle* on which she lived, provided with a clear view of her front door.

When he got there, he stood, leaning against a wall, for more than two hours before she left the building. She looked both ways when she stepped out, but Brunetti was hidden by the darkness in which he stood. She turned right and he followed her, glad he was wearing his brown shoes, the ones with the rubber heels and soles that muffled his footsteps. Hers, striking out from the high heels of her shoes, left a trail as easy to follow as if she were in constant sight.

Within minutes, he realized she was moving in the direction of either the railway station or Piazzale Roma, keeping to the back *calli* and away from the vaporetti on the Grand Canal. In Campo Santa Margherita, she cut off to the left, in the direction of Piazzale Roma and the buses that went towards the mainland.

Brunetti stayed as far behind her as he could without losing sound of her. It was after ten now, so there were few people on the street and almost no sound to obscure the steady, determined click of her heels.

When she came out into the Piazzale, she surprised Brunetti by crossing it, walking away from all of the spaces where the buses stopped. On the other side, she walked up the stairs and into the municipal parking garage, disappearing through the large open doorway. Brunetti hurried across the Piazzale but stopped outside the door, trying to see into the dim interior.

A man sat inside the glass booth to the right of the door. He looked up when Brunetti approached him. 'Did a woman in a grey coat just come in here?'

'Who do you think you are, police?' the man asked and glanced down at the magazine that lay open in front of him.

Wordlessly, Brunetti took his wallet from his pocket and pulled out his warrant card. He dropped it on the open page. 'Did a woman in a grey coat come in here?'

'Signora Ceroni,' the man said, looking up as he handed Brunetti's card back to him.

'Where's her car?'

'Fourth level. She'll be down in a minute.'

The sound of a motor from the circular ramp that led to the upper parking levels gave proof of this. Brunetti turned away from the window and walked over to the doorway that led outside and to the road to the mainland. He placed himself in the centre of the open door and stood, hands at his side.

The car, a white Mercedes, came down the ramp and turned towards the door. The headlights caught Brunetti full in the face, blinding him for a moment, forcing him to narrow his eyes to slits.

'Hey, what are you doing?' the man called to Brunetti, climbing down from his chair and coming out of his booth. He took a step towards Brunetti, but just then the car's horn shrieked out, deafening in the enclosed space, and he jumped back, crashing against the doorjamb. He watched the car cover the fifteen metres between itself and the man in the doorway. He shouted again, but the man didn't move. He told himself to run across and push the policeman out of the way, but he couldn't force himself to move.

The horn sounded again, and the man closed his eyes. The sharp squeal of the brakes forced him to open them, and as he watched, the car swerved wildly on the oil-slick floor as it turned away from the policeman, who still hadn't moved. The Mercedes sideswiped a Peugeot Sedan parked in slot 17 and then swerved back towards the door, coming to a stop less than a metre from the policeman. As the attendant watched, the policeman walked up to the passenger door and opened it. He said something, waited a moment, and climbed into the car. The car shot off and through the door, turned left and towards the causeway, and the attendant, unable to think of anything better to do, called the police.

Chapter Twenty-Seven

As they started across the causeway, towards the lights of Mestre and Marghera, Brunetti studied Signora Ceroni's profile, but she ignored him and looked straight ahead, so he looked off to the right, to the lighthouse of Murano and, even farther out, the lights of Burano. 'It's very clear tonight,' he said. 'I think I can see Torcello out there.'

She sped up and was soon travelling faster than any of the other cars on the causeway. 'If I turned the wheel to the right, we'd go over the edge and into the water,' she said.

'I imagine you're right,' Brunetti answered.

She took her foot off the accelerator, and they slowed down. A car swept past them on the left. 'When you came to the agency,' she said, 'I knew it was just a matter of waiting for you to come back. I should have left then.'

'Where would you have gone?'

'Switzerland, and from there to Brazil.'

'Because of business contacts in Brazil?'

'I couldn't have used them, could I?'

Brunetti thought about this for a moment before he

answered, 'No, given the circumstances, I suppose you couldn't. Then why Brazil?'

'I have money there.'

'And in Switzerland?'

'Of course. Everyone has money in Switzerland,' she snapped.

Brunetti, who didn't, knew what she meant and so answered, 'Of course.' Then he asked, 'But you couldn't stay there?'

'No. Brazil's better.'

'I suppose so. But now you can't go.'

She said nothing.

'Do you want to tell me about it? We're not at the Questura, and you don't have your lawyer, I know, but I'd like to know why.'

'Is this police or just you?'

He sighed. 'I'm afraid there's no difference, not any more.'

She looked at him then, not for the words but for the sigh. 'What will happen?' she asked.

'To you?'

'Yes.'

'It depends on . . .' he began to say, thinking that it would depend on what her reason had been. But then he remembered that there were three of them, and so that wasn't true. Motive would matter very little to the judges, not with three men dead, and all apparently in the coldest of blood. 'I don't know. It won't be good.'

'I don't think I care,' she said, and he was surprised to hear the lightness with which she spoke.

'Why's that?'

'Because they deserved it, all of them.'

Brunetti was about to say that no one deserved to die, but then he remembered the tape, and he said nothing.

'Tell me,' he said.

'You know I worked for them?'

'Yes.'

'No, not that I work for them now. I mean for years, ever since I came to Italy.'

'For Trevisan and Favero?' he asked.

'No, not for them, but for men like them, the ones who ran it before they sold it to Trevisan.'

'He bought it?' Brunetti asked, surprised to hear her talk as though it were a store.

'Yes. I don't know how it happened. But what I do know is that, one day, the men who were running the business were gone, and Trevisan was the new boss.'

'And you were . . . ?'

'I was what you would call "middle management".' She used the English term, voice heavy with irony.

'What does that mean?'

'It means I was no longer peddling my ass on the street.' She glanced across at him then to see if she had shocked him, but the look Brunetti gave her was as calm as his voice when he asked, 'How long did you do that?'

'Work as a prostitute?' she asked.

'Yes.'

'I came here as a prostitute,' she said and then paused. 'No, that's not true. I came here as a young woman, in love with my first lover, an Italian who promised to give me the world, if only I'd leave my home and follow him here. I did, and he didn't.

'I told you I was from Mostar. That means my family was Muslim. Not that anyone in my family ever saw the inside of a mosque. Except for my uncle, but everyone thought he was crazy. I even went to school with the sisters. My family said I'd get a better education, so I had twelve years of Catholic schools.'

He noticed that they were driving along the right side of the canal that flowed between Venice and Padua, the road of the Palladian villas. Even as he recognized the road, one of the villas appeared on the other side of the canal, its outline faintly visible in the moonlight, a single light burning in the window of an upper floor.

'The story is a cliché, so I won't tell you about it. I was in love, I came here, and within a month I was on the streets. Without a passport, with no Italian, but I'd had six years of Latin with the sisters, learning all the prayers, so it was easy for me to learn. It was also easy to learn what I had to do to succeed. I've always been very ambitious, and I saw no reason why I couldn't succeed at this.'

'And what did you do?'

'I was very good at my work. I kept myself clean, and I became helpful to the man who controlled us.'

'Helpful in what way?'

'I'd tell him about the other girls. Twice, I told him about girls who were preparing to run away.'

'What happened to them?'

'They were beaten. I think he broke some of the

301

fingers of one of them. They seldom did us enough damage to make us stop working. Bad business.'

'How else were you helpful?'

'I'd give them the names of clients, and I think some of them were blackmailed. I was good at spotting the nervous ones, and I'd ask them about themselves and, sooner or later, they all ended up talking about their wives. If they looked like they'd be good targets, I'd learn their names and then their addresses. It was very easy. Men are very weak. I think it's vanity that does it.'

After a few moments' silence, Brunetti asked, 'And then what?'

'And then they took me off the streets. They realized that I could be much more useful to them in a managerial capacity.' Again, she used the English words, speaking almost without accent, into and out of the language with the ease of a seal slipping in and out of the water.

'What did you do in that "managerial capacity"?' he asked, matching her lack of accent.

'I'd talk to the new girls, explain things to them, and advise them to do as they were told.' She added irrelevantly, 'I learned Spanish quickly, and that helped.'

'Was it profitable?'

'The higher I rose in the organization, yes. I saved enough in two years to buy the travel agency.'

'But you still worked for them?'

She looked at him before she said, 'You never stop working for them, once you start.' She stopped at a red light but didn't turn to him. Hands locked on the top of the wheel, she looked straight ahead.

'None of this bothered you? Doing all of this?'

She shrugged and, when the light changed, shifted into gear. They drove on.

'The business was expanding tremendously. There were more and more girls every year, every month, it seemed. We'd bring them in . . .'

He interrupted her. 'Is that what the travel agency was for?'

'Yes. But after a time, it almost didn't make sense to import them, so many were coming in from the East and from North Africa. So we changed our organization to adjust to this. We'd simply pick them up after they got here. It cut down tremendously on overheads. And it was easy enough to get them to hand over their passports. Well, if they had passports. A lot of them didn't.' Her voice grew prim, almost officious. 'It's amazing how easy it is to get into this country. And stay here.'

Another villa came up on the right, but Brunetti barely glanced at it. 'The tapes?' he reminded her.

'Ah yes, the tapes,' she said. 'I knew about them for months before I saw them. That is, I knew about them in theory, knew that tapes were being sent up from Bosnia, but I didn't know what they were. Trevisan and Favero and Lotto, all of them were excited about them because of the profits they saw. All they had to do was pay a few thousand lire for a blank tape and reproduce it, and then, at least in America, they could sell it for at least twenty or thirty times what they paid for the tape. In the beginning, they just sold the master tapes. I think they got a few million lire for them, but then they decided that they wanted to go into distribution themselves: that's where they said the money was.

'It was Trevisan who asked me what I'd suggest. They knew I had a good instinct for business, so they asked me. I told them exactly what I thought, that I couldn't tell them anything until I'd seen the tapes. Even then, I was thinking of them as a product and the whole thing as a problem in marketing.' She glanced at him. 'I even thought of it that way, in those terms. Product. Marketing.' She sighed.

'So Trevisan spoke to the other two and they agreed to have me look at a few tapes. But they insisted that I do it with them; they didn't trust me, they didn't trust anyone with the master tapes, not once they realized how valuable they were.'

'And did you see them?' he asked when he thought she was not going to continue.

'Oh yes, I saw them. I saw three of them.'

'Where?'

'At Lotto's apartment. He was the only one who didn't have a wife living with him, so we went there.'

'And?'

'And we watched the tapes. That's when I decided.'

'Decided what?'

'To kill them.'

'All three of them?' Brunetti asked.

'Of course.'

After a moment, he asked, 'Why?'

'Because they enjoyed those films so much. Favero was the worst. He got so aroused during the second one that he had to leave the room. I don't know where he went, but he didn't come back until they were over.'

'And the other two?'

'Oh, they were excited, too. But they had seen them before, all of the tapes, and so they could control themselves.'

'Were they the same kind of tapes that I saw?'

'Did a woman get killed?' she asked.

'Yes.'

'Then it was the same as these. She's raped, usually repeatedly, and then she's killed.' For all of the emotion in her voice, she could have been describing training films for flight attendants.

'How many tapes were there?' Brunetti asked.

'I don't know. There were at least seven that I know of, not including the three I saw. But those were the ones they sold outright; these three were the ones they wanted to reproduce and distribute.'

'What did you tell them when you saw the tapes?'

'I told them I'd need a day or so to think about it. I said that I knew someone in Brussels who might be interested in buying copies for the Belgian and Dutch markets. But I'd already decided that I would kill them. It was just a matter of finding the best way to do it.'

'Why?'

'Why what? Why did I wait, or why did I decide to kill them?'

'Why did you decide to kill them?'

She allowed the car to slow in response to a car ahead of them that was slowing to turn off to the right. When the lights of the other car disappeared, she turned to Brunetti. 'I've thought about that a great deal, commissario. I think the thing that decided me was that they enjoyed the tapes so much; that surprised me, that they would. And I realized, as I sat and watched the three of them, that they not only had no idea that there was anything wrong in watching the videos, but they didn't think it was wrong to commission them.'

'Were they?'

She turned her eyes back to the road. 'Please, commissario, don't be dull. If there were no market for such things, they wouldn't be made. Trevisan and his friends created a market, and then they saw that it was supplied. Before I saw the tapes and saw what was on them, I'd heard Trevisan and Lotto talking about sending a fax to Sarajevo to order more of them. They were as casual as if they were calling up to order a case of wine or to tell their broker to buy or sell some stock. It was business for them.'

'But then you saw the tapes?'

'Yes. But then I saw the tapes.'

'Did you think about whether it was wrong to murder them?'

'That's what I'm trying to tell you, commissario. It wasn't wrong. It was right. I never questioned that, not from the beginning. And before you ask, yes, I'd do it again.'

'Is it because the women are Bosnian? Muslim?'

She made a sound he thought was a chuckle. 'It doesn't matter who the women are. Were. They're dead now, so it makes no difference to them what happens, poor things.' She thought about his question for a moment. 'No, that didn't make any difference.' She took her eyes from the road and looked at him. 'People talk about humanity and crimes against humanity, commissario. The newspapers are filled with editorials, and politicians talk and talk and talk. And no one does anything. All we get is talk and noble sentiments, and still things like this go on; women get raped and murdered, and now we make movies and watch it happening.' He heard her anger, but it made her speech slower, not faster.

'So I decided to stop them. Because nothing else would.'

'You could have come to the police.'

'And what, commissario? Have them arrested for what? Is it a crime, what they were doing?'

Brunetti didn't know and was ashamed to admit it.

'Is it?' she insisted.

'I don't know,' he finally said. 'But you could have exposed them and their business with the prostitutes. That would have stopped them.'

She laughed out loud. 'How dull you are, commissario. I had no desire to stop the prostitution, none at all. I make a very good living from that. Why would I want to stop it?'

'Because of what's done to the women, the same thing that happened to you.'

She spoke more quickly now, out of irritation, not anger. 'It would happen to them wherever they were. They'd be whores and victims in their own countries.'

'Aren't some of them killed?'

'What do you want me to do, commissario, tell you I'm taking vengeance for all the poor dead prostitutes of the world? I'm not. I'm trying to tell you why I did it. If they were arrested, everything would have come out. I would have been arrested, as well. And what would have happened? A few months in gaol while they waited for a trial, and then what? A fine? A year in gaol? Two? You think that's enough for what they did?'

Brunetti was too tired to argue ethics with this woman. 'How did you do it?' He'd settle for facts.

'I knew Trevisan and Favero were having dinner, and I knew which train Trevisan always took back. I took the same train. The first-class carriages are always empty at the end of the trip, so it was very easy.'

'Did he recognize you?'

'I don't know. It was all very fast.'

'Where did you get the gun?'

'A friend,' was the only explanation she gave.

'And Favero?'

'During the dinner, he went to the bathroom, and I put barbiturates in his wine. Vin Santo. I made him order a half-bottle after dinner because it was sweet and I knew it would cover the taste.'

'And at his house?'

'He was supposed to drive me to the railway station so I could get a train back to Venice. But, halfway there, he fell asleep at a red light. I pulled him over and changed seats, then drove the car back to his house. He had one of those automatic door openers for the garage, so I opened the door, drove in and left the motor running, then pulled him back under the wheel and hit the button to close the door. I ran out of the garage as it was closing.'

'Lotto?'

'He called me and said he was worried, wanted to talk to me about what was happening.' Brunetti watched her profile as it appeared and disappeared in the light of the infrequent cars that passed them. Her face remained calm through all of this. 'I told him it would be better if we talked out of the city, so he agreed to meet me in Dolo. I told him I had some business on the mainland and would meet him on that back road in Dolo. I got there early, and when he pulled up, I got out of my car and into his. He was in a panic. He thought his sister had killed Trevisan and Favero, and he wanted to know if I thought so, too. He was afraid she was going to kill him. So all of the business would be hers. And her lover's.'

She pulled off to the side of the road and waited for a car behind them to pass. When it did, she made a U-turn and headed back the way they had come.

'I told him he could be sure there was nothing to fear from his sister. He seemed relieved to hear that. I don't remember how many times I shot him. Then I got back in my own car and drove back to Piazzale Roma.'

'The gun?' he asked.

'It's still in my apartment. I didn't want to throw it away until I'd finished with it.'

'What do you mean?'

309

She glanced at him. 'The others.'

'What others?'

She didn't answer, shook her head in a negation he sensed was absolute.

'Didn't you think that, sooner or later, you'd be found?'

'I don't know. I didn't think about that. But then you came to the agency and I told you I didn't drive, and then I started to think about all the other things, aside from the glasses, I had done that were wrong. I suppose people saw me on the train, and the man in the garage knew I was out in my car the night Lotto died. And then tonight, I knew it was over. I thought I could get away. Well,' she added, 'I don't know if I thought it so much as I hoped it.'

Some time passed, and then Brunetti was aware of passing the first villa he had seen, though it was on his side of the road now. Suddenly she broke the silence. 'They'll kill me, you know.'

He had been half asleep in the warmth of the car and the unaccustomed motion. 'What?' he asked, shaking his head and sitting up straight in his seat.

'Once they know I've been arrested, once they know I killed them, they'll have no choice but to eliminate me.'

'I don't understand,' Brunetti said.

'I know who they are, at least some of them, the ones I didn't kill. And they'll make sure I don't talk.'

'Who?'

'The men who make the tapes – Trevisan wasn't the only one – and run the prostitutes. No, not the little

310

men on the street, the ones who push them around and collect the money. I know the men who run the whole thing, the import-export in women. Only there's not a lot of export, is there, aside from the tapes? I don't know who they all are, but I know enough of them.'

'Who are they?' Brunetti asked, thinking of the Mafia and men with moustaches and southern accents.

She named the Mayor of a large town in Lombardy and the President of a large pharmaceutical company. When he whipped his head around to stare at her, she smiled a grim smile and added the name of one of the Assistant Ministers of Justice. 'This is a multinational business, commissario. We're not talking about two old men who sit in a bar, drinking cheap wine and talking about whores; we're talking about boardrooms and yachts and private planes and orders that go back and forth by fax and cellular phone. These are men who have real power. How do you think they managed to get rid of the notes of Favero's autopsy?'

'How do you know that?' Brunetti demanded.

'Lotto told me. They didn't want anyone looking into Favero's death. Too many people are involved. I don't know all their names, but I know enough of them.' Her smile disappeared. 'That's why they'll kill me.'

'We'll put you in protective custody,' Brunetti said, brain leaping ahead to the details.

'Like Sindona?' she asked sarcastically. 'How many guards did he have in prison, and video cameras on him twenty-four hours a day? And still they got poison into his coffee. How long do you think I'll last?'

'That won't happen,' Brunetti said hotly, and then it occurred to him that he had no reason to believe this. He knew that she had killed the three men; yes, but all the rest remained to be proven, especially all this talk of danger and plots to kill her.

Some sort of emotional radar passed the change in his mood to her, and she stopped talking. They drove on through the night, and Brunetti turned to watch the lights reflected on the canal on his right.

The next thing he knew, she was shaking him by the shoulder, and when he opened his eyes, he saw a wall directly in front of him. Instinctively, he raised his arms to cover his face and pulled his head down on to his chest. But there was no impact, no sound. The car was motionless, the motor silent.

'We're back in Venice,' she said.

He pulled his hands away and looked around him. The wall in front of him was the wall of the parking garage; on either side of him were parked cars.

She reached down between the seats and released her seat-belt. 'I suppose you'll want to take me to the Questura.'

When they arrived at the *embarcadero*, Brunetti saw a No. 1 just pulling away. He looked at his watch and was amazed to discover that it was after three. He hadn't called Paola, hadn't called the Questura to tell them what he was doing.

Signora Ceroni stood in front of the boat schedule and peered at it. Unable to read the list of times, she pulled out her glasses and put them on. When she had read through them, she turned to Brunetti and said, 'Not for forty minutes.'

'Would you like to walk?' he asked. It was too cold to sit in the open *embarcadero*, and at least walking would keep them warm. He knew he could call the Questura and have a boat sent to get them, but it would probably be faster to walk.

'Yes, I would,' she answered. 'I won't get to see the city again.'

Brunetti found this melodramatic but said nothing. He turned to the right and started along the embankment. When they got to the first bridge, she said, 'Do you mind if we walk over the Rialto? I've never much liked Strada Nuova.'

Saying nothing, Brunetti continued along the embankment until they came to the bridge that led to the Tolentini and the way through the back streets of the city towards the Rialto. She walked at a moderate pace and appeared to pay no special attention to the buildings they passed. Occasionally, Brunetti's quicker pace carried him ahead of her, but then he would stop at a corner or the foot of a bridge and wait for her. They came out beside the fish market and went down towards the Rialto. At the top, she paused for only a moment, looked both to right and left at the Grand Canal, empty now of all boat traffic. They came down off the bridge and headed through Campo San Bartolomeo. A nightwatchman went past them, leading a German shepherd on a leash, but no one spoke.

It was almost four when they got to the Questura.

When Brunetti pounded on the heavy glass door, a light came on in the guard room to the right of the door. A guard, rubbing sleep from his eyes, came out and peered through the glass. Recognizing Brunetti, he opened the door and saluted.

'*Buon giorno, commissario*,' he said and then looked at the woman who stood beside his superior.

Brunetti thanked him and asked if there was a woman officer on duty that night. When the guard said that there was not, Brunetti told him to call whoever's name was first on the roster and tell her to come to the Questura immediately. He dismissed the guard and led Signora Ceroni across the entrance and up the stairs towards his office. The heat had been turned down, so the building was cold, the air damp. At the top of the fourth flight, Brunetti opened the door to his office and held it for her, allowing her to pass inside in front of him.

'I'd like to use the bathroom,' she said.

'Sorry. Not until a female officer gets here.'

She smiled. 'Afraid I'll kill myself, commissario?' When he didn't answer, she said, 'Believe me, I'm not the one who's going to do that.'

He offered her a chair and went to stand behind his desk, looking down at its surface, shuffling through some papers. Neither of them bothered to speak during the quarter-hour it took for the officer to show up, a middle-aged woman who had been on the force for years.

When the policewoman came into his office, Brunetti looked across at Ceroni and asked, 'Would you like to make a statement? Officer Di Censo can witness it.'

Ceroni shook her head.

'Would you like to call your lawyer?'

Again, that silent negation.

Brunetti waited a moment and then turned to the policewoman, 'Officer, I'd like you to take Signora Ceroni to a cell. If she changes her mind, she may call her lawyer and her family.' He looked at Ceroni when he said this, but she shook her head again.

Turning his attention back to the policewoman, he said, 'She is to have no other contact, either with anyone in the Questura or with anyone outside. Do you understand?'

'Yes, sir,' Di Censo said and then asked, 'Am I to stay with her, sir?'

'Yes, until someone relieves you.' And then to Ceroni, Brunetti said, 'I'll see you later this morning, signora.'

She nodded but said nothing, stood and followed Di Censo from the office, and he listened to their heels disappearing down the stairs: the officer's steady and strong, Signora Ceroni's those same sharp clicking sounds that had led him to Piazzale Roma and then to the killer of the three men.

He wrote a short report, giving the substance of his conversation with Signora Ceroni, her refusal to call her lawyer or to give a formal confession. He left it with the officer at the door with orders for him to give it to Vice-Questore Patta or to Lieutenant Scarpa when either of them arrived at the Questura.

It was almost five when he slipped into bed beside Paola. She stirred, turned towards him, draped an arm over his face, and muttered something he couldn't understand. As he drifted off to sleep, his memory played back for him not the image of the dying woman but instead that of Chiara holding up her dog, Bark. Dumb name for a dog, he thought, and then he slept.

Chapter Twenty-Eight

When Brunetti woke the following morning, Paola was already gone but had left him a note saying that Chiara seemed all right and had gone off to school normally enough. Though he took some comfort in this, it was not enough to quell his abiding grief for his child's pain. He had coffee, a long shower, more coffee, but he was unable to shake off the dullness of body and spirit that lingered from the events of the night before. He remembered a time when he could spring back from sleepless nights, or from horror, with no effort, could push himself for days when in pursuit of truth or what he thought of as justice. No more. If anything, the spirit that drove him now was fiercer, but there was no denying the diminishing powers of his body.

He turned away from these thoughts and left the apartment, glad of the biting air and busy streets. As he walked past a news-stand, even though he knew it was impossible, he glanced at the headlines for mention of last night's arrest.

It was almost eleven by the time he got to the Questura, where he was greeted by the usual salutes and nods, and if he was surprised that no one came up

317

to congratulate him for having, single-handedly, brought in the killer of Trevisan, Favero and Lotto, he gave no sign of it.

On his desk he found two notes from Signorina Elettra, both telling him that the Vice-Questore wanted to speak to him. He went immediately downstairs and found Signorina Elettra at her desk.

'Is he in?'

'Yes,' she said, looking up but not smiling. 'And he's not in a good mood.'

Brunetti stopped himself from asking if Patta was ever in a good mood and, instead, asked, 'What about?'

'The transfer.'

'The what?' Brunetti asked, not really interested but always willing to delay having to speak to Patta; a few minutes with Signorina Elettra was, to date, the most pleasant way he had discovered of doing that.

'The transfer,' she repeated. 'Of that prisoner you brought in last night.' She turned aside to answer her phone. '*Si*?' she asked, and then, quickly, 'No, I can't.' Saying nothing further, she hung up and glanced back up at Brunetti.

'What happened?' he asked quietly, wondering if Signorina Elettra could hear the pounding of his heart.

'There was a call earlier this morning. From the Ministry of Justice, saying she belonged in Padua and they wanted her taken there.'

Brunetti leaned forward and spread both hands on her desk, supporting his weight with them.

'Who took the call?'

'I don't know. One of the men downstairs. It happened before I got in. Then about eight, some men from Special Branch showed up with some papers.'

'And did they take her?'

'Yes. To Padua.'

Horrified, Signorina Elettra watched as Brunetti drew his hands into fists, his nails leaving eight long scratches on the polished surface of her desk.

'What's wrong, commissario?'

'Has she got there?' he asked.

'I don't know,' she said and looked down at her watch. 'They've been gone three hours, a little more. They should be there.'

'Call them,' Brunetti said, voice hoarse.

When she did nothing, merely stared up at him, astonished at the change, he repeated, voice louder now, 'Call them. Call della Corte.' Before she could do anything, he grabbed her phone and punched out the numbers.

Della Corte picked it up on the third ring.

'It's Guido. Is she there?' Brunetti began with no explanation.

'*Ciao, Guido*,' della Corte answered 'Is who where? I don't know what you're talking about.'

'I brought in a woman last night. She killed all three of them.'

'She confessed?' della Corte asked.

'Yes. All three.'

Della Corte's whistle of appreciation came down the line. 'I don't know anything about it,' he finally said. 'Why are you calling me? Where'd you arrest her?'

'Here. In Venice. But some men from Special Branch

came and picked her up this morning. Someone in the Ministry of Justice sent them to get her. They said she had to be held in Padua.'

'That's nonsense,' della Corte exclaimed. 'She should be held in the place she's arrested until she's formally charged. Anyone knows that.' Then, after a pause, he asked, 'Has she been charged?'

'I don't know,' Brunetti said. 'I don't think so; there's been so little time.'

'Let me see what I can find out,' della Corte said. 'I'll call you back as soon as I know anything. What's her name?'

'Ceroni, Regina Ceroni.' Before Brunetti could say anything else, della Corte was gone.

'What's wrong?' Signorina Elettra asked, voice deep with alarm.

'I don't know,' Brunetti said. Without another word, he turned and knocked at Patta's door.

'*Avanti.*'

Brunetti pushed open the door and walked quickly into the room. He forced himself to remain silent, hoping to get an idea of Patta's mood before he had to explain anything to the Vice-Questore.

'What's this I hear about that woman being transferred to Padua?' Patta demanded.

'I don't know anything about it. I brought her in last night. She confessed to killing all three of them: Trevisan, Favero and Lotto.'

'Where did she confess?' Patta asked, confusing Brunetti with the question.

'In her car.'

'Her car?'

'I followed her to Piazzale Roma. I spent a lot of time with her, and then I brought her back here, to Venice. She told me how she did it. And why.'

Patta seemed uninterested in either. 'Did you get a confession from her? Was it witnessed?'

Brunetti shook his head. 'We got back here at four, and I asked her if she wanted to call her lawyer. She didn't. I asked if she wanted to make a statement, but she refused, so I had her taken to a cell. Officer Di Censo took her down to the women's section.'

'Without making a confession or a statement?' Patta demanded.

There was no sense in delaying. 'No. I thought I'd get one this morning.'

'You thought you'd get one this morning,' Patta repeated in a nasty singsong.

'Yes.'

'Well, that's not going to happen, is it?' Patta asked, making no attempt to disguise his anger. 'She's been taken to Padua.'

'Did she get there?' Brunetti interrupted.

Patta cast his eyes tiredly to one side. 'If you'd let me finish speaking, commissario . . .'

Brunetti nodded but didn't bother to speak.

'As I was saying,' Patta began and paused long enough to make the point that he had been interrupted, 'she was taken to Padua this morning. Before you bothered to get here and without her having made a confession, practice which, as I think you know, commissario, is essential to the most routine police procedure. But she was taken to Padua, and I hope you know what that means.' Patta paused here, archly dramatic, waiting for Brunetti to admit to the full extent of his incompetence.

'Then you think she's in danger?' Brunetti asked.

Patta squinted in confusion and pulled his head back. 'Danger? I don't know what you're talking about, commissario. The only danger is that Padua is going to get the credit for this arrest and for her confession. She's killed three men, two of them men of great standing in this community, and credit for her capture is now going to be given to Padua.'

'Then she's there?' Brunetti asked, voice sharp with hope.

'I have no idea where she is,' Patta began, 'and, quite frankly, I don't much care. As soon as she was taken out of our jurisdiction, she ceased to be of any interest to me. We'll be able to halt our investigation of the murders – there is at least that – but all of the credit for her arrest is going to be given to Padua.' Patta's anger was raw. He reached across his desk and pulled a file towards him. 'I have nothing else to say to you, Commissario Brunetti. I'm sure you can find something with which to busy yourself.' He opened the file, bent his head, and began to read.

Back in his office, Brunetti gave in to his impulse and dialled della Corte's number. No one answered. He sat. He got up and walked to the window. Then he came back and sat at his desk again. Time passed. The phone rang and he picked it up.

'Guido, did you know something about this?' della Corte asked, voice wary.

Brunetti's hand was slippery with sweat. He switched the phone to his other hand and wiped his palm on the leg of his trousers. 'What happened?'

'She hanged herself in her cell. They brought her back here about an hour ago and put her in a holding cell while they tried to locate a tape-recorder for her confession. They didn't bother to take her things from her, and when they got back to the cell, they found she'd used her panty-hose to hang herself from the heating vent.' Della Corte stopped speaking, but Brunetti said nothing.

'Guido? Are you there?'

'Yes, I'm here,' Brunetti finally said. 'Where are the men from Special Branch?'

'They're filling out forms. She told them on the way out that she killed the three men.'

'Why?'

'Why did she tell them or why did she kill them?' della Corte asked.

'Why did she kill them?'

'She told them she'd had affairs with all of them in the past and had been blackmailing them for years. Then all three of them told her they wouldn't pay any more, so she decided to kill them.'

'I see,' Brunetti said. 'All three?'

'That's what they say.'

'How many of them are there?' Brunetti asked.

'The men from Special Branch?'

'Yes.'

'Three.'

'And they all say the same thing? That she killed them because she couldn't blackmail them any more?'

'Yes.'

'Did you talk to them?'

'No. I got all this from the guard who found her.'

'When did they start to talk about her confession?' Brunetti asked. 'Before or after she was dead?'

'I don't know,' della Corte said. 'Does it matter?'

No, Brunetti realized, it didn't matter, for all three of the men from Special Branch, he was sure, would tell the same story. Adultery, blackmail, greed, and revenge: these were vices that would adequately explain what she had done. In fact, they were probably more believable than rage and horror, and the icy lust for retribution. The word of three officers of the Special Branch was hardly to be questioned.

Brunetti said, 'Thank you', and put the phone down softly. He sat and searched for scraps, for any thread of evidence that would pull another person to the truth. In the face of Ceroni's confession and suicide, the only tangible evidence was the phone records for the offices of the dead men. And what of that? Calls to various legitimate businesses in a number of countries, to a seedy bar in Mestre. It was little more than nothing and certainly not enough to merit investigation. Mara, he was sure, was back on the streets now, probably moved to some other city. And Silvestri would tell whatever story he was ordered to tell by the people who gave him drugs. Or he could just as easily be found dead of an overdose. Brunetti still had the videotape, but to trace it back to the Trevisans would mean asking Chiara to talk about it, to remember it, and he would not do that, no matter the consequences of his refusal.

She had warned him, but he had refused to listen. She had even named the man who would send her killers. Or perhaps there was someone even more powerful than him involved in this, another respectable man who, like the centurion in the Bible, had but to say, 'Go' and someone went. Or three such servants went to do his bidding.

From memory, he dialled a number of a friend who was a colonel at the Guardia di Finanza and briefly explained about Trevisan, Favero and Lotto and the money they must have been receiving, and hiding, for years. The colonel said they'd look into Signora Trevisan's finances as soon as they had time and personnel available. When Brunetti put the phone down, he felt no better. He put his elbows on his desk, lowered his head into his cupped hands, and sat that way for a long time. He had brought her in before dawn, but by eight o'clock the men from Special Branch had already come to get her.

He pushed himself up from his desk and went down to the officers' room two floors below, seeking Preside, the man who had been on guard duty when he brought Signora Ceroni in. He had gone off duty at eight, but in his logbook he had noted, '6:18 a.m. Lt Scarpa takes over day shift. Comm. Brunetti's report to Lt Scarpa.'

He left the room and stood for a moment in the hall, surprised that it took a few moments to feel entirely steady. He turned and walked towards the stairway that would take him from the Questura, forcing his mind away from the knowledge that remained behind him there. He started down the stairs, thinking of Signora Ceroni and of their strange journey through the night. He realized that he would never understand why she had done it. Perhaps you had to be a woman. He'd ask Paola. She usually understood things. At that thought, Brunetti's heart came back to him, and he left the Questura, going home.